Praise for *The Body in the News*

"Samantha Newman is back and more unputdownable than ever! Yellen is at the top of her clever, suspenseful game in THE BODY IN THE NEWS. Readers will be as delighted as I was." *Pamela Fagan Hutchins, USA Today bestselling author of BIG HORN, SWITCHBACK, and The Delaney Pace Novels*

"When I read The Body Business, the first book in author Gay Yellen's Samantha Newman Mysteries, I found a series I could count on for the perfect amateur sleuth read—an engaging cast of characters, stellar writing, and a whodunit that kept me turning pages. I finished book #3, THE BODY IN THE NEWS, wishing the next book was already available." *Lois Winston, author of the bestselling Anastasia Pollack Crafting Mysteries*

"Samantha Newman is the kind of gal I'd love to have as a neighbor or friend. She's clever, resilient, and funny. Her life is messy and dramatic and exciting, but she has the wits to survive almost anything. THE BODY IN THE NEWS presents her biggest challenge yet. Heart-warming and gripping at the same time, the story kept me cheering for her to solve the mystery and reach her best life." *Saralyn Richard, author of BAD BLOOD SISTERS and the Detective Parrott Mysteries*

Learn more at GayYellen.com

D1525081

THE BODY IN THE NEWS

A SAMANTHA NEWMAN NOVEL

Gay Yellen

GYDR PRESS
www.GYDR.com

This book is a work of fiction. Any references to historical or
current events, real people, or real places are used fictitiously.
Other names, characters, places, and events are products of
the author's imagination, and any resemblance to actual
events, persons or places are entirely coincidental.

Cover design: Heidi Dorey

The Body in the News/ Gay Yellen. −1st ed.
ISBN 978-0-9978915-4-6

To my readers, without whom this book would not exist.

Table of Contents

A murder is the culmination of
a lot of different circumstances,
all converging at a given moment
at a given point.

~Agatha Christie

CHAPTER ONE

Pies-O-Plenty

Shoehorned inside his cramped and windowless office, I watched Lloyd Sedgwick scrawl and erase ever-changing versions of an outline for his latest KHTS-TV investigative report. It was due first thing today, and by five a.m., he was hopelessly late. Despite the meat-locker chill in the room, beads of sweat dotted his forehead as he stood at the whiteboard behind his beat-up desk.

I should have walked out hours ago. But with a dwindling bank account and no home to call my own, I needed this job like a duck needs feathers.

Back when the sign on my office door read Samantha Newman, V.P. of Media Relations for a global human resources firm, KHTS-TV used to interview me every now and then about the employment outlook in Houston. I had been working my way up the corporate ladder until my company suddenly imploded in a scandal that made national news, which left me among the ranks of the unemployed.

As the final curtain came down on my old employer, I handed the inside story of its demise to Lloyd, and it became his biggest scoop of the year. My role in the affair gave me a kind of whistleblower status, so KHTS hired me, and Lloyd became my reluctant mentor.

He was supposed to be teaching me the ins and outs of his profession, but instead of sharing, he guarded his work like it was Fort Knox gold. He usually tackled subjects like government incompetence and corporate greed, but all I'd managed to glean so far was that his new report focused on flood control— or rather, the lack of it— in vulnerable parts of our KHTS-TV viewing area.

I wasn't keen on starting a new career from scratch, but the taint of my former bosses' crimes had rendered me virtually unemployable. The TV job was the only offer I got. Luckily, KHTS had the smallest viewership in town. I figured hardly anyone would notice if I failed.

At last, Lloyd set the marker down. He fished the last chili pepper pork rind out of the sack on his desk and chewed it while he reviewed his latest changes. I allowed myself to hope that he had come to the end at last.

But no. He exploded in a stream of unprintable words, and in a final act of destruction, he crushed the empty snack sack in his fist and swiped it across the whiteboard. Words became smears.

Tamping down an urge to scream, I rearranged my backside on the cold metal chair. Shrinking my arms up into my sweater, I ventured one more suggestion. "What if you—"

He waved me off. I tried again. "Why not show what you have to Jay Patel in the morning? Let him help with whatever is bugging you."

Lloyd shot me a dark look, but as he scanned the board, his wiry caterpillar eyebrows shot up. He seemed to be contemplating my suggestion. My spirits rose again.

Then he frowned. "Nah, I don't like the set-up." He erased the entire top section.

I tried a different tack. "How about a break? You could probably use one."

He peeled himself away from the whiteboard. "Yeah, okay. Pizza sounds good."

Pizza? "I was thinking more like go home, shower, change clothes..."

"Nah, I'm good."

Before you could say pepperoni, he'd whipped out his phone and ordered from his favorite place nearby. Not the best in town, but Pies-O-Plenty delivered around the clock, and they were just down the street.

Lloyd had them on speed dial. In no time, he had ordered his usual: a large sausage and hamburger, with pineapple, onions, and jalapeños.

As a recent casualty of his dietary quirks, I prayed I still had an energy bar in my bag. But I needed to escape first, if only for a few minutes.

I stood. "I'm going to the ladies' room."

The trek to the restroom helped restore circulation to my legs, but a quick splash of water on my face was a poor substitute for the steamy shower I craved. In the mirror, my face resembled the damp paper towel I'd just tossed in the trash.

There had to be a way to make this job work. I made a circuit of the darkened hallways, trying to recalibrate my frustration level before slogging back to that refrigerator of an office.

In my absence, Lloyd had erased more from the whiteboard. I stood at the door in disbelief. "You've got to be kidding!"

He turned from the board. "Beg pardon?"

"You've been chasing your tail for hours."

"No I haven't. Just reorganizing a few things."

With a reasonable amount of sleep, or food, or warmth, I might have been able to choose my words more carefully. "What you're doing is wasting time."

His face went crimson. "Excuse me?"

"Let me help you, Lloyd. I may be new to your business, but I'm pretty good at making a complex subject understandable for a general audience."

"I don't need your help."

"But this could be a teaching moment for you. The sooner I learn, the sooner I can—"

"Steal my job entirely?" His jaw muscle flexed. "Think I'm fool enough to let you do that?"

Oops. I hadn't dialed that into the equation. It took all my will power to check my tone. "I was going to say, 'the sooner I'll be out of your hair.' I could never replace you, Lloyd."

His face purpled. "Like hell. You're young. Ambitious. Perky. Why else are you here?"

Perky? Before the walls imploded, one of us had to back off. "I'm here to learn from you, period. What's the harm in helping each other?"

Before Lloyd could respond, Moe, the night security guard, walked in.

"You guys order pizza?"

A young delivery person slouched in Moe's shadow. Lloyd waved him in.

Moe eyed the box, looking like he wanted a slice, too. When no invitation came, he clapped his hands and backed away.

The delivery guy wasn't big on eye contact. As he set the box on the little café table by my chair, the bag with our jumbo sodas slipped from his hand and landed with a splat on the floor. He stared down at the overturned sack, seeming unsure of what to do about it. Maybe he'd been up all night, too.

Before I could move in to help, Lloyd righted the soggy bag, set it on the table, and went for the pie. He scooped a slice toward his mouth and chomped down.

I started for the leaky bag, but the delivery guy had me blocked. As he fumbled around inside the bulging pocket of his baggy pants for what I figured was the receipt, something else fell out and clunked to the floor.

A gun.

Major parts of my critical thinking screeched to a halt. The pizza guy froze, too. We both stared down at the weapon for what felt like a millennium.

Oblivious to the gun, and to the puddle that had formed at his feet, Lloyd pulled a remarkably intact soda from the sack. My heart raced as I tried to teleport a silent alarm to him: Gun! *Gun! GUN!* Evidently lacking in the ESP department, he busily squeaked a straw into the lid of the cup.

I lunged for the weapon, but the pizza guy grabbed it first and aimed it at each of us in turn.

Lloyd finally came to the party. He raised his hands in surrender. The soda tumbled from his grasp.

"Whoa there buddy. Put that thing down before you hurt somebody."

The guy's aim stopped at Lloyd. "Don't talk." His voice was high-pitched, almost child-like.

"Okay, but—"

"Don't talk!" The gun shook wildly in his hand.

Lloyd paled. The pugnacious journalist—with his sights set on earning an Emmy or a Peabody before he turned fifty—lowered his eyes to the cola circle that had expanded around his Clark Kent socks. When had he taken his shoes off?

In the momentary lull, I studied our young assailant. Skinny body swimming inside a soiled, oversized jacket. Baseball cap with a Pies-O-Plenty logo, pulled down low. Thick black hair swept underneath. Face in shadow. Tan neck, shiny with fear.

Despite the gun, the punk seemed more nervous than homicidal. Either way, somebody had to try to diffuse the situation.

I spoke as calmly as I could. "Is there something we can do for you?"

The gun swiveled my way. I can't tell the difference between a BB gun and a Beretta, but pointed at me, this one looked like a cannon. I fought for control over the wobble in my voice. "You could get in trouble with that thing. Why not put it away for a minute so we can talk."

He seemed to be considering my offer as the three of us stood gaping at each other. I could almost hear our hearts pounding outside our chests.

Finally, he lowered the gun and spoke, so softly it was hard to make out the words. "I already been to the radio station. They won't help. I gotta get my story out, and nobody listens."

Me, shakily: "We'll listen, if you put the gun down."

He looked pretty shaky, too. "I wanna talk to the boss in charge."

Lloyd pointed at me. So did the gun. "Samantha Newman, right there. She's the one you want." And then, I swear, he giggled.

Some joke. I briefly contemplated seizing the weapon and shooting Lloyd myself.

Moe showed up in the doorway. "Say, if there's any pizza left, I'll polish it off for ya."

The punk's body tensed. His back was to the door, so Moe likely couldn't see the weapon. I gave mental telepathy another try.

I'm not sure if Moe got the message, but something made him take a step into the room. He glanced from me to Lloyd. "Everything okay in here?"

The pizza kid raised his head. His dark eyes were big as baseballs as he eased the weapon into his jacket pocket.

Hoping Moe could recognize body language, I joined Lloyd and raised my hands in the universal surrender pose. "This young man says he has an important story to tell, and if we don't broadcast it, he'll be very, very angry and he might do something we'll all regret."

The kid shifted from one foot to the other, keeping his back to Moe and his gun hand inside his jacket. "The boss. I'll only talk to him."

Moe stood there, eyes blinking like a pen light on a modem.

I tried again. "Could you please make a call? It's an e-*mer*-gen-cy."

This time, Moe seemed to get the picture. "Oh! Uh, sure, uh, you guys just sit tight and I'll call, okay?" He disappeared down the hall.

I took a chance and slowly lowered my arms. "See, we're going to help you. There's no need for the gun anymore."

The kid scowled. "I knew you wasn't nobody." He pulled the weapon from his pocket and pointed it at Lloyd. "You either."

With Lloyd frozen in place, a few scenarios raced through my mind before I landed on one. "You know, our boss probably won't get here for at least an hour. That's a long time to stand around, don't you think? Why don't we all sit, and you can tell us your story while we wait. Give us a head start, so when the boss shows up, we're ready." I sounded surprisingly calm.

At last, our assailant bowed his head and lowered the gun, letting it dangle loosely in his hand. Without the weapon aimed at us, I relaxed enough to refocus on him. It struck me how small he was. Smaller than Lloyd or me, for sure. Maybe I could—

I lunged for the weapon.

The little hoodlum was too fast. He swung the gun away, but not before I caught his arm and clamped my hand around his wrist.

He started twisting and squirming like live bait on a hook. We wrestled around for a minute or so, until a slick of sweat loosened my grip. He kept flailing and trying to wrench his arm away, but somehow I managed to hold on. We were both breathing hard.

The longer we struggled, the more I feared I'd lose what little control of him I had. In a desperate attempt to grab the gun with my free hand, I threw him off balance. He fell, and took me down with him.

We landed hard in an awkward jumble on the floor, just as the crack of a bullet ripped past my eardrum.

CHAPTER TWO

Punchline

Dead silence, except for the skull-shattering whine in my head. I couldn't move. Nobody moved, as if we were freeze-framed.

Lloyd whimpered. "Jesus, sweet Jesus, I've been shot!" He had collapsed in the middle of the soda spill. Watery brown cola soaked his shirt. A red blotch blossomed at his shoulder.

The kid's face was turned to the wall. His ribcage heaved with violent gulps of air. The gun had fallen between us. While he sobbed, I reached over and snatched it.

I had the upper hand, until the weapon began to wobble in my sweaty grip. What if I had to use it?

On shaky knees, I managed to stand. Bracing the gun with both hands, I aimed it down toward the little hoodlum. He rolled face up, wracked with spasms of despair. The Pies-O-Plenty cap fell back, exposing his face to the light.

I blinked and tried to make sense of what I was seeing: dark eyes, wide and wet. Snub nose, soft jawline. A pink heart tattoo the size of a valentine mint rested just above a delicate collarbone. His jacket was splayed open, revealing a lavender boat-necked tee shirt with cartoon princesses and the word *Frozen* written in sparkly purple script across the front, over the unmistakable shape of budding young female breasts.

I blinked again. The pizza boy was a *girl*.

Lloyd moaned. He had managed to raise himself to a sitting position and lean his back against a leg of the table. Blood oozed down one side of his cola-soaked shirt. He gasped. "The little creep shot me!"

I turned his way, the gun's aim traveling with me. Moe burst in. "Did I hear a gunshot?"

I pointed to Lloyd. "He's wounded. Get an ambulance and call the police."

Moe's eyes bulged at the sight of the weapon in my hand. "Oh, golly! I called the boss like you asked. Told him you needed him. I thought that's what you meant. Anyhoo, Mr. Patel is on the way."

Lloyd groaned, "I need help *now*!" Blood was slowly seeping into the pool of cola beneath him.

Moe started toward Lloyd, but the puddle forced him back. "Don't worry, Mr. Sedgwick. I'll get help here in a jiffy." He eyed me again. Gaping at the gun that was still in my grasp, he raised his hands and backed out the door.

It would have been super nice if he'd hauled the little hoodlum to a secure place until the police arrived, and taken the weapon with him.

In truth, the kid didn't look to be a flight risk. She was still crying, though her sobs had slowed to four or five a minute.

I tiptoed through the soda spill to check on Lloyd up close. A nasty combination of odors rose around him: iced cola, hot blood, flop sweat. His eyes struggled to stay open.

I set the gun down outside the puddle but close enough to grab, and stripped off my sweater. Best I could, I wound it around his shoulder and tied the arms together to secure it.

He opened his eyes, looked at me, and closed them again. I patted his good shoulder. "Hang in there, buddy."

In case I'd misjudged the kid's ability to flee, I grabbed the gun before I pulled myself up and tiptoed out of the muck. Keeping an eye on her, I planted myself in the chair behind Lloyd's desk and set the weapon down within what I hoped would be quick-draw distance if necessary.

Lloyd's blood covered my hands, and bloody cola had soaked my jeans from the knees down. As we waited for the ambulance and police, a huge case of déjà vu came over me. Here I was again, an accidental witness to another random crime, like the punchline of a bad cosmic joke.

Lloyd slumped down a couple of inches. He was moaning and panting rapidly. Our assailant rose onto her elbows and looked around. When she caught sight of Lloyd, she renewed her bawling.

I picked up the gun and pointed it at her. "That's right. Look at him. You did that."

Her tear-swollen eyes widened at the sight of the pistol. She scooted backwards to the wall. "You gonna shoot me?"

Despite the predicament the little lowlife had put us in, a twinge of sympathy snuck through. I'd expected her to be tough, defiant. But the tremor in her voice and the terror in her eyes showed a glimmer of remorse.

The gun weighed heavy in my hand. I wanted to put it down again, but I couldn't risk it. "Just stay where you are. Don't run. Don't make me try to stop you."

I hoped she was scared enough to obey.

After what felt like hours, Moe brought the emergency medics to the door. As he backed away, he said, "Watch out. She's got a gun."

All eyes turned to me.

The three EMT's—a tattooed gym-rat by the looks of his biceps, plus a ponytailed redhead with freckles speckling her face and arms, and a bald older guy— all glanced at Lloyd before their focus returned to me and the weapon in my hand.

I gestured toward the girl on the floor. "It's her gun. I was just keeping it until the police showed up."

Lloyd coughed and struggled for air. The younger EMTs looked to the bald one.

He held them back. "Look, lady, either we wait for the cops to secure the scene while your friend bleeds to death, or you put the weapon down and step away so we can help him."

"Of course." I set the gun on the desk and nudged it away from me. My knees buckled as I tried to stand, but I managed to force my legs straight and back away.

The bald EMT kept his eyes on me as he pulled on a glove, picked up the gun, and carried it out the door. While the kid sobbed and Lloyd wheezed, the female tech entered the spill zone to check his vitals while the third tech rolled a gurney up to the edge of the puddle.

Time raced forward, then slowed to a crawl in a cycle of alternating realities. Then it stopped altogether. Had it been hours or minutes ago that Lloyd and I were squabbling over his report? Hours or minutes since his pizza order had turned into this nightmare?

After the paramedics hooked Lloyd up to oxygen and a saline drip and wheeled him out, Moe stood guard outside the door. I returned to the desk and collapsed into the chair. The kid remained on the floor, eyes closed, back to the wall, beating her head against it. Except for the soft thuds of her skull against the sheetrock, all was silent, until she raised her tear-soaked eyes to me.

"I didn't have no choice. They made me do it."

I glared down at her. "Made you? Who?"

She shook her head. "You wouldn't understand. Nobody does."

From outside the door, a commanding voice changed the subject. "Police! Drop your weapons! Hands up! Nobody move!"

Two of them leapt into the room, guns drawn, crouching low and aiming at all corners until they focused on me and the girl. She lifted her hands high. So did I.

Though their arrival hardly calmed my pounding heart, I was relieved to see them. "Thank goodness you're here."

The burly one aimed his weapon at me. "Stand up and step away from the girl."

"Sure, but you should know—"

He closed in on the desk. "I said stand up and move away!"

"I'm only trying to tell you—"

"Stand up!" He yanked me out of the chair and pinned me against the wall, his face so close, I caught a whiff of breakfast burrito on his breath.

Keeping his gun pointed at me, he backed off a few inches. "Do. Not. Move. Understand?"

I nodded and clamped my jaw shut. Why was he treating me like a criminal?

His partner tugged the girl by her jacket and backed her next to me. Her cheeks ran with tears.

Moe showed up in the doorway again. He blanched at the state of the room. "Ooo-wee, what a mess! At least Mr. Sedgwick's on his way to the ER. You okay, Miss Newman?"

"I will be, soon as you explain to the officers that I'm a victim too."

Moe sucked in some air. "Well, I would, except I already told them I saw you with the gun. And before they left, the ambulance guys said you were still holding it when they came in, so..."

How many times can a person's brain metaphorically explode before it actually blows a gasket? "But the gun is hers," I explained. "It went off when she dropped it. I only picked it up to—"

The big cop gripped my shoulder again, squeezing bones. "Four witnesses put the gun on you. That's enough to haul you in."

I caught a glimpse of hand restraints as he yanked them from his duty belt. Seconds later, they were on me.

CHAPTER THREE

Puppies at Noon

It's not every day you get handcuffed and hauled off to jail. I protested all the way to the police station, which got me nowhere. I've watched enough crime shows on TV to know that at some point, I had the right to a phone call. That kept me reasonably sane for a while.

They swabbed me up and down and handed me a set of jail scrubs. A female officer escorted me to a bathroom to clean up. Blood and cola had glued my shirt to my chest, and plenty had soaked through. I yanked a wad of paper towels from the dispenser, wet them and wiped off what I could, but the stickiness remained. I peeled off my jeans, which wasn't easy, due to the goo that had seeped in up to my knees. A total clean-up was beyond the power of the foamy hand soap.

I stared at my reflection. Mascara streaked my cheeks. Uncombed since yesterday, my hair had formed clumps that jutted out from my head at odd angles.

My guard held open a plastic bag for me to drop my ruined clothes into. "I'm a victim here," I complained.

She gave me a that's-what-they-all-say eye roll and escorted me to an interrogation room where she planted me on a hard metal chair and exited, shutting the door behind her.

No telling how long I'd been there when a guy about my age breezed in. By his shirt and tie, slacks and jacket, I guessed he was a detective, though he didn't bother with introductions. He dropped some papers on the table—most likely the responding officer's rendition of why I was hauled in—and sat across from me. It took so long for him to read through the report, he could have been translating the *Mahabharata*.

I harrumphed. "When do I get my phone call?"

He handed me his card and smiled. *Smiled.* Then he had the nerve to ask, "How are you today?"

"How am I? I've been insulted, assaulted and stripped nearly naked. Thanks for asking. How long before I can get out of here?"

He checked his papers. "Far as I can see, you haven't been charged."

Relief drained a milliliter of the anger rolling through me.

He checked another paper. "Yep, we just need a formal statement from you before you go."

For the next few minutes, I gave him a statement, with a side serving of sarcasm.

Despite my attitude, he handed me his card, and another smile. "Thanks for your cooperation. I'll have your personal items brought in. You can call someone to pick you up."

He turned to the one-way mirror and circled the air with his finger, then stood and paced around the table, studying my file while we waited for my things to arrive.

Soon as I retrieved my phone, I turned it on. A pack of messages popped up. I bypassed them and tapped the RoadSquire app for a driver to pick me up.

The detective kept pacing and reading. "Make sure your friend brings clothes. We'll be keeping yours for testing."

Lovely. Not that I'd want the bloodied things back, but a driving service couldn't bring fresh clothes, and no sane person was likely to let me inside their car in my prisoner scrubs and general state of ickiness.

Recalibrating, I returned to my messages, hoping a friendly chauffeur would appear among them.

My boss, Jay Patel, popped up first. Next was Jojo, the part-time hair and makeup guy. Jay Patel, again. Then Maura Tustin, Lloyd's producer. She was probably chomping at the bit to get my take on the shooting for a soundbite. With no better news-worthy disaster to report, the schedule could deteriorate into a puppy-rescued-from-manhole or boa constrictor-found-in-toilet kind of news day.

I checked the time. Eleven-forty. It would be puppies at noon today.

I thumbed down to Jay Patel's last message:

Call asap.

My car—I'd named it the Ferret in honor of its plucky attitude and exceptional ability to get into and out of tight spots—was still in my assigned parking space at KHTS. Patel would no doubt be happy to send someone to pick me up, and maybe even come himself. But then I'd have to endure more questions. And asking him to bring clothes for me? A non-starter.

Hoping for a better solution, I let the messages stew and scrolled through my contacts.

First, Carter Chapman, my now-you-see-him, now-you-don't boyfriend. He was off to who-knows-where for another hush-hush consulting job for the

CIA, the U.S. Cyber Command, or some other high-profile client. A few years back, he'd designed a crime-solving interface that became a game-changer for local, national and international law enforcement organizations. He made a ton of money from it, and now he mostly tackles gnarly cyber-security issues for big players on the world stage.

At least that's what I hoped he was doing, and not disappearing into one of his former if-I-tell-you-I'd-have-to-kill-you missions. He had promised me those days were over. I believed him, mostly.

I scrolled down the alphabet to Gertrude Gold. The day I hired Gertie to be my secretary at my old executive job, she became my best friend, despite the fact that she's twice my age. Since I was orphaned at eighteen, and she was middle-aged and childless, I suppose we filled those empty spaces for each other. Gertie would normally be my go-to in this kind mess, but she was currently off on a European cruise with her new husband, Louis.

My circle of friends had flatlined. As a last resort, I opened the KHTS roster to see if I'd forgotten a generous soul. I hadn't been there long enough to know all the staff, but maybe a potential friend would pop up.

The detective rounded the table again. He stopped behind me and leaned in close enough for me to feel his breath on my neck. Was he flirting, or had he been peeking at my contacts list? I twisted around and gave him the stink-eye.

He seemed unfazed. "If you don't have anyone, I can arrange a ride for you. Matter of fact, I'm about to go on lunch break. I could take you home."

Hot tears sprang in my eyes. "I'm not as pitiful as you think, Mister..." I read his business card for the first time... "Detective Jebediah B. Hanks. Several people would be happy to pick me up. It's just that my closest friends are all out of town, and I, well, I..."

"Don't want just anyone to see you like this? Understandable. If you are uncomfortable accepting a ride from me, I can get a female officer to escort you. And it's Jeb, please."

Something genuine in his tone made me look at him without anger blinding me. Clean-cut. Smooth, tanned skin. Caribbean blue eyes. Mesmerizing.

In a split second, Carter Chapman's soulful amber-brown eyes took over, then dissolved. My face flushed.

Hanks raised an eyebrow. "So, is that a yes?"

I took a deep breath, recovered my wits, and called Maura Tustin.

CHAPTER FOUR

Doughnuts

An hour later, Maura found me at the police station. Water dripped from her raincoat and umbrella, and she was huffing like a sprinter. "Between the friggin' weather and the maze I had to navigate to find you... well, anyway, I got here fast as I could." She reached into her gym bag and pulled out a purple tee and brown sweat pants. "Hope this works."

Maura was about my height and on the plump side. Her gear looked a couple of sizes larger than anything in my closet, and smelled only fifty-percent fresh. But they were cleaner than I was at the moment, and they beat the jailbird suit, for sure.

After I changed, we headed downstairs to the exit. Beyond the glass doors to the parking lot, rain poured down diagonally in wind-driven sheets so dense it was hard to make out anything past the sidewalk. We were doomed to be drenched within ten feet of the building.

We made a run for it. It was slow going in the flip-flops Maura had brought for me. Pellets of pea-sized hail pounded my head and shoulders. By the time I caught up to her old blue Prius, I was soaked to the bone and freezing.

Rain splatted onto the passenger seat when I opened the door. The car's interior smelled like the bubblegum Maura constantly chewed, plus a nose-wrinkling combination of odors from the remains of several take-out cartons. The back seat was littered with coffee-stained styrene cups, crumpled soda cans, snack bar wrappers, and other unidentifiable detritus. I plucked a balled-up Torchy's Tacos sack from the passenger seat and tossed it to the back. Dripping wet, I got in.

The car's windshield wipers clacked like mallards heading south. Once Maura maneuvered past a flooded intersection that had traffic backed up for blocks, she started unloading questions about the shooting. "So, fill me in before we get to the station."

Ugh. "I'm still processing what happened. I really need to go home."

She gave me a side glance from behind her sparkly yellow cat-eye glasses. "Thing is, the schedule's running on empty today. I mean, how long can we talk about the weather? Plus, Patel wants our viewers to hear from you, asap. We have to be out front with our own breaking news. Lloyd's out of commission, so you're the only eyewitness."

Lloyd. So deep inside my own predicament, I'd blanked out his awful trauma. "Is he okay?"

She shrugged. "Word is, he's still in surgery. C'mon, Samantha. We need your take, pronto, before another station scoops us."

"What about Moe? He was there, too."

I could see the eye roll behind her glasses. "It's gotta be you."

"Can't you just quote me? I feel like I might shatter into a million pieces any minute now. I need to go home."

I gave her the address of The Wellbourne, Carter Chapman's luxury condo in the Museum District. The place wasn't exactly "home." I was living there only until the house I rented— Gertie's cozy little pre-marriage bungalow, actually—was put back together after the last big hurricane blew through town. That was almost a year ago, and since Carter refused to charge me rent, my independent streak had me feeling like a freeloader.

Maura continued to head to the TV station, but at the next corner, her plum-glossed lips tightened and she changed direction toward The Wellbourne.

I squished down low in the passenger seat, shut my eyes, and contemplated the ironies swirling in my head. There's a huge difference between working in the news business and being in the news. At the moment, I wouldn't give a dime for either one.

Water, hot and pulsating, thumped my head, pounded the nape of my neck, and streamed down my back, sending microshocks of relief rolling through me. I could have stayed under that merciful stream forever, or at least until my fingers shriveled. But Maura had insisted on coming up to the condo with me, and she was waiting in the kitchen.

I toweled off and shuffled across the master bedroom. In the walk-in closet, I yanked a long-sleeved tee and leggings out of a drawer, threw one of Carter's old flannel shirts over the tee and rolled up the sleeves. It still held a hint of him and his sprawling Central Texas ranch, Serenity. Earth, trees, grass, fresh air. I lifted it off my shoulders and breathed it in.

Maura was in the kitchen on her phone, speaking with someone at KHTS. Jay Patel, by the sound of it. "Yes sir," she said. "I'll bring her with me." When she saw me, she ended the call.

A box of Shipley Do-Nuts sat on the counter beside her. Normally, I can smell those lovelies a block away. I must have been off my game earlier, not to have sensed them in the car. The old taco bag and who knows what else had likely masked their heavenly aroma.

She opened the lid. "Stress relief. Thought you might need it." Nestled tightly inside, twelve sugar-glazed beauties glistened.

I was just getting to know Maura. As Lloyd's producer, she seemed to be kind of a half rule-keeper/half risk-taker, and some days it was hard to know which half I was dealing with. Her dead-pan demeanor was tough to read, especially with half her face obscured by those huge glasses. That she might be a thoughtful, caring person had never occurred to me. But as I inhaled the yeasty, sugary fragrance of her offering, I considered making her my new best friend.

We sat at the kitchen island in near silence, hugging our mugs of coffee and scarfing up half a dozen doughnuts apiece. Apparently, Maura was in need of a little stress relief, too.

Fueled by caffeine and heaps of fat and sugar, I was ready enough to face the issue at hand. "Was that Jay Patel on the phone?"

Maura licked a speck of sugar glaze from the corner of her mouth. "Yeah. While you were in the shower I sent in some copy to post on the website. Your status. Lloyd's status. They'll run new audio over old footage of him until we get there. At least we won't get scooped."

I could guess how it would play: *Breaking news. Our own KHTS investigative journalist, Lloyd Sedgwick, shot and in serious condition...* or critical condition? Or worse?

I convinced Maura to go to the station without me, and texted Patel with a promise to be there first thing in the morning. I expected him to be ticked off, but he responded with concern. He even offered to make an appointment for me with a trauma counselor to head off potential PTSD.

What had happened only hours ago was definitely traumatic, but it didn't feel post to me. I didn't want to analyze it. I wanted it to disappear.

I replied with:

Just need a nap, thanks.

I clicked the phone off. Enough of the world for now.

Exhaustion pointed my body toward the bedroom. I tottered down the hallway, collapsed onto the bed and shut my eyes.

Suddenly, the awful scene began to replay in my head: Lloyd's blood. The fear on his face before he lost the struggle to stay conscious. His heavy rag doll body when they lifted him onto the gurney.

The doughnuts threatened to spew. I swallowed hard, which seemed to work. Afraid the horror would repeat itself if closed my eyes again, I left the bedroom and retraced my steps to the kitchen. I dumped the rest of the coffee down the drain, grabbed a club soda from the fridge and took a couple of swigs. Why were my hands shaking?

Something about my right hand seemed especially off. I stared at it until the problem came into focus: my mother's ring wasn't on it. It had always been a tad loose on me, but I wore it anyway, ever since the day the coroner handed it to me, after the fire destroyed our home and took Mom, Dad, and my little brother with it.

Then I remembered. The police had confiscated it this morning along with everything else. It should have been returned along with my wallet. I grabbed my bag off the counter.

The ring was in there. I slipped it on and spun it around my finger a couple of times with my thumb. Gradually, my pulse slowed to near normal.

The apartment felt emptier than usual. Carter traveled a lot, and used the condo mostly as a landing place in the city whenever he needed to be here for a local corporate client or his private charitable foundation. It was an easy ninety-minute drive from his home base at Serenity—his ranch in Central Texas—and an even shorter trip by helicopter.

Too bad he wasn't here now. I could use a dose of him tonight.

I wandered out of the kitchen, set my phone on the beveled-glass coffee table in the vast living room, and flopped onto the nubby sofa. The floor-to-ceiling windows opened onto a wide balcony, offering a hundred-eighty-degree view of the city.

The rain had moved on, and the sun was making a comeback. In the distance, a column of black smoke thickened as it rose just east of downtown. The sooty plume wafted upward, caught an air current, and meandered over the snaggle-toothed skyline. Probably from an illegal tire dump, or a warehouse full of flammable material. Or something worse, like a chemical fire near the port.

I figured I should alert someone at KHTS, in case they weren't on it already. It could fill part of the news void for a couple of days while Lloyd...

Lloyd. Maura had said he was in surgery, and not out of the woods yet. Half of me wanted to call and check on him. The other half wasn't ready. Maybe I wasn't out of the woods yet, either.

The pillar of smoke grew thicker and darker as it rose. I turned my phone on and checked the KHTS web feed. Nothing there yet about the shooting, and nothing about the fire. I texted an alert to Maura.

I'm not sure how long I sat there, mindlessly following the progress of the smoke, until a buzz from my phone startled me. The phone fell from my hand and clunked heavily onto the bleached hardwood floor.

When the screen lit with Gertie's caller ID, my heart lifted. I scooped it off the floor. "Gertie! Where are you?"

"Home, dear. Louis had a bad tummy problem— you know how overly-rich cruise food can be. Once we docked in Reykjavík, we caught the first plane home. Arrived yesterday and went straight to the doctor. He's better today, though we're both rocky with jet lag. We just turned on the TV for the first time and saw a news report about the shooting at your station. It didn't involve you, did it?"

"Define 'involve'."

"Oh dear." Gertie was always able to read me, even in my silences. "Are you at work?"

"Not today."

"I'm coming over." She disconnected before I could protest. Not that I would have.

Ready or not, I had to know what KHTS had announced to the world. I dragged myself off the sofa and plodded down the hall to the bedroom. Before I clicked the TV on, I scooted under the covers.

Our little station usually aired syndicated talk shows, game shows, and reruns of old sitcoms on weekday afternoons. But today, the screen belonged to Alicia Sultana, goddess of the KHTS evening news. In a navy blue suit jacket accented by a beaded bib necklace, she was live at the news desk in a split screen with the fresh-faced Francine Bascom. Wearing her usual peasant skirt and jean jacket, the young reporter was standing in front of Ben Taub Hospital, where most of the city's victims of violent crime were treated.

As I attempted to catch up to what they were saying, the *Breaking News* ticker at the bottom of the screen caught my eye.

Investigative reporter in guarded condition. Stay tuned to KHTS for more...

CHAPTER FIVE

Deadline

Gertie arrived out of breath, with two full grocery sacks and a small cooler. The sleek River Oaks stylishness she had acquired when she married Louis Kleschevsky was missing, and my old familiar friend, a slightly frumpy Gertie stood before me. It hurt a little to see her so bedraggled.

Her face crumpled when she saw me. I must have looked a tad undone myself.

I carried the sacks to the kitchen and set them down. We hugged. I held on until she pulled away and peered into my eyes. "Samantha, you could have been killed!"

I focused on the groceries. The first sack held fresh produce. Mandarin oranges, bananas, apples, apricots. As I transferred them to the wire bowl on the breakfast island, a couple of mandarins slipped from my hand and plopped onto the floor, each rolling in a different direction. For some reason, I couldn't think what to do about them.

Worry lines crossed Gertie's forehead. "Why don't you sit while I put everything away?"

I retreated to a barstool and watched her unpack a roasted chicken, couple of green drinks, a zip bag of popcorn kernels, bottle of cranberry juice, half-gallon of ice cream, a tin of spearmint tea, and what looked like a sweet potato casserole with baby marshmallows on top.

"You didn't have to bring all this."

"After what you've been through, you need decent food." She lifted two more foil-wrapped packages from the cooler. "I baked most of these and froze them before we left on the cruise. Want something now?"

Usually, when I'm under pressure, I inhale every foodstuff in the immediate vicinity. But I still felt a little off. "Maybe later."

Gertie stowed the sweets in the freezer and wiped her hands on a dishtowel. "That should tide you over for a couple of days." Her frown returned. "Have you heard from Carter?"

"No. Don't expect to, really. I've no idea where he is, but it's probably on the other side of the world."

"You know he's always wired in."

"Nothing really terrible happened to me. Nothing he can do anything about, anyway, so—"

The kitchen phone rang. For a moment I allowed myself to hope that the planets had aligned and delivered a call from Carter. But it was only the Welbourne concierge announcing a new visitor.

"Who?"

My face fell at his answer. "He wants to come up?"

I disconnected. "My boss is here."

Gertie pursed her lips. "We haven't had time to talk yet."

"It's okay. Go home and take care of Louis. I'm not up to talking anyway."

I walked her to the elevator. We hugged again until the doors slid open.

Jay Patel stepped out of the elevator and Gertie got on. Under different circumstances, I would have introduced them, but I let social graces slide and waved goodbye to my friend as the doors shut.

"Hello, Jay." I took a deep breath and turned back to the apartment.

He followed, explaining his visit to my backside. "Apologies for the intrusion, Samantha. I know you want to rest, but we need to talk before you come in tomorrow."

I led him into the living room and waited while he took in the impressive space. His journalist's gaze fell on the nubby silk sectional, the blond hardwood floor, the posh Persian rug, and the wide balcony with its full view of downtown Houston. I could imagine his thoughts, calculating how I could possibly afford such luxury on my starting salary. "Nice place you have here."

"Thanks." I dropped into a side chair.

He sat on the sofa and seemed to be waiting for me to say more. If I told him the place wasn't mine, I'd have to explain whose it was. Since Carter Chapman had a professional aversion to revealing personal information, I let the topic die.

Despite my temporary pique, I liked Jay Patel. His kind black eyes and soft-spoken demeanor were a welcome relief after the insatiable greed of my former employer. Jay had given me a chance to redeem my reputation from the ashes. I owed him a lot, but it didn't include explaining my current living arrangement. That tale is long enough to fill a novel or two.

I'd never encountered my new boss outside of work, where he ruled with upbeat confidence. Now, he seemed more like a guppy longing for the safety of its own aquarium. "Uh, was that your mother back there?"

"Just a friend." I rotated Mom's ring around my finger, a habit I fall into whenever my nerves are jangled. I caught Patel staring at it and pressed my thumb on it to hold it in place. "If you've come to check on me, I'm okay. Just a little unnerved, is all."

"I would have called, but I was at the hospital to see Sedgwick, and since you live nearby..."

"How is Lloyd?"

Patel blew out some air. "Well, he's lost a lot of blood."

I shuddered.

"Sorry." He lowered his eyes. "Anyway, they're saying he should recover. He made it through surgery, but with the blood loss... It must have been awful for you, too. If you need a mental health day, I'd understand."

"Thanks, but as you can see, I'm okay. Really." I stood.

He remained seated. "One more thing, Samantha. As soon as Sedgwick is strong enough, I'm told that he'll be transferred to a skilled nursing facility for physical therapy. He'll be there for at least a week or two. So, there's the matter of the deadline for the project you two were working on. Which was today."

"Sounds like he'll be able to work on it soon enough. I'll take the work to him while he's healing. If you could give him a few more days..."

"Here's the thing. I want you to wind it up asap. If it's as ready as Sedgwick told me it was last week, there won't be much for you to do."

My boss had no idea how little Lloyd had shared with me about the project. If I told him now, it would sound like I was badmouthing a defenseless and vulnerable colleague.

"I'd rather wait for Lloyd's help."

Patel rose from the sofa. "Tell you what. Get some good rest. We'll talk when you get to the station tomorrow."

Jay Patel's visit left me jittery. I still didn't feel like eating, but my stomach was growling.

I opened the fridge. Despite Gertie's bounty, nothing called to me. I opted for a green drink. After a couple of swigs, I made popcorn, dumped it into a bowl and padded to the bedroom. It was past time for the start of the evening news. I climbed into bed to watch.

Alicia Sultana was on camera again, her face a portrait of concern. I'd missed the opening of the report, but at least I caught the end. "The unidentified shooter is in custody, awaiting charges. No further word on the journalist who was working with Lloyd Sedgwick when the shooting occurred."

She called me a journalist, a description that didn't feel quite right. Not yet anyway. At least she hadn't said my name. I turned off the bedside lamp and scooted down until my head found the pillow.

As soon as I closed my eyes, my phone buzzed with the best kind of interruption. Carter Chapman had emerged from whatever black hole he'd been traveling through.

"Heard you had a rough day."

The concern in his voice brought tears to my eyes. "Kinda."

"Sorry I'm not there."

"I'm okay."

"I'll be heading back to the ranch for the week. Let me pick you up on the way."

Being with Carter in the gently rolling hills of Central Texas would feel better than the trauma counseling Jay Patel offered.

"My boss says I have to finish Lloyd's report asap. It's already past deadline."

"I worry about you."

"Don't. I'll be too busy to get into any trouble."

"What you've been through, it's not easy to put aside. Believe me, I know."

"I'm just a little tired right now. I'll be fine once I get some sleep."

"I hope you're right. Anyway, I'll be there soon. Rest well."

After we said goodnight, I flipped through the television for something mindless to fall asleep to. Everything seemed annoyingly grating. I switched it off. If only I could switch off my brain as easily.

No way I could complete Lloyd's project anytime soon, not when I knew so few details to start with. What could I say to my boss that wouldn't make me sound like a weasel, or a coward, or a quitter?

Beyond the balcony, the downtown skyscrapers glittered against a darkening sky. I lay back and stared at the ceiling, hoping an answer would find me.

CHAPTER SIX

I'm Fine

Pain shot through my shoulder as I rolled over to grab my phone before it buzzed itself off the nightstand. Yesterday's tussle with the pizza kid must have wrenched something out of place. I mumbled a hello.

"You're late. Jay and I are waiting." Maura sounded none too happy.

I struggled to a sitting position and checked the time. Eight-thirty. I'd slept the entire night.

"I uh… ouch!" I switched the phone to my other hand. "Sorry. I'll be there soon as I can."

I braved it and put one foot on the floor, raising my arm to test the shoulder. It barely made it to a three o'clock angle before the pain caught hold.

Except for a moment of agony while pulling a tee over my head, getting dressed was a snap. My business wardrobe had been obliterated by the floodwaters that breached Gertie's house, but since I wasn't on-camera yet, pretty much anything worked at the station. The tee, jeans, and a black blazer, and I was good to go.

I took a moment at the mirror to practice a bullet-proof smile that I hoped would fend off any conversation about yesterday's events, trying for one that said: I'm fine. See how fine I am? No need to ask, okay?

It went a little crooked.

With no time for breakfast, I eyed the left-over green drink and popcorn on the nightstand. Both looked reasonably edible. I carried them with one hand and grabbed my work bag with the other. My shoulder barked all the way to the elevator.

Then it hit me: my car was still where I'd parked it in its assigned slot at the TV station. Normally, Carter's Tesla would be my back-up. But he'd driven it to Serenity Ranch a couple of weeks ago, just before he went dark.

I tapped the RoadSquire app and headed downstairs to wait.

KHTS-TV was a small, independently-owned station and a far cry from the slick network affiliates in town. As our tagline boasted, we put the "local" in local news. Housed in the former home of a defunct community newspaper, its flat, one-story roofline sat just below a canopy of oaks at the commercial edge of an older neighborhood, midway between Greenway Plaza and The Galleria.

Jay and Maura were deep in conversation in his office. He waved me over to join them at his desk. As I set my bag down, I caught the news crawl on a wall monitor: *Investigative journalist Lloyd Sedgwick: slow recovery ahead.*

I fell into a chair and let that sink in while Patel brought me up to speed. "Maura and I are reworking the schedule for Lloyd's report. He's still due to be transferred to a physical therapy facility in a day or two."

Relief poured over me. "Sounds positive. Once he's in rehab, I can take him whatever he needs to finish."

Patel shook his head. "We're already behind schedule. Which is why, as I said last night, I'm charging you with getting the piece ready to air."

"But I... I'm not—"

"I understand your reluctance, Samantha, but for reasons I cannot disclose, this story can't wait. I am confident that you, with Maura's assistance, can bring it home."

I believed that Jay was on my side. After all, he'd hired me when no one else would. But he had no idea how unprepared Lloyd had left me.

"I need more time, Jay. And I want Lloyd's okay before it airs. It's his piece, after all."

Patel's face darkened. "With or without him, I'm counting on you to bring it home. Work with Maura. Get it done."

Lloyd Sedgwick was an old school reporter. I suspected that he'd squirreled away his hand-written notes somewhere. What I hadn't known was that they had already been transcribed to digital, until Maura brought a load of printouts to me, sorted into folders. They would be my first peek at anything of substance.

She commandeered a small conference room for me to work in. Like Lloyd's office, it was windowless, but at least it was roomier and warmer. There was seating for six around an oval table in the center and a storage credenza along one wall. Before leaving to tackle her other duties, Maura set our first meeting for the afternoon. Not enough time to read through everything, but it gave me a couple of hours to begin.

I read myself cross-eyed until she returned.

She asked me to bring her up to speed on where I was so far. I tried to conjure the last iteration of the outline Lloyd had been working on, and threw in a few details I'd gleaned from the printouts. By the time I finished, I realized she'd been testing my command of the subject.

I blushed. "I know there are a few gaping holes. I wish Lloyd had shared more details with me."

She gave me a tight smile. "No worries." Before she left for a meeting, she gave me a list of specific info to gather.

Like diving into a bottomless pool, I held my breath and picked up new folder.

A dozen pages in, my head was pounding. I tried to ignore it and opened my laptop to take notes. That's when something dawned on me.

The material from Maura contained only basic research, which was forcing me to start the report from scratch. But given Lloyd's deadline, he must have had at least a rough draft sketched out. Since I hadn't seen it among the papers from Maura, it could still be on his computer, which I hoped was still in his office. Another peek at that outline on the whiteboard could be helpful, too. Even smeared and incomplete, it could start me in the right direction.

I dreaded being in that room again, but I had to get inside. At least a short walk down the corridor would give me a chance to stretch my legs and work out the soreness in my shoulder.

A familiar voice stopped me before I could round the corner. "Hey, Sammy-am!

It was Jojo, the hair and makeup guy, in his usual raggedy jeans and Ziggy Stardust T-shirt. He was the first person to befriend me at KHTS.

He made a sad face and opened his arms. "Come give us a hug." His bony frame against mine felt good.

He pulled away and gave me the once-over. Clucking like a mother hen, he fussed with my hair, finger-combing it to one side and back again, then tugged at the lapels of my blazer, reset it on my torso, and patted the shoulders in place. Though his touch was light, it triggered fresh pain.

"Are you okay?"

I gave him the new smile. "I'm fine."

He rolled his eyes. "Not buying it, babe. But at least you look less catawampus. Now we need to get that karma readjusted."

"I wish."

"Seriously, one call and it's done." He pulled his phone from his jeans. "My friend is the world's greatest—"

"Thanks, but not now. I have to focus."

"Say when, okay? She's good, believe me." He re-pocketed the phone. "Where are you headed?"

"Lloyd's office. Patel is making me finish his report, and I can't do that until I get to his files."

He waggled a finger at me. "You can't. They put that yellow police tape over it yesterday. Besides, you've been hit by a giant asteroid this week. Give yourself some time."

His phone buzzed. "Oops, Queen Alicia needs me. Ta-ta for now."

While Jojo obeyed Alicia Sultana's summons, I trudged back to my makeshift work space and tried to re-engage with the flood regulations. Minutes later, my concentration failed me again.

Lloyd had toiled over this project for months. Clearly, it was impossible to finish it in a matter of days without him. Maybe, in his weakened state, he could be persuaded to guide me through. I tapped his number to see if he was ready for a visit.

"Who's calling?" A woman's voice.

I was momentarily stunned. He'd never mentioned a wife, and I didn't remember seeing a family photo or a wedding ring. Maybe a sister? A nurse?

"I'm Samantha. Newman. I work with Lloyd at KHTS."

"What do you want?"

"I'm calling to see if he's up for a visit today."

There was a pause before she spoke again. "He can't be bothered with business now."

"I understand. It's just that I was with him when he was shot, and I—"

"You were with him?" Another pause, longer this time. "I see."

She disconnected. But she hadn't said no. I could still go to the hospital and appeal to Lloyd's reasonable side—assuming he had one. Fingers crossed, I'd get his help.

Wait a minute. Who was I kidding? Lloyd would never hand his precious baby over to me. Before I faced another battle with him, I needed to see if his laptop was still on his desk. Jojo said the room had been sealed, but I went to check for myself.

Luckily, no tape barred the door. I took a deep breath and opened it.

The little room had never looked so tidy. Every surface was scrubbed bare, but the whiteboard remained undisturbed, except for Lloyd's angry smear. I snapped a photo of it with my phone. Now, to search for his research notes, grab the computer, and anything else relating to the report.

His laptop wasn't on his desk. Thinking it might be stowed inside along with the rest of his files, I circled around and reached for a drawer. But when my fingers touched the pull, the whole nasty scene exploded to life again: the sobbing kid, the gun, Lloyd, the blood.

I had to get out of there fast, but not before I found what I was looking for. I took a deep breath, yanked a clean trash bag from the wastebasket and opened every drawer. Without taking time to sort through, I dumped the contents of every drawer into the bag and lugged the sack back to my work space.

My heart was beating halfway outside my chest as I dragged the sack across the floor to the conference room. After a few deep breaths, I bent over to peek inside. Masses of markers, highlighters, paper clips and other work rubbish blanketed the top. I dug through layers of junk to reach some papers, folders, and spiral notebooks filled with handwritten notes. One by one, I pulled them out and tossed them onto the table.

My shoulder complained, but I dove in again. This time I excavated fistfuls of ballpoint pens, red pencils, a stapler, a yellow squeeze ball, and a two-inch stack of business cards held together with a rubber band. No laptop, but there was plenty of other material to sort through.

Anything that could be related to the report went into a separate pile. Everything else got dumped back into the trash bag. Time to begin.

I started with the spiral notebooks. By the dates of the entries, they appeared to be Lloyd's original research. I found a blank notebook to make my own notes in, then opened the one of his with the earliest date.

Lloyd's penmanship was nearly indecipherable. Squinting at each word helped a little, but after ten minutes of torture over his bunched-up chicken scratch, I was half blind.

I remembered seeing a candy bar or two among the junk still inside the trash bag. I stuck my head in and raked my hand along the bottom. The candy bar proved elusive, but I did find another folder with loose pages inside. In his tiny script, Lloyd had scribbled *Love Letters* on the tab. A very tempting distraction, but probably a waste of time. I set it aside and dove in again.

Still no laptop, but I did manage to rescue a Snickers bar. Working on a comforting mouthful, I texted Maura and Patel to ask if one of them had Lloyd's computer. Then I went back to work.

By five-thirty, I'd made a little progress. I stowed the folders on the top shelf of the credenza. The half-empty trash sack went in on the bottom. At least I felt somewhat organized.

Maura replied that she didn't have the laptop. It occurred to me that it might have made its way back to Lloyd. Despite his crabby attitude and the surliness of the woman who'd answered his phone, I had to get him to hand it over. I slid a few folders into my work bag and headed to the hospital.

CHAPTER SEVEN

Zigzag

A t the nurses' station on Lloyd's floor, I stopped to ask how things were going with him. They confirmed that he was due to be transferred to a physical therapy facility in a day or two. With that piece of good news, I hoped to find him in a decent mood.

I zigzagged through a chaos of attendants pushing dinner carts and medical machines to get to his room, then took a moment to quiet my nerves before I knocked.

No one answered, but I could hear the TV through the door. I knocked louder.

No reply. I pushed the door open a crack and called out. "Lloyd?"

Nothing. I opened the door a crack wider. The bed was empty. On the other side of it, I saw two bare feet splayed at odd angles on the floor. Unless I'd interrupted a yoga session, something was off.

I tiptoed in. The feet belonged to a pair of stocky legs carpeted in curly hair. I took a step closer. His face was turned away, but by his shape, it was definitely Lloyd on the floor. Bed linens covered his stocky torso, like he'd fallen out of bed and taken them with him. I spoke loud enough to rouse him. "Lloyd, are you okay?"

Still no response. The back of my neck prickled.

I sped out to the hall and yelled for help. A nurse and an aide left what they were doing and rushed over. They checked his pulse, wrestled his limp body up and onto the bed, then shooed me out of the room.

I waited in the busy corridor while a steady stream of technicians wheeled monitors and machines in and out. The nurse came out and asked me how Lloyd came to be on the floor. Once I explained that he was like that when I walked in, and no, I wasn't family, everyone pretty much ignored me.

A doctor arrived and everything got quiet. A few minutes later, people started to file out, pushing past me with their equipment. One of them stopped long enough to say they would be moving Lloyd to ICU for more testing. No way to see him after that.

The adrenaline I'd mustered on the way to the hospital had vanished. Bone tired, I drifted back through the maze of elevators and hallways to the parking garage, found the Ferret, and headed into the night.

Moving back into Carter's high-rise condo had forced me to face two issues. The first problem was accepting his offer of free rent for a second time. I also had to renegotiate a truce between my fear of heights and the lofty view from thirteen floors up. But given the past couple of days, the place was starting to feel like a refuge.

I dropped my work bag in the kitchen and slumped down the hall, stripping off my clothes as I went. A good long shower and bed were tops on my wish list. I was down to bra and panties when I heard a man's voice coming from the bedroom.

Carter?

I peeked in. He was pacing along the balcony doors and speaking to someone on his phone. When he saw my state of undress, he did a double-take.

Clasping my jacket to my nearly naked body, I waved.

He turned away and spoke into his phone. "Hey, buddy, something's come up that needs my immediate attention. Call you later." He tossed the phone onto the bed and wrapped me in his arms.

And just like that, the ills of my world fell away. Despite our occasional disagreements and separations, that's how it's been from the first time we touched, almost two years ago.

We clung tight, breathing each other in, until I felt a tug on the blazer that was still sandwiched between us. His breath tickled my ear. "Can we get rid of this?"

I dropped the jacket and collapsed into him.

He caught me and held me to him. "Whoa there. Are you all right?"

Question of the week. "Just another really bad day. I was heading for the shower to wash it down the drain."

"Okay if I help?"

"Help?"

"If you recall, I washed a bag's worth of potato chips and who knows what else off you the last time you had a bad day."

The memory floated in. Me, unconscious on the balcony where he'd found me, after an ill-fated ice cream pity party. Then, me, under the steady patter of water, and Carter, tenderly washing my hair, soaping my body, literally showering me with love.

I smiled, remembering. It was an offer I couldn't refuse.

I stood under the warm spray while he poured a dab of shampoo on his hands and swept it onto my head, massaging all around until my hair was full of lather. Then he moved it to the side and gently rubbed my neck. His touch was so silky I almost swooned.

He rinsed my hair and began soaping my body nose to toes with a luscious milk-and-honey scented bar, gently kneading the sorest places as he went. I doubt Cleopatra's famous baths were more luxurious.

I reached for the soap to reciprocate, but he stopped me. Taking my face in his hands, he shook his head. "This one's all for you."

"But—"

He put a finger to my lips. "Grab a towel. I'll be out in a sec."

Carter found a clean shirt and khakis in the closet. I pulled on a tee and shorts, and we ambled into the kitchen to forage for food.

He opened the fridge. "You cooked?"

My lack of culinary skills was a running joke between us. Obviously, he recognized the signs of Gertie's bounty. He retrieved the roasted chicken and a brick of cave-aged cheddar and set them on the kitchen island. We ate like hungry dogs.

Carter rose to clear the dishes. "We should talk about the shooting."

Poof! went our perfectly lovely evening. "I'm sure you've seen the reports."

"Your take is what matters to me."

"Maybe tomorrow."

"Let's start tonight. I need to know that you're okay."

As I spun out the sad tale from the beginning, the whole thing felt oddly distant, as if I were reporting from a drone hovering over the scene. I ended the story where Maura sprang me from jail. "That's pretty much it."

Carter put his arms around me. "I'm sorry I wasn't here for you."

"You're here now. That's enough."

"Is it?" He gave me a funny look, as if he expected an answer. "I never feel good about leaving you, Sam."

"I'll try to be less lovable next time." I dug into in the freezer for Gertie's home-baked treats and lightly nuked a selection. "Goodies, if you want some. Or we could save them for breakfast."

He pinned me with his irresistible amber eyes and reached for my hand.

I knew that maneuver. "You're leaving tonight?"

From the time of his first vanishing act, every part of me wished he wouldn't go, but I never wanted him to feel guilty about it. The cyber work he did for corporate and government entities was critical, urgent, and mostly classified. I didn't have to like it, but I understood.

"It isn't for a client," he said. "First thing tomorrow, they're coming to survey a couple of locations for a small bridge across the creek that will give us faster access from the ranch to the new therapy retreat for troubled families. There's a history of indigenous artifacts along the banks in that area, so we have to be careful not to disturb anything important. Besides, you said you were too busy to play with me. You were kinda wrong about that." He kissed my forehead. "I don't have to go yet, if you want to play some more."

I fell into bed as soon as Carter left. During the night, I dreamed I was with him at his ranch, riding full canter atop Hollywood, the honey palomino, toward the bluff that overlooked the creek and the site of the new retreat on the other side. Tall prairie grasses undulated like ocean waves all around Carter as he rode ahead astride Remington, his chestnut Appaloosa. He was waiting for me at the top of the rise, and as I caught up to him... my phone buzzed with a text from Jay Patel.

For a confusing moment, I was caught between sunny Serenity and the dark bedroom. When the dream dissolved, I read the message:

Need u here asap

CHAPTER EIGHT

Glazed

It was still dark outside when I dragged into Jay Patel's office. He and Maura were waiting for me, again. I tossed my bag onto the loveseat and slumped into the chair next to Maura. Patel poured coffee and scooted a mug to me. His suit looked like he'd slept in it.

Mercifully, there were doughnuts. Maura's contribution, no doubt. I tried to read Patel's face, but got nothing. Maura reached for a glazed goodie and nibbled at it. The three of us were locked in an awkward silence.

Patel started to speak, then stopped, like he didn't know how to begin. He started over slowly, as if each syllable was painful to pronounce. "I can't begin to fathom this on a personal level, but we have to absorb it somehow and keep going."

His dark, bloodshot eyes found Maura's, then mine. "I called the hospital this morning to check on Lloyd, and…" He shook his head, unable to continue.

Maura's eyes filled. "He's not…"

"He's hanging in there, but…" His voice went ragged. "Apparently, he stopped breathing last night. His heart and brain functions could be compromised."

I choked down a wad of doughnut.

Patel turned to me. "We'll all be working under a lot of strain, I know, but we have to fight on. That report is all yours now, Samantha. I want to air it next week. Don't let me down."

Maura paled and straightened her glasses. She knew how unprepared I was, but she remained silent.

Before he let us go, Patel instructed her to prepare a tribute to Lloyd's body of work, "Just in case."

Stoic as ever, she pulled a tissue from her pocket and dabbed her eyes. "What should we say about his current condition?"

He hung his head and massaged his temples. "I don't know."

"But what if—"

He shot up, his dark eyes blazing. "Figure it out, for Pete's sake. Do your fricking job!"

Maura's face turned beet-red. She exited without a word.

I slunk back to my work space, hoping Lloyd's condition wasn't as dire as Patel had made it seem.

In my high-powered executive days, I was a whiz at making complex employment statistics understandable for the layman. But the dynamics of flood control were foreign to me, and Lloyd's research was labyrinthine. To bring it all home in a matter of days seemed impossible.

After hours of wrangling with an infinity of flood factoids, I found myself staring at the same piece of paper for who knows how long without comprehending a word. I gave up. Might as well have some lunch.

Patel had ordered an extravagant lunch buffet from Kenny & Ziggy's deli: roast beef, turkey, and pastrami, three kinds of sliced cheese, rye, wheat and pumpernickel breads, slaw, pickles and condiments for making sandwiches. Plus an array of Dr. Brown's sodas and desserts: rugelah, cookies, and cheesecake.

The usual lunchtime hubbub was subdued. People huddled over their meals. I made a half-sandwich of pastrami on rye, grabbed some condiments, a cream soda, and an apricot rugelah and headed back to my work space to eat in peace. I almost crashed into Patel as he was exiting my room.

He looked as startled as I was. "I was just... I, uh, I came to see you, but you were—"

"Getting lunch. Thanks for the deli, by the way. What's up?"

"Well, for starters, I, uh, just wanted to say how much I appreciate your hanging in there. I'm sorry if I've been pushing you too hard."

This was my chance to explain the predicament Lloyd had put me in. Whatever was driving Patel to rush Lloyd's report, it didn't seem wise to leave the entire job to a newbie like me.

I set my lunch on the table. "As a matter of fact, Jay, we need to talk."

He looked at his watch. "Great. Let's do it next week when you hand in the report. I have a meeting downtown in twenty minutes and a two-day conference tomorrow. See you Monday." And with that, he was gone.

Monday? I needed to scream, or hit something, or both. I shoved a stack of folders off the table and watched as they sailed across the room, their newly freed pages floating to the floor.

That felt somewhat satisfying, so I gathered the pens and markers and flung them, one by one, hard against the wall. That was even better, so I swiped at the rest of the papers. They flew up and formed a blanket over the entire chaotic jumble.

Breathing hard, I paused to contemplate the mess before an urge to break something, anything, came over me again. I briefly considered the potential impact my deli lunch might have if I smashed it against the wall, but then I remembered the trash bag that still contained a good amount the rubbish from Lloyd's desk. I yanked it from the bottom of the credenza, grabbed fistfuls of the junk, and rained all of it down over the rest.

I was out of ammunition, but fury still held me in its grip. I lunged for the door and ran to catch Patel before he made it out of the parking lot, ready to spew a heap of wrath at him.

By the time I got outside, he was speeding away in his cherry red Porsche.

The double doors banged open as I burst into the lobby again. Momentum propelled me straight into the reception desk. On duty this afternoon, Donna Sue Bisbee, a part-time receptionist, gasped. I murmured an apology and sulked back to my work space.

Jojo was standing in the doorway, gaping at the aftermath of my little tantrum. I joined him to survey the scene. Somehow, the glorious field of destruction hit my funny bone. I started cackling hysterically.

Jojo yanked me inside and shut the door.

"Ouch!" I rubbed my shoulder.

"I had to shush you before somebody calls the psycho squad."

He started to pick up the mess. I tore a folder from his hand and threw it across the room. "I don't need help. I just need..." My mind went blank.

He eyed me for a second, then pulled his phone from his jeans and tapped a number. "Hey Cass, whatcha doin' this evening? A friend is in dire need of a karma adjustment. Say around five-thirty?"

I shot him a scowl and a thumbs down.

He waved me off. "Great. I'll text the info." He disconnected.

"I don't have time for anything extracurricular."

"Sure you do. Medical emergency."

"Is she a doctor?"

"A healer. Same thing, only better. Now let's clean up this mess."

"I'll do it myself."

He scanned the destruction and raised an eyebrow. "You sure?"

"I'm fine. Really." To prove how fine I was, I calmly gathered the highlighters and neatly aligned them by color on the table. Then I gave him the smile.

"Sorry, hon, not buying it. Holler if you need me."

Alone again, I looked over the mess. It was a masterpiece of chaos, a perfect portrayal of how I felt. I considered walking out and shutting the door behind me. Then curiosity took hold. It was possible that something important still lay among the junk.

I picked through the pile carefully, examining each item before tossing it. My shoulder sparked fire.

Toward the center of the heap, my eye caught on a pocket-size voice recorder that Lloyd likely used for interviews. It wasn't his laptop, but it could be useful. I stashed it inside my work bag along with the rubber-banded stack of business cards.

The *Love Letters* folder had fallen intact. I set it aside and gathered up the rest of the scattered pages to return to their rightful folders. What remained on the floor went back into the trash bag. Order had been restored, more or less.

I was suddenly famished. Good thing I hadn't messed with my plate of deli goodies. I popped open the can of cream soda and took a swig, then slathered the contents of a mustard packet on the bread, added the pickles, and chomped down. Heaven.

As I ate, I reviewed the situation. My work bag was full of potential, but Lloyd's laptop still hadn't surfaced. Maura said she didn't have it. Patel hadn't responded to my text, and I'd missed my chance to ask him in person. I texted him about it again. If it wasn't with him, my guess was that someone might have delivered it to Lloyd at the hospital.

I fretted over whether to call Lloyd's phone again. Instead, I sent a message saying how sorry I was for his setback and asking about the laptop.

The reply was instantaneous. STOP, it read, as if I were some random spammer. I was beginning to think Lloyd's report was cursed, and me along with it.

I was stewing over what to do next when an intern came to the door to say I was needed in the broadcast studio. I took a quick swig of cream soda and followed him there.

Studio lights were focused on the small conversation pit where most sit-down interviews were staged. Maura and a handful of staff members stood outside the pool of light.

In a burgundy silk jacket and black leather pencil skirt, Alicia Sultana occupied one of the two upholstered armchairs on the set. Her lips moved as she studied the screen on her tablet. Brad Hudson, who rode the anchor desk with Alicia, was vacating the chair opposite her. His high forehead glistened with perspiration.

Brad was the same vintage as the regal Alicia Sultana. Far as I knew, he had always played second fiddle to her at KHTS, but he seemed comfortable there. His basso-profondo voice and silver fox good looks lent authority to everything he read. Word had it that thousands of stay-at home-housewives of a certain age tuned in regularly to listen to his operatic delivery and gawk at his manly features.

Maura motioned to me. "Your turn for the tribute to Lloyd." She pointed to the empty chair opposite Alicia.

"Me? On camera? Now?"

Maura slid her glasses up to her forehead and massaged the bridge of her nose. "Alicia will lead you through a few questions about what it's like to work with Lloyd."

Oh no. "I'm not dressed for it."

"You're a working journalist. Sloppy works. Just sit and say something nice."

Before I could find a better excuse, Jojo emerged from the darkness. "Let's check you under the lights." He walked me to the chair. As he smoothed my skin tone with his magic powders, he offered advice under his breath. "Just pretend you're talking about a friend. Make something up, if you have to. It'll be over quicker than a root canal."

Bless him for making me smile. I nodded to Alicia and sat. She nodded back. A pinched expression crossed her usually immobile features. I didn't know how she felt about Lloyd, but it seemed like our tête à tête would be tough on both of us, perhaps for similar reasons.

Alicia opened with a doozy. "Coming from outside the television world, what has it been like to work with Lloyd Sedgwick?"

It took some mental gymnastics on my part to form an acceptable reply. "Like I'm back in high school again."

Alicia forced a laugh. "And what have you learned from him so far?"

Uh, nothing? A second later I found an answer. "The importance of research."

"You were with him the night of the shooting. Can you tell us a little about it?"

I froze.

Ever the pro, Alicia took over. "I know it must have been frightening, but I'm sure our viewers would be interested in your eye-witness account."

Every time the scene replayed in my mind, my chest tightened, and this was no exception. I cleared my throat. "Rough. It was... rough."

She waited for more. Somehow, I hit on an audience pleaser. "He was brave."

Alicia smiled. "And that was the last time you saw him?"

Uh-oh. No way I'd answer that. "I wanted to visit him in the hospital, but his wife said it wasn't a good idea."

A low gasp came from somewhere off camera. Alicia sat up and leaned toward me, her eyes narrow and glittering in the lights. "His wife?"

"Well, I called his phone to ask if it was okay to visit, and a woman answered. She seemed very protective of him, so I just assumed it was someone close to him. I suppose it could have been a nurse."

After the interview, I stopped at the staff kitchen for fresh coffee. A few employees were in there, taking a break, too.

While I was busy with the coffee, someone at the table spoke up. "It's disgusting how everybody's talking so nice about that rat."

"Yeah, and he's not even dead yet," another voice chimed in.

"I heard he's got a hit list on people he doesn't like."

"Too bad the pizza kid missed."

I made a hasty exit.

It was almost five, and I had to be at the condo in half an hour to meet Jojo's "healer" friend. I stuck a few files in my work bag and moved the rest of the stack inside the credenza. The *Love Letters* folder was still on the table. I tucked it into the bag, too, and grabbed my keys.

CHAPTER NINE

Cassandra

W hatever I expected to see when I opened the door to greet Jojo's friend Cassandra, it did not include the tiny furry creature perched atop her head. At first, I thought it was a squirrel, but it was small as a mouse, and way more adorable, with pale gray, velvety fur and big round shiny black eyes that took up half its face. Its wide-set ears swiveled my way. So cute, it made me laugh.

At the sound of my voice, the little thing scrambled down the back of her neck and poked his face out from under her earlobe. She tilted her head to give me a better view. "This is Apollo. He's harmless, I promise. Hope you don't mind."

I led her into the living room. As she scanned the space, I had my first good look at her. A gauzy flowered sundress hung loose on her petite frame and grazed the tops of her hiking sandals. Caramel skin. Freckles. Frizzy hair, parted down the middle, almost colorless at the temples, darkening to russet toward the tips of two long French braids that rested on her collarbone.

She turned toward the balcony and studied the skyline beyond. "Nice view, but is there somewhere more intimate, with fewer distractions?"

I mentally rewound. I hadn't made the bed this morning, and it was almost certain I'd left a small popcorn trail in my haste to get to work. Also, I was pretty sure that yesterday's clothes hadn't made it to the dirty laundry hamper yet.

The library was an oak-paneled room next to the entry. Its built-in bookshelves, brimming with books and old LPs, spanned the walls, offering a comfortable cocoon-like vibe. I led her there.

She dropped her paisley hobo sack beside the chess table and tapped her phone. An ethereal flute melody, punctuated by ocean waves, whale song, and occasional metallic tings filled the air. I winced as she tugged the reluctant Apollo from the braid he was clinging to and stuffed him into a pocket in her skirt.

"Don't worry," she said. "Apollo is a sugar glider. They're super-chill, but our world is a big stressor for them. He should be flying through the branches in a rainforest with his buddies. For now, taking naps in warm places helps him stay centered."

She gave her pocket a gentle pat. "Please sit wherever you're comfortable."

I chose the buttery-soft suede cloth sofa. Cassandra took a chair from the chess table and sat facing me. Her steady, direct gaze made me a little antsy, especially when her eyes fell on Mom's ring.

I stopped myself from spinning it. "Bad habit. Sorry."

"Tell me about the ring. Is it old?"

"It was my mother's."

"Nice." She resettled herself in the chair. "Jojo mentioned that you're in some distress."

"The week's been a nightmare, but I'm fine, really." I flashed the new smile.

"What about your shoulder?"

My hand flew to the problem joint. "Well, yes. Didn't Jojo tell you about it?"

"No, but I felt..." She tapped her own shoulder. "Let's back up a minute. Did Jojo explain how I work?"

"Not really."

A tiny furrow appeared across her forehead. "I'm often able to sense another person's pain. And sometimes I'm able help resolve their discomfort without traditional medical intervention. If you're willing, we can explore that possibility."

I suspected I was in for an onslaught of hocus pocus. I reminded myself that Cassandra was Jojo's friend. I had to be nice. "Okay."

She closed her eyes, took a deep breath, and focused on me again. "Jojo said your colleague suffered a gunshot. Where was he wounded?"

"In the shoul... In the sho—" I could not complete the sentence. "Look, a gun was fired. I wrestled with a kid for it. I probably hurt myself then."

"Perhaps. But could we stay open to another possibility?"

"Which is?"

"Pain can also arise from sympathy over witnessing the suffering of others. Or emotional trauma. Or guilt."

"Like survivor's guilt?" I rubbed at the ache. "I thought you were supposed to make me feel better."

"To help you heal, you may have to endure a bit more discomfort, until we discover its true source. Let's do some breathing to start."

She demonstrated how I was supposed to breathe: exhaling through the mouth, then allowing new air to naturally filter through my nose down to my lungs.

I managed to produce a couple of shallow sucks. "I don't think this is going to work."

Her pocket changed shape as the napping Apollo shifted inside, but she didn't budge. "Pain is part of being human. It can lead us to discover new truths about ourselves, if we're willing to explore the possibilities. The hardest part is to begin."

Something about the music and her mellow demeanor kept me on the sofa. "Okay, I'll give it a try."

She asked me to close my eyes. "Discomfort can manifest itself through different modes. I'd like you to concentrate on the color of your pain. And then, what it tastes like, if you can."

Cue the hocus pocus. Just to humor her, I shut my eyes and tried. Darned if I didn't begin to see a blurry red blob appear behind my lids as the taste of salt and copper filled my mouth. Freaky. I opened my eyes and left the chair.

"Something came?"

"Kind of, but this really feels like torture."

"Let's try again, only this time we'll go for something soothing."

Reluctantly, I returned to the sofa. She led me through another round of breathing, and I did better with it.

She shifted in her chair. "Good. Now this time, try to visualize a place where you've felt most at ease, past or present. See it, smell it, feel it. Put yourself there as you breathe."

Eyes shut, I searched for a place, any place where I remembered feeling calm. What came to me was our kitchen back home. All of us—Mom, Dad, my little brother and me—were pitching in to get dinner on the table. But that scene quickly morphed into the last time I saw that room, all ash and destruction.

My eyes flew open. "I can't."

"If your thoughts become too uncomfortable, return to your breathing, then try again," Cassandra urged.

Eyes closed, I searched for a better place. This time, I landed at Serenity. I was riding Hollywood, the palomino, catching up with Carter at a bluff overlooking the creek. He plucked a leaf from a low bough of an old sweetgum tree, crinkled it in his hands, and gave it to me to breathe in its earthy green fragrance. Sunlight peeked through the branches, and I could feel the heat rising from the horse's neck. Somewhere above, a mockingbird advertised its musical repertoire.

I could have stayed there forever, but the connection faded. I opened my eyes.

Cassandra smiled as she studied me. "You found it." She started packing up. "You learned that exercise quickly. Practice it. Go back to that place whenever you're feeling anxious. Let it resonate and settle in."

She checked on Apollo, still snoozing in her pocket. "Apollo and I are going to Axelrad for some gentle socializing with friends this evening before we retreat from the city. Why don't you come? It's only a few blocks away, full of music and positive energy, and we can walk from here. I think it might help you relax."

I weighed the prospect of confronting Lloyd and his harridan of a gatekeeper at the hospital against accepting Cassandra's offer. There was no denying that she and her little buddy had lowered my stress level a notch or two, despite my resistance. It would be nice to hold onto the feeling a little longer.

I figured I could always stop at the hospital and see Lloyd on the way to work in the morning.

CHAPTER TEN

Jazz Night

I'd never been to Axelrad, a popular beer garden and music venue just south of downtown. But from the balcony at the condo, if the breeze was just right, I could sometimes catch faint samplings of live music coming from their outdoor stage.

The sun was easing toward the horizon as Cassandra and I walked the backstreets to avoid the hubbub of rush hour traffic on Alameda Road. She hummed a tune I didn't recognize while Apollo rested quietly inside her pocket. I was grateful for the absence of conversation.

After a few blocks, she pointed ahead to a two-story brick structure on the corner. From a distance, it looked to be just another old house within the original 1837 boundaries of Houston's Third Ward. But thanks to the keen eyes and generous hearts of its current owners, the old Axelrad place was no longer among the dead and dying. Far from it.

Beyond the front door that once had welcomed neighbors to a small grocery on the ground floor, the reimagined house was hopping. At the bar, thirsty patrons queued up three- and four-deep to order from a copious list of craft beers and specialty drinks. Barkeeps danced around each other behind the bar, taking orders and drawing brews from the carved wooden folk-art characters that adorned the taps.

The tables inside were filling fast. In shorts and jeans, half the crowd looked like neighborhood regulars. Others were clearly downtown professionals just off work: men with shirtsleeves rolled and women in pencil skirts and heels.

Cassandra led me toward the back door. "We can get something to drink after I find Denny."

She pushed the door open, revealing acres of beer garden. At the far end, a bandstand backed up to the rear wall of a neighboring pizzeria. For Axelrad patrons, the wall served as a movie screen. At the moment, old-timey cartoons were playing on it.

Toward the left edge of the yard, a joyous whoop rose from a small crowd gathered around a beanbag toss. To our right, low-slung hammocks were occupied by chilled-out humans swaying in the lingering sunlight.

At a scattering of picnic tables, patrons shared a variety of food from nearby vendors: pizza, pasta, tacos, curry, crepes, pho—a culinary mishmash that mirrored the ethnicities of the clientele. Assorted ages, social classes, and backgrounds intermingled in a microcosm of the city itself. Cassandra was right about the positive vibe.

Cassandra waved to a lanky guy with stringy blond hair near the stage. He abandoned the soundboard he'd been fiddling with and headed toward us. She beamed. "Samantha, this is my partner, Denny. He's on keyboards tonight."

Denny's open smile revealed a jumble of teeth. He tucked a wayward strand of hair behind his ear and extended a hand. "Nice to meet you."

At the sound of his voice, Apollo roused and scampered up Cassandra's torso. Then he spread his appendages, launched himself, and paraglided onto Denny's neck.

Denny laughed and bent his head toward Apollo in a hug. "Want to sit in with the band, buddy?"

As if he understood the invitation, Apollo climbed up past Denny's ear, stretched his gliding membranes and flattened himself astride the musician's bald spot. Clinging to a few strands of Denny's hair on either side, the curious creature seemed quite happy to be there.

Denny kissed Cassandra on the cheek and headed back to the outdoor stage.

Cassandra looked radiant as she watched them retreat. "Denny's a music teacher by day, jazz guy by night. He's great with Apollo."

It was Jazz Night, and as the sun began its final swoon, the band assembled onstage. A lone tree in the center of the yard came alive with colorful neon branches, morphing the open area into a magical nighttime playground. We bought drinks and food at a food truck near the parking lot, then found seats at a table across from a family of four. The kids were eating chocolate/banana crepes and playing with Lincoln Logs.

I felt a tap on the back. "Can I squeeze my tush in here?" Jojo asked.

He wiggled onto the bench between Cassandra and me and scooped a chip full of guacamole from my plate. "Mmm... I need a brew. Be right back."

Just as the band started up, my phone vibrated with a message from Jay Patel. I took a peek.

Suddenly, a horrifying shriek rose above the band's opening notes and reverberated through the crowd. "No! No! No!"

It had come from me.

The family at our table stopped eating. The band quit playing. A hundred eyes turned in my direction as I tried to fully grasp what I'd read.

Everyone was staring at me. I hid my face in my hands. My heart pounded in my ears.

Jojo was back. "Sammy, what's wrong?"

I showed him the message:

Sedgwick dead.

Jojo walked me back to The Wellbourne, both of us lost for words. He came upstairs with me and made tea. Cupping our warm mugs, we sat at the breakfast island, deep in our own thoughts.

After a while, something on the countertop caught Jojo's attention. "Is that what I think it is?" He pointed to a small Mason jar sitting next to the pantry. He picked it up and set it between us. Inside was a cream-colored candle. "Looks like ones that Cassandra makes."

He closed his eyes and sniffed. "Mmm... definitely hers. The scent is divine. Calming, too. She must've left it for you, lucky girl." He pulled a Zippo from his jeans, lit the candle, and turned off the lights. "Nice, huh?"

When Jojo left, I slumped toward the bedroom with the candle in my hand and set it on the nightstand. Its scent bore soothing hints of sweetgum leaves, earth and wild grasses, like a warm breeze at Carter's Serenity Ranch.

But as I slid under the covers, my mind returned to Lloyd. If I'd never reached for the gun, would he still be alive?

CHAPTER ELEVEN

Password

After a sleepless night, I dragged in to the KHTS lobby. My work bag felt like a fifty-pound medicine ball. Soon as I got to my work space, I set it down and worked my fingers open and shut to get the blood circulating before emptying everything out on the table.

I had to stop hoping that Lloyd's computer would miraculously appear and start cobbling my own report together. Working non-stop from now through the weekend, maybe I could have something serviceable by Monday.

Before I got started, a sizeable dose of panic threatened to stop me cold. I headed to the break room for coffee.

Brad Hudson was at a table, hunched behind a newspaper copy of the *Houston Chronicle*. He mumbled a greeting from behind the business section. I didn't feel much like talking either.

My phone pinged with a text from Maura, asking to meet asap.

When I got back, she was already there, leaning against the door frame and sobbing uncontrollably. She didn't notice me until she paused to wipe her wet cheeks.

"Gah!" She fell back against the door and grabbed her chest. "Thanks for letting me know you were here!"

"Sorry. Didn't mean to scare you."

She patted her damp face. "My fault. I let myself go for a minute there."

"I'm sure we're all feeling it. You especially, having worked so closely with Lloyd for so long."

She gave me a strange look.

Had I said something wrong, or was she about to lose control again? "Can I get you something? Coffee?"

"If I drink any more this morning, I'll float to Galveston." She snuffled into the tissue. "Let's just dig in."

I opened my laptop and showed her the beginnings of the work I'd started. She glanced at it without comment, then picked up a folder from the table and opened it. At the sight of Lloyd's handwriting, she slumped into a chair and started crying again.

Her phone chimed, interrupting the tears. She sat up and glanced at the screen. "Drat. Gotta go." She dropped the folder on the table and pointed to the laptop screen. "It needs more meat."

More meat? "Look, Lloyd's research was encyclopedic. I am absolutely drowning in flood factoids. To turn them into something coherent by Monday seems impossible, especially when I can't get my hands on his computer."

Maura's face scrunched up, and she started sobbing again. Eventually, she pulled herself together and left.

For the rest of the morning and most of the afternoon, I worked to gather "more meat" from the seemingly infinite puzzle pieces: state and local water management rules, and residential construction regulations, developers' landscaping and drainage schematics, mandated insurance company coverage and their policies and responses to flood claims, and numberless other moving parts. Sorting them out seemed nearly impossible. Maybe that had been Lloyd's problem, too.

I vaguely remembered leaving one last candy bar inside the trash bag. As I reached into the credenza, my hand grazed something hard and metallic. Something that wasn't in there before. I peered in for a closer look.

There, on top of the trash bag, sat a laptop with Clark Kent and Superman decals pasted over every inch of it. It was unmistakably Lloyd's.

I wobbled to the floor, my eyes glued to the elusive object as a cyclorama of questions whirled in my brain. Where had it been? Who put it in there? And why did it show up in my credenza?

Voices in the hall snapped me to attention. I stood up so fast I nearly blacked out. When the voices faded, I seized the laptop, rushed it to the table, and shut the door to the room. After a couple of Cassandra-style deep breaths, I booted it up.

Password. Of course there was.

I ran my fingers through dozens of combinations of *lloyd sedgwick* and got zilch. I added the station's call letters and ran through a dozen more possibilities. I tried every permutation I could think of, even *open sesame*.

Nothing worked. I slammed the lid down on the infernal machine and glared at it. A half-dozen Clark Kents glared back.

My phone buzzed, ending the staredown. It was Carter. "Tough news about Sedgwick. You okay?"

"I would be, if it weren't for a giant asteroid that keeps messing with me."

"A what?"

"Just quoting a friend. But honestly, it's beginning to feel that way. Lloyd is dead, and Jay Patel is gone for the rest of the week. I thought maybe Jay would change plans and come back today, but he's still a no-show. I don't know what I'm doing, and I'm so upset I can't see two feet in front of me. I feel like a failure."

"What if you packed up everything and brought it to Serenity?"

"I can't. I just found Lloyd's computer, which might solve everything, if I can figure out his password."

"We're pretty good with that kind of thing around here. It's a laptop, isn't it? Bring it with you."

"Except I should probably stay here in case Patel shows up."

After we disconnected, I returned to the trash bag for the candy. With a mouthful of Snickers to fuel me, I was ready for another go at Lloyd's password. The superheroes glared at me. I glared back. And then I had an idea.

I tore off another bite of Snickers and reopened the laptop. After a silent prayer to the gods of all things digital, I typed in *clarkkent*.

I was in! My pulse kicked up a notch as dozens of icons popped onto the screen.

I opened one titled *Lexluthor* and watched it blossom into another dizzying catalog of documents. I clicked on a few of them to make sure I was on the right track, then started scrolling, only to discover they were exact duplicates of the printouts Maura had given me.

For the entire rest of the day, I examined the other items in the document files, and still found nothing even remotely resembling a report.

I shut the laptop and pushed it away. With a dull thud, it bumped against Lloyd's voice recorder, which suddenly started playing in the middle of an interview. The room filled with Lloyd's raspy tenor. "...and yet you claim you were unaware of the problem before the storm hit?"

His voice stopped my heart and sent me time-traveling back to our last all-nighter together before the pizza delivery, when the biggest problem at hand was his looming deadline. Hearing him speak now gave me chills. I killed the volume and turned the recorder off.

With the laptop looking like a dead end, I was beyond weary and sick of the whole project. Instead of discovering more "meat" for Maura, I struck dry bones.

And yet, I couldn't give up. For Gertie and the thousands of others who had lost their homes. For the sake of my job. And for Lloyd.

Even though he had been awful to me, I felt genuine grief for him. Selfish as he was, he had done some good his life: saved an old cemetery, called out public schools for mold, exposed fraud wherever he found it. His life meant something to people who never met him. Given time, maybe we could have found common ground.

Or not. I was still angry at him for being such a jerk, which made me feel like a jerk, too.

It was still light when I got to the condo. I dropped my work bag in the kitchen and slogged to the bedroom to peel off my clothes. A quick shower was a must, then food, and another attempt to cobble together some semblance of a report.

The fridge offered up the left over roast chicken from Carter's visit, and the rest of the bottle of white we'd opened. I considered skipping the wine in favor of a cranberry soda, but my jangled nerves voted for wine.

One glassful left only an ounce or so in the bottle. I drank a little down, then topped off the glass and set it on the island. While I ate and drank, I contemplated a plan of attack for organizing the material.

By the time I returned to the laptop, it was clear that the wine had been a bad decision. Instead of finding a path through the maze of material, I was even more lost than before.

Tomorrow, I promised myself. Tomorrow would be the day I'd get it done.

CHAPTER TWELVE

Blast from the Past

I arrived at the station early Friday morning and had just finished laying my work out on the table when Donna Sue buzzed me from the reception desk.

"This caller says he's a police detective, but he won't give me his name. Okay to put him through?"

Expecting it to be Jeb Hanks, the blue-eyed detective who had offered me a ride home from jail the day of the shooting, I took the call.

Unfortunately, it was different voice from the past.

"Ms. Newman, this is HPD Detective Buron Washington. I called to speak with Jay Patel, but apparently he isn't available. Since you and I share some history, I thought I'd chat with you."

Chat? Last year, the relentless and tenacious detective had been lead investigator in the murder of my next door neighbor. Right out of the box, he'd put my name on his list of suspects. Only after I helped him unravel the truth of that case, did our relationship improve to a wary kind of trust. Still, I never thought our paths would cross again.

"Is this is about the shooting? I thought Detective Hanks was on the case."

"He doesn't work homicide."

Homicide? A chill ran down my neck. "Please don't tell me you're charging that poor little pizza kid with—"

"This is not about the shooting."

Not the shooting? "I don't understand."

"I'm sorry to say that while your colleague was recovering in the hospital, it appears that he was murdered by a person or persons unknown."

Murder. An ugly word. So is gob-smacked, which was the best way to describe me at the moment. The sight of Lloyd crumpled on the floor returned, sending a swarm of emotions through me. My mind went blank.

"Do you need a moment?"

"I'm okay."

"How well did you know Mr. Sedgwick?"

"He was supposed to be training me for my new job here."

"Which is?"

"Well, Lloyd is... was... an investigative reporter, and Jay Patel wanted me to learn from him."

"Interesting. What about your personal relationship?"

"Personal?"

"How well did you get along?"

Oh boy. "Lloyd was kind of prickly. I don't think he got along with anyone particularly well. What makes you think he was murdered?"

"This discussion should continue in person, after Mr. Patel returns my call."

"I'll make sure he does." I disconnected fast.

Hearing Buron Washington pronounce the word *murder* again sent me into overdrive. I bolted to the restroom and stared into the mirror, with all kinds of disturbing thoughts bouncing around in my brain. It took a while for my pulse rate to dip closer to normal.

Back in my workspace, I booted up Lloyd's laptop and forced myself to focus on the flood report. I was double-checking his *Documents* folder when I heard a gasp.

Maura was in the doorway. She pointed to Lloyd's computer. "You found it?"

"For all the good it does. Everything I've seen so far is identical to the material you gave me. I haven't gotten to any more meat yet."

Her face tightened. She strode to the table. "Well, since you don't need it, I'll take it off your hands."

I pulled the laptop closer and folded my hands over it. "I think I'll keep it a little longer, just in case."

Her eyes were glued to the laptop. "But you said you couldn't find anything."

Somehow, we had descended into a curious tug-of-wills. It would be completely reasonable for her to end up with it, given how closely she'd worked with Lloyd on his projects. Still, I wasn't ready to let it go. "I need to be sure I didn't miss something."

Her eyes stayed fixed on the laptop. For a nanosecond, she looked ready to snatch it and run. Instead, she began to cry and stumbled out.

The superheroes glared at me from Lloyd's laptop like I was the worst person in the universe. But I had a mission to accomplish, and the clock was ticking. I shut the door.

Before I could refocus, a message from Carter pinged my phone:

Coming to Serenity tonight?

My heart twisted. At least one person in the world didn't hate me. I replied:

Too much work.

Carter:

It's almost the weekend. Take a break.

Me:

I need one.

Carter:

Do it. I'll be waiting.

After the most hellacious week ever, I was itching to escape. But how?

My mind worked on overdrive. I grabbed a flash drive and loaded the entire *Lexluthor* flood file onto it. Once that was accomplished, I wouldn't need to drag those reams of paper around anymore.

I exchanged the thumb drive for the paper files in my work bag. Before stashing them inside the credenza, I shuffled through to make sure their digital twins were on the flash drive.

All of them matched except for the *Love Letters* folder. Seemed like a waste of time, but before I passed on it entirely, I decided to take a peek.

The opening sentence of the first letter was a heart-stopper: *Quit badgering me, you nitwit, or I will come there and split your skull open.* Definitely not from a fan.

Nor was the next letter. *You lying sonofabitch,* it began.

Lovely. I paged through a few more. They dated back years. Some were typed on business stationery. Others, hand-written, looked like they'd been dashed off in a fit of rage. The kinder ones called him a hack, a sham, a fake.

The worst was this: Y*ou're a dead man walking.* Halfway through, my pulse was racing.

Hate mail. Murder. What kind of snake pit had I fallen into?

CHAPTER THIRTEEN

Washed Away

Hoping to avoid another confrontation with Maura, I made my escape at lunchtime. With Patel out until Monday, there was nothing to keep me at the station.

My route to the condo usually took me past Gertie's old neighborhood. It was about time for the rebuild to be finished, and I hadn't checked on her little bungalow in weeks. The sooner the place was restored, the sooner I could move back in. I made the two-block detour, hoping for the best.

Too many homes on Gertie's block still bore sad reminders of the devastation the last hurricane had wrought upon this and dozens of other Houston neighborhoods. Some sat derelict and abandoned. Empty lots remained where others had been razed down to bare earth. A few intrepid owners had rebuilt on some of them from scratch. Several houses had been jacked up a few feet in hopes of riding out future storms above the water. Gertie's was one of those.

I was with her and Louis when they first inspected the damage. The sight of it hit like the bad news it was. Outside, her lovely garden, always bright with seasonal flowers, was completely washed away.

Inside, every stick of furniture the front rooms had floated up with the rising water and, soaked in nasty muck, lay beached at random angles when the water flowed out again. Three feet up the walls, a sickly brown waterline spanned the room like toxic wainscotting.

Worst of all was the stench, a noxious mix of sewer water, road grease, rotting plants and animal offal.

Louis had tried to make a joke. "At least there aren't snakes." We were all too sad to smile.

Now, with so many familiar homes gone, it was difficult to get my bearings. I braked the Ferret when I thought I'd reached Gertie's, and lowered my window to take it all in.

Raising the entire house had created a higher roof line, which gave the place a more imposing profile. The old tan brick had been glazed over in oyster white, and the wood trim—once a muted green—was painted glossy red.

I mounted the steps. The front door didn't have lock yet, so I stepped inside. Once I glimpsed the vaulted entry, I knew. The cozy bungalow I loved had vanished.

The place was up-to-the-minute trendy. Walls had been removed, and I could see through the once-intimate living room, past a gleaming steel-clad kitchen island, all the way to the shiny glass-tiled wall above the cooktop.

It was a new house, open, fresh and bright. And sterile. Gertie's place, the one I cherished, was gone forever. I couldn't bear to see the rest. I ran down the steps and sat in the car for a solid minute, blinking back tears.

Soon as I shut the front door to the condo, I dropped my work stuff in the kitchen.

My stomach growled. I opened the freezer and removed a couple of brownies, perfect to power me through until dinner at the ranch with Carter. While I ate, I made one last go at Lloyd's computer.

Munching on a mouthful of brownie, I scrolled through the rest of the document folders, hoping to find a draft of the report. Hope dimmed as I neared the end.

Carter called. "I'm making a great dinner for us. Are you packed yet?"

"Almost. I'll just peek at one more file, then I'll be on the road."

I had intentionally skipped over the *Miscellaneous* folder earlier, for fear it would be a giant rabbit hole. While I finished the brownies, I decided to opened it. A dizzying array of files appeared on the screen. If I ran through them quickly, I figured I'd have more time to relax at Serenity.

I was opening the umpteenth document when my phone buzzed.

Carter. "Did you get a better offer?"

I checked the kitchen clock. Almost ten p.m. The rabbit hole had sucked me in.

"Cripes! I lost track! Did I ruin dinner?"

"Nope. It was delicious."

"I'm so sorry. It's just that I'm lost in the weeds with this report. I can't find what I need to finish it, and I'm really, really, really sick of the whole thing. I mean, will KHTS viewers care about the fine points of every regulation, or the 100- and 500-year flood maps that failed to predict the multiple disasters of the past decade?"

"I worry about you, Sam. A person needs time to decompress from a trauma like you've been through. It might be good for you to talk to someone."

"I have a therapist."

"You do? Who?"

I was pretty sure Cassandra's credentials wouldn't impress him. "I'm okay. It's just a little nuts right now. I'll come tomorrow, if you still want me."

"Always."

When we disconnected, I returned to the laptop. The *Miscellaneous* folder was open to where I'd left off. Nothing looked familiar. Apparently, I'd been zombie-scrolling for who knows how long before Carter's call. I powered down and shuffled to the bedroom.

I fell into bed and clicked the TV. KHTS was airing our tribute to Lloyd. It began with Alicia, then Brad, then me—all of us saying nice things. Alicia called him hard-working. Brad said Lloyd was like a brother.

I hated how I'd massively sanitized our relationship, especially the way I described his behavior on the night of the shooting. When I said he was brave, I'd meant to be kind, but it galled me that my little fib was now on record. I'd have to live with it, along with all my other mixed-up feelings about my fallen colleague.

CHAPTER FOURTEEN

Whataburger

A clap of thunder jolted me awake. For a split second, I was back in Lloyd's office, at the moment the gun fired. My eyes flew open.

I checked the time. Six a.m. Beyond the balcony, heavy clouds billowed on the horizon. Not optimal for a drive to Serenity.

The weather app on my phone predicted a fast-moving storm moving in from the northwest, which meant I'd be heading right into it. The good news was, I was going in the opposite direction from its path. Maybe it would pass over quickly.

I dressed, grabbed my overnighter, and headed to the kitchen to fill my travel mug with coffee. With Lloyd's computer and recorder, and my own laptop in my work bag, I dashed down to the Ferret. Before leaving the garage, I set up Lloyd's recorder so I could listen to his interviews while I drove.

By the time I left the city limits, the rain had let up, and I could see the road again. I took a quick sip of coffee and turned on the recorder. It caught Lloyd at the start of an interview with an elected official about whether the residential building codes in his jurisdiction were strictly enforced.

Suddenly, traffic ground to a halt. The sea of cars up ahead blocked my view of what was causing the holdup. More vehicles were jamming in behind me. No one was going anywhere anytime soon.

I put the Ferret in park and punched up the next interview. Lloyd was questioning a real estate developer about the devastation that the last major storm had wreaked on one of his planned neighborhoods. Had the man known about the flood risk before he acquired the land? Had he disclosed it to prospective home buyers?

The developer launched into a round of circular reasoning. His evasions caught my attention. Lloyd's too, as he probed for concrete answers. Things got pretty testy between them.

I was so deep into their argument, I hadn't noticed that more than a few cars ahead of me were peeling off toward the next exit—a sign that the standstill wasn't likely to end anytime soon. I set my blinker to the right and inched the Ferret over, car by car.

As the line crept upward on the ramp, a thick shelf of charcoal clouds came into view beyond the highway. Down below, dozens of emergency lights were flashing at the underpass. I had exited just in time.

Most cars on the ramp were turning right at the first corner, probably lured by the orange and white-striped billboard announcing a nearby Whataburger. It seemed like a reasonable place to wait for the storm to clear, so I followed the crowd and managed to pull the Ferret into the last available parking space.

I texted Carter to say I'd be late and grabbed the recorder, hoping to listen to more of Lloyd's interviews inside.

All the tables were filled. I joined the line anyway, behind a family of four. The two kids were debating the merits of a strawberry versus a chocolate shake while their parents discussed alternate routes to Washington on the Brazos, the birthplace of the Republic of Texas. Since Carter's ranch was in that direction, I listened.

The man in line behind me butted into the conversation to warn the parents that the storm was expected to stall right over us. In worn-out jeans, cowboy-style work shirt and a Texas Aggie cap, he looked like a local who knew something about the situation.

The food line finally dwindled down to me. I asked for a "junior" and a Dr Pepper, took the orange-striped tent card with my number on it, and proceeded to the soft drink dispenser.

All the tables were still occupied, so I wedged myself against the wall next to a trash can and waited for an opening.

The man in the Aggie hat passed by me on his way to join two others at a window booth. After he greeted his friends, he motioned across the noisy crowd to offer me the fourth seat.

The men all looked like ex-footballers. Unsure if there was enough space for both my cheeks to fit on the bench, I set my drink and tent card on the table, thanked them and headed to the restroom. Predictably, there was a line there, too. By the time I returned, my order had arrived.

The three men were deep into their double-meat-double-cheese burgers. I considered gathering my food to eat in the Ferret until I realized they were talking about a new housing development nearby. I perched on the edge of the seat to hear more.

Apparently, the guy in the Aggie cap had recently sold his acreage to a developer. "Yep, gone to the highest bidder," he was saying. "Between the cost of feed these days and those do-gooders givin' beef a bad rap, I'm tired of fightin' the odds. Kept a parcel big enough for the house and the horses and sold the rest. Three weeks after, the guy had skinned the dirt, concreted the pond, and put up a sign."

I nibbled at my burger while they commiserated over the stresses of the cattle business. By the time I'd finished eating, the men had, too. I followed them out. At the door, I thanked the Aggie and asked where his former property was.

"If you're heading to the city, you can't miss it. Got a sign in front says Hyssopp Cove Estates, big as Jesus. Half a mile south down the feeder road and you're there."

I recognized the name of the development from Lloyd's list of interviews, though I hadn't listened to that one yet.

Heavy raindrops pounded on the concrete and on the windshield of the Ferret as I slid inside. Storm clouds hung ominously over the highway heading northwest, but back toward the city, sunlight was peeking through. I took that as a sign and texted Carter about the flooded highway and the chance I wouldn't make it to Serenity He replied with a grumpy-faced icon. Then I reversed direction to check out the new housing development.

CHAPTER FIFTEEN

Nothing Illegal

It was easy to spot the turnoff to Hyssopp Cove Estates with the enormous billboard and the giant neon-colored inflatable robots gyrating wildly along the service road. A culvert between the road and the property had been prettied up with an overlay of broken rock. Limestone pillars flanked the main entrance.

Inside, the land was flat and barren, with no hint of the Aggie's former cattle ranch. Along the only paved street, small signs boasted *Friendly financing! Pick your own lot! Buy NOW!*

A fountain, only slightly larger than a backyard hot tub, burbled in the center of a roundabout. About thirty feet beyond it stood a lone trailer with a sign that identified it as the sales office. No homes were built yet, at least none that I could see.

I stopped in front, next to a banner announcing *Amazing Amenities!* The only other vehicle in sight was a black Cadillac SUV with a longhorn rack adorning its hood. I parked next to it.

Before I left the car, a middle-aged man—looking like he never missed an all-you-can-eat night at the local steakhouse—bounded out.

"Hiya, ma'am. Name's Kyle." His beefy hand swallowed mine as he jerked it up and down like the lever on an old-timey water pump.

Inside the trailer, renderings of model homes covered the walls. Kyle grinned and handed me his card: Kyle Hyssopp, Real Estate Development. "Are you lookin' to own a piece of paradise?"

"Isn't everyone?"

"I sure hope so." He wedged his sizable frame behind a desk covered with colorful brochures and other promotional material. "Have a seat, and I'll show you what we got here."

Sharing the cramped space with the mountain of flesh that was Kyle Hyssopp felt too much like being back in Lloyd's office. "Thanks, but, I'd rather stand."

His eyes narrowed. "Suit yourself. What kind of heaven you got in mind? We have floorplans to suit any wallet."

"Actually, I was just on my way into town and saw your sign and I—" I *what*? I had no idea if he was a good guy or a bad guy, or why he was on Lloyd's list. He didn't look like a murderer, but then again, what does a murderer really look like?

He was waiting for me to finish the sentence. Rethinking my approach, I decided on a more direct one. "Do you know Lloyd Sedgwick?"

Kyle's smile disappeared. "Hmm..." His fingers tapped the desk as he appeared to search his memory. "Nope, can't say as I do."

"He's a reporter for KHTS-TV in Houston."

Kyle shifted in his chair. "Maybe I seen him on the TV?"

"Possibly. Anyway, he's... he was working on a report about the new housing developments around here, and Hysopp Cove is on his research list."

Kyle's phone pinged. He gave it a quick glance and clicked it off. "So, you're not interested in buying out here?"

"Just curious, really."

"You trying to dig up dirt?"

Sounded to me like he did know who Lloyd was. I hedged. "Just wanting fill in some blanks. Lloyd is... unable to continue, and I'm supposed to be finishing his work. I thought if you two had met, you could share with me what you two talked about."

"Except I don't recall talking to him. Sorry, honey. And if you're not a buyer, I need get back to my business here."

I stood my ground. "Just one question."

"Which is?"

"I've heard that some housing developments might knowingly be situated on flood prone property. Do you know of any?"

A laugh came from deep in his belly. "Heck, girl, it's almost all flood-prone around here. But unless the county or the state says we can't build, and until people stop wanting to own affordable real estate, we'll take what the Good Lord gave us and make hay while the sun shines."

He pointed toward the small window behind me. "See that fountain out there? Did you notice the stone channel at the front when you came in? That's our flood control, all according to code. If it's good enough for the powers that be, what's the problem? Ain't nothing illegal in it."

I was dumbfounded by his candor. And he wasn't finished.

"Looky here. Ten years ago, I wanted to develop a property a couple miles north of here. Once my investors found out it was in a floodplain, they got cold feet, and somebody else bought it out from under me. Built a shopping center on it. It's flooded twice already, but everybody's collected insurance, and they're open for business as usual. Long as folks want new homes, office buildings and shopping malls, we're gonna build 'em. We make money, they make money, and the state collects taxes. Floods come, floods go, but people stay around and rebuild. It's human nature."

The phone on his desk erupted with an old country western song I didn't recognize. He took the call. "Hey rascal! Yeah, I've got a pretty little lady here from the TV. What? Yeah, some story they're doing. Hold on a sec."

He set the phone down and stood, hooking his thumbs into the pockets of his jeans. "So... I gotta get back to work here."

Clearly, this was the brush off. I gave him my number in case he decided to open up.

The storm had passed with only a light sprinkle. Before driving away, I sat in the Ferret and let Kyle's opinions percolate. He had elevated Lloyd's tedious facts to a striking social commentary on the foibles of our culture: unrestrained growth and its consequences—both positive and negative. In Kyle's world, there were no bad guys, only the natural order of things.

It was a new perspective for me to ponder, though he had definitely lied about knowing Lloyd.

CHAPTER SIXTEEN

White Poppies

Before I left Hyssop's property, I stopped to reconsider my original plan to be with Carter for the weekend. I had my work with me, and I was halfway there.

I sent him a text and turned west again toward Serenity Ranch.

It seemed like no time before I reached the exit for the private road to the manor house. I followed the gentle roll and rise of the land as it curved upward beneath a canopy of century-old oaks. I was brimming with anticipation.

Once the Ferret broke free of the overhang, the three-story limestone mansion came into view.

The house, a classic Texas Greek Revival, was as old as the trees. A wide veranda with stately white columns wrapped around its perimeter. Between the columns hung baskets of white bougainvillea, their branches trailing downward toward a baluster railing. Broad front steps led up to a portico and hand-carved oak double-doors.

I stopped the Ferret in front and stepped out onto a wet carpet of leaves. The rain-cooled air felt freshly-washed. In a checkered shirt, work jeans, and boots, Carter bounded down the front steps and wrapped his arms around me.

I melted into him like warm butter. We held on, until he jerked his head back and made a face. "Whataburger? Really? After I slaved over a hot oven for you?"

"A girl needs what a girl needs when she needs it. Besides, the burger was lunch. I haven't had breakfast yet."

That made him smile. "Get your boots on while I dish it up."

I dashed up the front steps ahead of him and headed for the grand stairway while he busied himself in the kitchen.

He had already set the riding boots at the foot of his bed. Though he called them mine, he had bought them for his wife, Katherine, as a birthday surprise. Sadly, she and their twins were killed by a drunk driver before she ever put a foot in them.

The first time Carter took me riding, he had offered the hand-tooled beauties for me to borrow. They fit like they were mine.

I tugged them on now and headed down the staircase, curving past old maps of the historical territories that eventually became Texas.

The top map was the most recent: Texas as it was when it became the twenty-eighth of the United States of America. In descending order through the centuries, the next one down depicted the Republic of Texas, the sovereign nation that existed for nearly a decade before it joined the U.S. It was followed by an older map of the land as a part of the Mexican empire. Next came the territory first claimed by Spanish conquistadors, followed by another of the French claim.

At the very bottom of the stairs was a map that displayed the state's earliest human inhabitants, with indigenous tribal names and locations of settlements that once thrived here. In their collective splendor, the maps demonstrated a centuries-old geopolitical history of Texas, a kind of heroism replete with greed, larceny, bloodshed, and courage, much of which had played out within a few miles of Serenity.

I crossed the grand foyer toward the high-ceilinged kitchen, where shiny copper pots hung above a cooking island and whitewashed cabinets flanked the walls. Tiny motes danced in sunlight as it spilled through a window above the sink. On the old wooden farm table, big enough to seat ten, someone had placed a Mason jar filled with golden coreopsis, purple thistles, and white poppies.

I sat at the table while Carter dished slabs of French toast from the oven onto two plates. He looked up and grinned. "Hey, beautiful."

"Hiya, handsome."

He cupped a dish of baked apples between two oven mitts and set it over a trivet on the table. The aroma reminded me of the apples my Mom used to make.

He brought the coffee and added a pitcher of cream. "This should do for now. Let's eat while it's warm."

Is it just me, or is there something utterly irresistible about a man who knows his way around a kitchen? It almost doesn't matter what he's cooking. The mere sight of Carter smearing peanut butter and jelly on a slice of bread makes me want to be the sandwich.

Okay, maybe it is just me.

He kissed my forehead, and took a seat. "I have good news and bad news."

He must have read my frown. "Sorry. I heard about the murder investigation. I know you weren't fond of the guy, but are you okay?"

Hoping to avoid eye contact, I poured cream over my apple and watched it swirl into the syrupy sauce. "Still processing."

"Want to talk about it?"

"I'd rather hear your bad news."

"Not bad news, really, just a slight change of plans. The horses are spoken for this morning. We'll be taking the Jeep."

"And the good news?"

He flashed a Cheshire Cat grin. "That comes later."

We took a freshly-laid gravel road that ran beside the horse trail toward the bluff. The route took us past four live oaks that guarded the little cemetery where Carter's wife Katharine and their twins were buried. He visited their graves often, and still carried grief from that unspeakable loss. It was in their memory that he'd formed his charitable foundation.

Their grave marker reminded me of another family in mourning here. "How are Tom Mason and the kids?"

Carter's forehead furrowed. "Doing well. Tom's managing the construction for the new retreat, and T.J. is slowly coming out of his shell. Seems to enjoy helping his dad."

"And Lizzie?"

"I know she misses her mother, but nothing keeps that little girl's spirit down for long."

I squeezed his hand. "You've done a wonderful thing, taking them in."

"I'm the lucky one. It's a great family, and the kids get along with Ralph's two. They all understand what it's like to be motherless."

Carter's right-hand cyber-geek, Ralph Velasco, had arrived with his children and his mother, Dottie, through the federal witness protection network, after an eastern crime syndicate murdered Ralph's wife. Carter's kindness toward them was born from his own personal loss, and sustained by his private mission to help heal the world.

We arrived at a low ridge overlooking the creek that flowed between the ranch and the retreat. Carter parked under the sweetgum tree where he'd first mentioned his plan for the land on the other side. Above us, the tree's sturdy branches spread its broad green leaves like open hands. He let the engine idle while we walked to the bluff.

I scanned the opposite bank. "I can see a rooftop or two."

"We've made good progress. There's a special new building I want to show you later."

We returned to the Jeep and circled back past the big house and down the tree-lined entrance to the farm-to-market road. From there, it took a minute to reach the new site.

Carter stopped at a gravel parking area in front of a half-finished two-story structure shaded by old trees on each side. "This will be the main gathering place."

Taking the steps up to the wrap-around porch, he spread his arms. " Out here, we'll have tables and chairs where families can play games, eat, talk, or just sit and listen to the birds, or watch the stars come out. Things they don't get to do in the city."

He led me through the unfinished interior, naming the spaces as we went. Industrial kitchen, dining hall, a series of activity rooms and a space for offices. At the rear entrance, he pointed to a circle of six smaller structures about thirty yards away.

"Four of those will be family cabins. They're duplexes, so we'll be able to take up to eight families, though we'll start with only three or four until we get up to speed. The other two cabins will serve as offices for our on-site counselors."

I touched his shoulder. "It's really happening, isn't it? Your dream made real."

"It's a start." He took my hand. "There's a missing piece or two. Matter of fact, you can help me with that."

CHAPTER SEVENTEEN

Hollywood

By the time we retraced our steps, four young riders were approaching the main lodge. Lizzie Mason and Kerry Velasco jumped off their horses and raced toward me.

The children were close in age, and competitive in most things, including their exuberant expressions of affection for me. Their body-squeezing hugs were a joy, but I had to pry them away to breathe.

Freckled-faced Lizzie beamed. "Samantha, guess what! I'm gonna be a junior girl guide when the retreat opens!"

Not to be outdone, Kerry chimed in. "So am I!" He blushed. "For boys, I mean."

Lizzie grabbed my hand. "Come see our new house!"

Kerry took my other hand. "Let's show her the treehouse first."

Carter laughed. "Guys! We'll all be together later. Right now, we have a swap to make. I'm trading the keys to the Jeep for the horses."

He dangled the key in front of T.J., Lizzie's older brother. The high-schooler glanced at Kerry's sister, Courtney, whose eyes lit up.

T.J. dismounted. "Seriously? You'll let me drive it?"

Carter squinted at the lanky teen. "If the state of Texas says you're legal to drive, you might as well get some practice."

Before T.J. could grab the key, Carter yanked it away. "Rules first. Not over fifteen miles an hour on pavement, ten on the gravel. Take the kids with you. And make sure everybody's buckled in."

"But you only need two horses," Lizzie complained.

Kerry piped up. "Yeah, I wanna stay with you and Samantha."

Carter shook his head. "I need the two of you to go with T.J. and your big sister and make sure they behave." He put the key in T.J.'s hand. "Young man, you are responsible for precious cargo, including yourself. Be safe."

T.J. tried to hide his excitement behind a solemn expression. "Yes sir. Thank you sir." His father Tom, a recently retired Army Ranger, had trained him well. We waved goodbye as they drove away.

Carter mounted T.J.'s horse and grabbed the leads of the other two. I approached Hollywood slowly, hoping she would recognize me. When I stroked her cheek, she answered with a soft whinny and stepped nearer, bowing her head so I could reach between her leathery ears for a scratch. She smelled wonderful.

Tears sprang in my eyes. I blotted them with my sleeve, but more streamed down, too many to wipe away. I pressed my face against Hollywood's powerful neck, and gave in to the flow.

I felt Carter's hand on my shoulder. "What is it?" he whispered.

I couldn't answer.

When the house I grew up in burned to the ground and took my parents and little brother with it, I shed a lifetime of tears. It still haunts me to think I might have saved them, if only I'd been there.

Then my two best friends were murdered. After that, I swore I'd never cry again. Now this would be my last cry. The absolute last. Might as well make it epic.

While I emptied myself of tears, Carter sat on the ground with me. "Please say something, Sam. Talk to me."

I calmed myself enough to speak. "I saw Lloyd. In the hospital. He was dead."

"You were there?"

"I didn't know it then. I thought he'd fallen out of bed, until Buron Washington called yesterday. I felt like he was ready to accused me of murder all over again. And Gertie's old house is... gone. Seems like everything good in my life disappears." I blotted my face with my sleeve. "Better not get too close to me, or you'll be gone, too."

"Is that what you're afraid of?" He peered into my eyes. "Don't worry, Sam. I'm not going anywhere."

I blotted my eyes with the back of my hand. "I think I'm going crazy."

"You've been crazy since the day we met. But this was a hell of a week for you." Carter's eyebrows knit. "What did Washington say?"

"That Lloyd was murdered. I'm sure my name's on the suspect list, but from what I know, there are at least a handful of other possible killers, including my co-workers at the station. I don't know who to trust."

I couldn't tell from Carter's expression if any of this was news to him. "Let's get you back to the house."

He boosted me up to Hollywood's saddle, and we began a slow, silent amble back to the big house with the two other horses trailing behind. The pale blue sky was streaked with wispy-thin clouds. The sun stung my eyes.

The minute we stepped into the grand foyer, we heard the kids' voices coming from the kitchen. Lunch time.

Carter squeezed my hand. "If you're not up to joining them, Dottie can fix plates for us to eat on the veranda."

I went upstairs to wash my face while he organized lunch for us outside.

I only picked at my chicken and dumplings. Neither of us spoke. Time passed quietly, accompanied by birdsong, rustling leaves, and the soft tinkle of water flowing along the rocks that lined the lap pool below.

After a while, Lizzie and Kerry came running out the door, full of giggles as they raced off to their next adventure. Soon after, T.J. and Courtney wandered out, holding hands. When they caught sight of us, they quickly separated. T.J. leapt down the steps and headed for Tom's truck, probably to join his Dad at the construction site. Courtney waved a shy hello and took off on foot toward the horse barn.

I gazed out through the oaks that shaded this side of the porch. If we could just stay here and not talk it would be perfect. But Carter restarted our conversation.

"I know you're dealing with a lot, Sam. Talking about it might help."

"I think I dumped everything out at the bluff."

"What upset you so much about Gertie's house? I thought the remodel was almost finished."

I shrugged. "I know it's silly, but the old house felt almost like my folk's place. Now it's all slick and brand new. And my new career has turned into a nightmare."

"Maybe it's time to quit."

"I'd be homeless and jobless again."

"You still have the condo. And me."

"But I'd be even more dependent on you. I hate feeling like a freeloader."

"You know that's not—" His eyes clouded. "Let's leave that for now. You're suffering. You may be strong, but you're not invincible. If you won't talk to me about it, we can find somebody who—"

Dottie appeared and eyeballed our plates. "Something wrong with lunch?"

I'd hardly touched the food, and Carter's was only half-eaten.

Hands on hips, she assessed the situation. "Well, I guess it'll keep." She took our bowls inside.

The day had soured, and it was my fault. I pushed away from the table. "I should go."

Carter took my hand. "Please stay, at least for the afternoon."

Sadness darkened his voice. I wanted to tell him I was okay, but words were hard. I cleared my throat. "I'm fine."

"How's that possible?"

"Just because I fell apart for a minute doesn't mean I'm helpless. I can't relax until I finish this report. And with Washington ready to investigate… coming here was a bad idea."

I pulled my hand away. "I should leave." I rose and started for the door.

Carter followed. "But Sam, you really need—"

I wheeled around to face him. "Don't tell me what I need! There's way too much going on. I only need to focus." I stormed inside to take the boots off and grab my things.

Driving away from Serenity, I replayed the ugliness I'd spat at Carter. Ever since the house fire took my family, I hated for people to pity me. I knew they meant well, but it made me feel like a victim, too, when I was struggling so hard to be brave.

Yet, Carter hadn't deserved the anger I'd let loose on him. What kind of person does that to someone who is only being kind?

CHAPTER EIGHTEEN

Scribbles

Thanks to the speed setting on Lloyd's recorder, I had listened to all his interviews by the time I returned to the condo. Though the people sounded like chipmunks going at each other, only one was too rapid to follow. I could always replay it later at normal speed.

I had silenced my phone when I left Serenity, so while I waited for the coffeemaker to do its thing, I checked for messages.

First, one from Gertie. "Samantha, dear, it's me. Just calling to see how you're doing, and if you need anything. I could come over and bring some—" Her cheery tone sounded suspiciously like a wellness check, most definitely at Carter's request. I cut the message off.

Next, Detective Washington. "I shall be at the TV station first thing Monday. I would like to see Lloyd Sedgwick's files when I arrive."

With little time left to double-check Lloyd's material before the police started pouring over it, I set to work in the dining room. Two hours later, I'd managed to cover a lot of ground.

Inside the *Love Letters* folder, I'd come across a ledger sheet that must have been misfiled. On it, in Lloyd's unreadable scrawl, were random numbers and mixed-up pairs of alphabet letters, perhaps an inventory of some kind. I was about to put the sheet aside when my eye caught on a toll-free phone number in the margin with the letters CC scrawled in pencil. On the off-chance that it related to the flood report, I tried the number.

Half a dozen rings later, a robo-voice answered. "Serenity personnel are unavailable to take your call." There was no prompt to leave a message.

Serenity? I redialed. Same response. Were the name and initials simply a coincidence, or did the CC refer to Carter Chapman and Serenity Ranch?

The question rendered me mildly catatonic, until my phone buzzed and jolted me back. Without thinking, I answered.

It was Gertie. "Samantha, dear. How are you?"

"Deep into work. Can we talk next week?"

"Let's talk now."

"I have to get this report done. Until then, I can't deal with anything else." I disconnected, and immediately regretted it. Even on my worst days, back when she was my secretary, I'd never treated her like that.

The phoned buzzed. Gertie again. "Do not hang up on me, Samantha. I know you're under pressure, however—"

"Sorry. I just need..." A hard knot in my throat made it impossible to continue.

Silence lingered until Gertie spoke. "What you need is help, and rest."

A rough laugh—more like a cackle—unraveled from deep in my chest.

"Dear girl, let me do something. Anything. Just name it."

The ledger sheet with the CC scribble and toll-free number on it caught my eye. Gertie could definitely help with that. Back when she was still my secretary, Carter had recruited her to spy on our shady employer, a task that she bravely accomplished. And so, after that company cratered, he hired her to work for his foundation. She knew his operation better than I did. If a connection existed between Carter Chapman and the CC on the ledger, she could find it.

"How about a little research? Would you check a phone number and see if it has anything to do with Carter's ranch... without asking him?"

"Of course."

Having Gertie's support again boosted my mood, even for this small task. As soon as we disconnected, I set the *Love Letters* file aside, booted up my laptop, and went straight to the report I'd begun writing for Maura.

What I'd written so far turned out to be more pages than I remembered. It had been a long day, and my energy was sagging, but I pushed through and started rereading from the beginning.

The next thing I knew, I was face down on the keyboard.

I peeled myself up and blinked at the computer screen. Nothing on it but an endless stream of blank pages. A small puddle of saliva and my aching jaw told me that I had fallen asleep on the space key.

Sunday morning, I rose in the dark with a heavy brain fog pressing inside my skull. Even a second mug of coffee wasn't enough to fuel me through another go at the report. I crawled back into bed, but in a short while the coffee kicked in and killed any chance for sleep.

I considered taking a shower to revive my senses. Then I got a better idea. I opened the balcony door and looked down. The crystal clear water of the swimming pool shimmered silver and pink in the morning sun.

In the time it took to put on my swimsuit and get downstairs, a middle-aged couple had ventured out to the pool and were basking in the first rays of the day. At the far end of the pool, they seemed content to ignore my presence.

I eased my body into the cool, clear water and swam lap after lap until my fingers shriveled and every muscle relaxed, including the ones in my shoulder. If only my life could be so smooth.

As I toweled off, a lounge chair enticed me to stay for a while. I spread the towel, lowered my body onto it, and closed my eyes, with only the gentle lapping of the water and the soft hum of an early Sunday morning for company.

The sound of a familiar voice and the squeals of overexcited children startled me. My eyes fluttered open to discover Pansy Gump—a Wellbourne resident and the self-appointed authority on proper decorum—chasing after two preschoolers like a mother hen with wayward chicks.

Despite Pansy's aggressive pride in her centuries-deep Texan heritage, she tended to enunciate like the Duchess of Kent. "Yoo-hoo, darlings," she warbled. "You must wait for your Grand-ma-*ma* and Grand-pa-*pa*!"

Her voluminous caftan flapped wildly as she dashed past me toward the kids. She dropped her enormous beach tote on a lounge chair under an umbrella and reclined on the one beside it. Her husband, Hubert, trailed behind, venturing a wave as he passed. All four were thickly smeared with white sunblock.

Ignoring their Grand-ma-*ma*, the kids cannonballed into the pool, which prompted the other couple to gather their things and retreat. When the little boy came up for air, he hurled a beachball at his little sister and missed. The ball skirted the water, bounced off the edge of the pool, and landed into my lap.

So much for peace and quiet. I hung my towel over my arm and walked the dripping ball over to Pansy. She lowered her Chanel sunglasses and gave my bathing suit the once-over. "Haven't you found a job yet?"

"Nice to see you, too, Pansy. And yes, I have a job. I'm working at KHTS."

Her frowny face turned wide with interest. "Ooh! Isn't that the station with that wonderful Brad Hudson?"

"I see him every day."

"Now there's a real man. So authoritative. And handsome."

Hubert rolled his eyes. I handed the ball to him.

Upstairs, I changed into a tee and shorts and headed to the dining room, ready to go another round with the flood report. I decided to polish off the easy stuff first and removed the rubber band that held the business cards together. Ones that seemed relevant, I stacked to my right; the others went to the left.

One card advertised *Next Exit to Love*, with a slogan that offered "Relief & Relaxation Off the Beaten Path," which seemed to involve an entirely different subject. Perhaps another time.

With fewer than a dozen cards in the right-hand stack, I started making calls. It didn't take long to figure out that Sunday morning wasn't the best time to reach a business by phone. I set the cards aside.

Waffling between returning to the work I'd fallen asleep over last night, or continuing to search for a draft of Lloyd's report, I used the one-two-buckle-my-shoe method to decide. Nine-ten-a-big-fat-hen landed on the report for Maura. *Ugh.*

I worked all day until I started to nod off, and went to bed with the nagging feeling that I'd overlooked something major. I slept roughly, with one question plaguing my thoughts.

What else did I need to save to finish the report before Washington showed up? What else... what else... what else?

CHAPTER NINETEEN

Purple Rain

When I arrived at KHTS Monday morning, my brain was still whirling like a Ferris wheel through a mental inventory of Lloyd's research. Had I duplicated absolutely everything I needed?

I hadn't made copies of the hate mail. The business cards were likely only minor research points. I grabbed them anyway, along with the *Love Letters* file and made a beeline to the copy room.

The ledger sheet with the CC and toll-free number stayed in my bag. No way I'd give that up until I was sure that the "Serenity" toll-free number had nothing to do with Carter or his ranch.

Back in my workspace, I added the originals to a stack in the credenza and slid the new copies into my bag. My heart was racing as fast as my brain. I forced myself to sit and take a couple of deep breaths.

An old puzzle wormed its way into my thoughts. When Lloyd's computer went missing, where had it been? Why did it show up in my credenza? Who put it there? Did it still hold evidence that pointed to his killer?

Some of the hate mail in the *Love Letters* folder had been printed from emails. There could be other email messages relating to the flood report that I hadn't seen. If I wanted one more crack at those before Detective Washington arrived, I'd have to hurry.

I booted up his laptop and scrolled back in time through tons of spam until I hit on an email from Maura that was dated the morning of the shooting. The subject line read *Purple Rain*, and it included an attachment. I clicked.

A document popped onto the screen. My pulse quickened as its pages loaded and I began to comprehend exactly what it was: a full draft of Lloyd's flood report.

Goosebumps pimpled my arms as I sped through the pages. The story it told was compelling and disturbing, and way too dense for a single television news spot. Hopeful that I could whittle it down to something manageable, I grabbed my notebook and started from the beginning, outlining the key points.

I was on a roll when footsteps in the hall reminded me that Washington could arrive any minute. I stopped outlining, copied the *Purple Rain* document to my thumb drive and loaded it onto my laptop, then returned to Lloyd's computer to search for whatever else might be in his emails. As a professional whistle-blower, I figured it was my duty to snoop.

While I searched, a new question began to niggle. It looked as if Maura had sent the *Purple Rain* document to Lloyd, and not the other way around. If she already had the report back then, why hadn't she given it to me?

I was pondering that question when she walked in. She pointed to Lloyd's computer. "Time to hand it over."

"But I just found Lloyd's report." I skipped over the fact that I'd found it in an email from her. "It was in here all the along, ready to go. And it's good. Long, but really good."

She paled, covered her face with her hands, and wailed. "Why can't I ever catch a break?"

"This is a break! We can get it on the air in the next few days for sure."

Her face turned red with fury. "You don't know anything! You waltzed in here thinking you could take whatever you wanted, and everybody else be damned. What do you care about people who've slaved for years in this business, hoping that maybe someday, somebody will notice them? You have no clue!" She flopped into a chair across from me and buried her head in her hands.

I offered her a tissue. Once it felt safe enough to speak, I began gently. "The report is ready, Maura. And it's an eye-popper. Let's focus on that. For Lloyd."

She raised her head and gaped at me. "For Lloyd? You've gotta be kidding! Lloyd's dead. There is no more Lloyd." She began to giggle, and not in a good way.

It dawned on me that I may have mischaracterized the reason for her outburst. "But his report—"

"Is mine. I wrote it."

"You? But it's Lloyd's."

She removed her glasses and stared at the ceiling as if searching for divine guidance. After a ragged breath, she reset them on her nose. The damp, shredded tissue fell apart in her hands as she spoke.

"Lloyd had a nose for finding a good story, and the determination to dig up info from a thousand sources. But he always had trouble bringing everything together in a clear narrative. As his producer, I felt like my job was in jeopardy if he failed. So I stepped in, took his research, wrote the reports, and sent them back to him."

"Are you saying he didn't—"

"I wrote them all, every single one." Her eyes held a strange gleam. Pride maybe. Or perhaps something worse.

My mind sped back to the night of the shooting, when Lloyd was struggling with the storyline. "Before Lloyd was shot, did he have this final draft?"

She shook her head. "I didn't email it to him until around seven that morning. He probably never saw it. I'd been begging him for months to give me credit for my work, at least as a co-contributor, and he'd always say, 'Maybe next time, honey.' I'd had enough of his frickin' ego. So I let him choke on it for a while."

It occurred to me that Washington probably hadn't spoken to Maura yet. Otherwise, she would be more careful with her words.

She eyed Lloyd's computer again, which made me curious. "When I couldn't find Lloyd's laptop, you said you didn't have it, but did you?"

Her lips tightened. "Why would I need it? I had the report. My report. With Lloyd out of the picture, I figured I could show my work to Patel, and he'd let me air it myself, instead of giving it to somebody else."

My neck prickled. That somebody else was me. I closed the laptop and rested my hands on it. Awkward silence ensued.

Her phone buzzed. She glanced at it and groaned. "Gotta go." Giving Lloyd's computer a wistful glance, she backed out of the room.

When my breath returned, I sat back and rethought Lloyd's reluctance to share his work with me. Now I realized he'd held out on me not only out of fear I'd take his job. He must have also feared that I'd find out he was a fraud.

Maura had kept the truth from me, too, even after Lloyd was gone. They both wanted me to fail. She still hoped I would.

Had she wanted Lloyd out of the picture bad enough to kill him? Was I next on her list?

CHAPTER TWENTY

The Warrant

I felt the presence of a person standing in the doorway: HPD Detective Buron Washington, looking buttoned-up as ever in a tailored gray suit and tie.

He offered a wry smile. "May I come in?" Without waiting for an answer, he approached the table, unbuttoned his suit jacket, and took a chair.

"I don't want to be rude, Detective, but I'm on a really tight schedule."

"I'll be brief." He extracted a file from his leather satchel and set it on the table in front of him. All business, as usual. "When we spoke on Friday, you said your relationship with Mr. Sedgwick was difficult?"

From experience, I knew to keep my answers brief. "I said he was prickly." My face heated. "Wait a minute. You can't possibly think... I had nothing to do with—" I crossed my arms and clammed up.

Washington wrote a note to himself. "I would appreciate your cooperation, Ms. Newman. At the moment, I am simply interested in what you know about him."

"Not much. I haven't been here long."

We were in a staredown until he changed the subject. "Can you show me to Mr. Sedgwick's work area?"

"Of course." I led the detective down the hall to Lloyd's office. His eyes lit on the whiteboard. "Is that what he was working on?"

"Yes."

He pulled out his phone and snapped a picture, then continued to scan the room. "Where are his work files?"

Drat. I wasn't ready to give up Lloyd's computer yet. I had to stall him.

"My boss isn't here, and I'm pretty sure he'd need a search warrant if you want to look at files."

Washington's stink-eye met mine. "That can be arranged. I'll be back shortly."

I had just started in on the *Document* files again when Brad Hudson stuck his head in. "Have you seen Patel?"

"I don't think he's here yet."

"Blast it!" He slapped the door so hard it ricocheted off the wall and returned to smack him in the face. Slightly dazed, he raked a hand through his salt-and-pepper coif and collected himself.

I expected him to leave, but he caught sight of something on the table. "My God! What are you doing with that?" He pointed to Lloyd's laptop.

"Patel wants me to finish Lloyd's report."

He paled. "Jay Patel gave it to you? Unbelievable!"

He stormed away, muttering to himself. Obviously, he was angry that I'd been assigned to Lloyd's report instead of him. After all, he would probably be the one to deliver it on camera.

In the meantime, I would guard the laptop with my life until I had everything I needed.

After lunch, Jay Patel was still a no-show, but Washington showed up, warrant in hand.

I opened the credenza and pointed to the paper files inside.

The detective peered greedily over them. "That everything?"

"It's what I have of Lloyd's original research and other items relating to his last report. For older stuff, you'll have to ask Maura Tustin." I wondered if I should mention my disturbing conversation with her this morning.

The detective focused on the stash in the credenza. "How did you come by all of this?"

"Jay Patel reassigned the report to me. Maura's his producer. You could ask her if she has anything more."

Washington leafed through a few folders, then called in a uniformed officer to remove the papers. Once that was accomplished, the detective's eyes pinned me like a splayed bug on a specimen tray. "Are you sure this is everything?"

I turned away and gave the room a thorough once-over while my brain raced through my options. I glanced wistfully at Lloyd's computer. My chance to mine more emails was lost.

"The laptop on the table with the decals on it is his. And the voice recorder, too."

Washington signaled to the officer to add the devices to the box, but his eyes stayed on me. "Anything else?"

"It's all I have."

His eyes bore into mine. "The least little thing, whether or not you think it's relevant, could be important."

I couldn't bring myself to mention Maura again. Searching for another bone to toss his way, I hit on the *Love Letters* folder.

I pointed to the box in the officer's hands. "There's a file in there you might want to look at first. It says 'Love Letters' on the outside, but it's really hate mail addressed to Lloyd."

The detective snatched the box and rifled through. He yanked the folder out and skimmed over the papers, his eyes stopping now and again on a few of them. "Could be something here."

"I hope so."

His eyes swept the room. "So, that's it?"

I nodded.

Washington dismissed the officer, who left with the full box. Then he turned to me. "Mr. Patel has not answered my calls, and did not honor my request to meet with me this morning. Can you think of any reason why?"

I shook my head. "Haven't seen or talked to him since he left Thursday."

"Is that unusual?"

"He's been really busy, and under a lot of pressure lately. Last week he said he'd be in meetings downtown."

"Meetings with...?"

"He didn't say."

Washington frowned. "Ms. Newman. During our encounter last year, you exhibited extreme loyalty to your friends, to the point of withholding facts from my investigation. I hope you'll refrain from such behavior this time, lest you get yourself in trouble."

"If memory serves, Detective, I provided the key information that helped you solve that case."

My comment raised a half-smile from him. "Perhaps you did." His expression turned stony again. "Nevertheless..."

"Don't worry, Detective. I'll do everything I can to help you catch Lloyd's killer."

Washington moved on to interview Maura and the rest of the KHTS staff. My worktable was bare. Patel was still a no-show, and my nerves were jangled to the max.

The doors to the empty credenza yawned open. I shut them and booted up my own laptop, then plugged in the thumb drive and opened the *Purple Rain* report.

Now that I knew about Maura's authorship of the document, I had mixed emotions. How could I, in all conscience, claim the report for myself?

My phone buzzed. The caller ID read TRIAD. My first thought was that an evil Chinese gang was targeting me. Given the way my life was going these days, it wouldn't be a great shock. Even if the letters stood for something only slightly less evil—like a robot calling to inform me that I'd won an all-expenses-paid vacation to Bora Bora—I let it go to voicemail.

Someone tapped on the door. I looked up to see Francine Bascom. She leaned in. "Do you have a minute?"

Fresh from earning her bachelor's in communications, Francine had started her on-the scene reporting job at KHTS a couple of months before I arrived. She took on all sorts of local disasters, including the one where I first noticed her, when she stood in front of the empty De Theret International Building and recited the multitude of criminal charges against my former employer.

"What's up, Francine?"

"It's about the girl who assaulted you and Mr. Sedgwick. I just interviewed her social worker this morning and—this is kinda interesting—she said she wanted to speak to you."

"The girl?"

"The social worker."

"Why?"

"She thinks you might be able to help the child's case."

"Me?"

"Says she's met you before, and she feels you might be willing to help."

The only social worker I knew was the college counselor who spoke to me after my family was killed in the fire. But that was in another state, and over a decade ago. "She must be confusing me with someone else."

"She seemed pretty confident about it. I gave her your contact info. I hope you don't mind."

I was still struggling to put that entire morning out of my mind, including the little troublemaker in the princess T-shirt. "I don't know. There's a lot going on right now."

"What are you working on?"

"Lloyd's last investigative report."

Francine frowned. "Enough said. I have to report from toxic gas leak sites and wade into nasty floodwaters for a living, but it's still better than dealing with Lloyd Sedgwick."

"You've worked with him?"

"For a nanosecond, until I told Patel I'd quit if I had to spend one more day in his dismal presence.

Luckily, a field reporter had just retired, so I lobbied for this job and got it."

Hmm. No wonder my predicament had me feeling like a chump. I was one.

Francine turned to leave, but stopped at the door. "By the way, do you know anything about the detective who's roaming around here? I saw him in the hallway and recognized him from a couple of murders I've reported on. He was looking for Maura. Do you know why?"

Not wanting to be the one to break the news, I shrugged. "Detective?"

"I'm going to see if I can run him down. He's homicide, so there's gotta be a story there. See you later."

My conversation with Francine killed what was left of my enthusiasm for dealing with the flood report. Instead, I checked my voicemail and listened to the TRIAD message. Turned out to be from the pizza kid's social worker.

Curiosity got the best of me. I called her back, just for kicks.

She started talking right away. "Thanks so much for returning my call, Ms. Newman. I'm Riva Ramirez, a Juvenile Probation Officer from the TRIAD Prevention Program. I've been assigned to the case of Valentina Garcia, the child who—"

Valentina. The pizza kid had a name. While I processed that, Ramirez continued. "I'd like to meet with you in person about Val's case in the next day or two. It's critical to her future."

The woman sure knew how to hook a person. "Why is my input so important?"

"It's a long story. I'd rather explain in person."

"This is not a good time."

"Anything you can give us. Please."

"I have to go." I disconnected and immediately felt a pang of guilt. Were my personal issues more urgent than helping a child in trouble? I checked the time. Three-fifteen. A sudden urge to get away and a hankering for the chicken fattoush salad at Barnaby's came over me.

I called Ramirez back. "Meet me at Barnaby's, the original, in half an hour."

CHAPTER TWENTY-ONE

Barnaby's

E ven at mid-afternoon, Barnaby's buzzed with its typical Montrose mix of diners. While waiting for Riva Ramirez in a booth at the back of the ramshackle diner, I meditated on the amusing canine portraits on the walls and the images of Barnaby, the owner's late beloved Old English sheepdog, frolicking among the clouds on the ceiling in a whimsical doggy heaven. If I ever have a real home again, I'm definitely adopting a dog.

A woman approached the booth. With wavy, dark hair and an open smile, she did not look familiar.

She sat across from me. "You don't remember me, do you?"

Friendly as she seemed, she'd come on behalf of the girl who had ruined Lloyd's life and turned mine upside down. I was determined to keep my guard up. "Sorry, I don't."

"I suppose we both look different these days. And you were under some stress then—"

Then? She didn't know the half of it.

A waiter came to take our order. Without looking at the menu, I chose the chicken fattoush salad, my favorite. She asked for a buffalo burger.

When the waiter left, she continued. "Last year, I was at The Wellbourne with my senior partner.

We were investigating the murder in the unit next to yours. I was Officer Ramirez then."

Aha. On that dreadful morning, she had been the only person who didn't treat Gertie and me like criminals.

I managed a smile. "So, what can I do for you?"

"Not for me. For Valentina. It's ironic that we met that day. It was my last day as a cop. I'd been studying for a degree in social work, and I switched jobs as soon as I got my certification. First case on my own? This one.

"When I saw your name in Valentina's file, I remembered how you'd spoken that morning about your best friend's funeral. How sad you were that you couldn't help her. And how you defended your other friend when we took her in for questioning."

A forlorn image of Gertie from that morning came flooding in. "In handcuffs. Like a common criminal," I added.

Ramirez blinked. "That was Detective Washington's choice. I agree, he could have handled it differently. Anyway, you seemed like a compassionate person. I'm hoping you'll help us get leniency for Val. May I continue?"

I crossed my arms. "Have at it."

She hesitated. "You're a TV reporter now?"

"Sort of."

"Could this conversation be off the record?"

I wasn't fully versed in journalistic protocol yet, but I did know how to keep a secret. "Sure."

"Last year, while Val and her two older brothers were in school, their mother was deported. The father isn't here either, which left the kids alone. Val's sixteen-year-old brother quit school and found work washing dishes at a seafood restaurant to support the younger two kids. Then the big hurricane wiped out the restaurant and flooded the ground floor apartment the kids shared with another family.

"To keep a roof over their heads, the boys hooked up with a neighborhood gang that hung out in the same apartment complex. The gang charged extra rent for Val, and demanded payment with either money or sexual favors. To cover her rent, the older brother took a second job delivering pizza on the graveyard shift. He took her to work with him so she'd be safe at night."

By the time our food arrived, my appetite had faded. I pushed the salad bowl away.

Ramirez continued. "Somehow, Valentina got it into her head to free the three of them from the situation herself. She knew your TV station was a regular late night delivery customer, so she made a deal with one of the gang members, saying she would rob the customers and give the cash to him. He gave her a gun and told her it wasn't loaded, and he made her swear not to tell anyone where it came from.

"At the TV station that night, Val begged her brother to let her take the pizza inside by herself. She never intended to rob anyone. She only wanted to get on television in hopes someone would help them escape the gang. You know the rest."

"She's definitely creative, but what makes you think I can help?"

"She's a good kid with a short life full of bad breaks, and now she could be charged with a serious felony. Even with a lesser charge, she'll get stuck in the juvie system for years. The only chance we have is to plead lack of intent and extenuating circumstances. I'm asking if you'll give us a statement to help her case."

I remembered how woefully inexperienced the child had seemed at wielding a loaded weapon, and nearly as traumatized as we were. I rubbed my eyes and exhaled. "I already gave a statement to the police after it happened."

"We're not asking you to contradict anything you said before. But if you could offer your sense of Valentina's demeanor, anything that could persuade the court to be lenient. She's certain she didn't pull the trigger. She says the gun went off after you tried to grab it."

My stomach twisted. I drilled into the images again. "The gun went off when we hit the floor. Maybe she didn't mean to shoot Lloyd, but she brought the gun."

"She was told it wasn't loaded."

I reviewed the sequence in my mind's eye again. It all had happened so fast. Was I remembering everything right?

Ramirez seemed to notice my confusion. "Perhaps neither of you was holding the gun when it discharged. If you'd just put that in a statement it would be very helpful. Like I said, I know you're a sympathetic person. Your memory of what happened could counter the worst of the charges against her."

"I need to think about this." I signaled the waiter for the check and slid out of the booth.

Ramirez stood, too, still pleading her case. "Val became mute after the shooting. I've managed to get her to open up to me a little. She's a smart kid who did a stupid, desperate thing that spiraled out of control. She'll have to face some consequences. I'm only trying to keep them to a minimum."

The waiter brought the receipt and biodegradable take-away containers. On the way out, Ramirez made a final plea. "You're Val's best hope for a decent future. Please think about it."

I walked out, got in the car, and sat there, dazed.

Suddenly, a car horn blasted in my ear. I looked up to see a guy in a Honda gesturing for me to roll my window down.

"Are you coming or going?" he yelled.

I was still parked at Barnaby's, with no idea how long I'd been sitting there. With an apologetic wave, I started the Ferret and pulled away.

CHAPTER TWENTY-TWO

Holy Shitake!

Images of the shooting chased me all the way back to the station. I tried to shake them off, but the awful scene kept replaying itself the way Ramirez suggested it happened. Could I be the one who put Lloyd in the hospital?

Carter would know. Hoping he had forgiven me for ruining the weekend, I called his number. He picked up on the first ring.

I took a deep breath. "I think I may be the reason Lloyd is dead."

"He was probably dead before you saw him on the floor in the hospital."

"No, I mean before that." I unspooled the highlights of my conversation at Barnaby's with Riva Ramirez. "I thought the gun went off after it hit the floor. But the more I try to remember, the more confused I get. What if, when I tried to take the weapon away from the girl, I inadvertently set the trigger? If Lloyd had never been shot, he wouldn't have been in the hospital like a sitting duck. Is it possible for a gun to go off like that?"

Carter was quiet for what seemed like a long time before he spoke. "It's unlikely that the gun discharged on its own."

"But possible?"

"However it happened, there's nothing to feel guilty about. You didn't introduce the gun to the scene. Truth is, if Sedgwick had been on schedule, neither of you would have been at the TV station in the middle of the night, and therefore, no pizza delivery or crazy mixed-up kid. If someone wanted the man dead, they would have found another way to get him."

As I processed Carter's reasoning, I considered how such different paths had brought the three of us— Lloyd, the girl, and me—together in that miserable room on that awful night.

Carter cut into my thoughts. "It is not in any way your fault."

"I keep trying to tell myself that."

"Look, let's talk this through when we're together."

"No prob. I'm fine. Really."

After we disconnected, I shook off my doubts and booted up my laptop. I had just plugged in the thumb drive with Lloyd's stuff on it when Francine came to the door. "Quick question."

I looked up. "Okay."

"I couldn't find that homicide detective, but guess what! He's been talking to people about Lloyd. Like maybe he was murdered at the hospital."

"Who told you?"

"I'm sworn to secrecy. But I also heard that Lloyd did have a wife, like you said."

"May or may not be true."

"Makes a person wonder, though. Homicide? Wife?" Her eyes sparkled at the thought. "I think I'll look into it."

"Go for it."

Once Francine moved on, my appetite kicked in. I opened the to-go package from Barnaby's and was about to dig into the chicken fattoush salad when Jojo stuck his head in.

He waved an envelope at me. "Special delivery for Ms. Sammy-am!"

I set the plastic fork aside and opened what looked like a personal letter. Inside was a single sheet of paper with only two words on it, scrawled with a thick red marker in big capital letters: *You're next.*

A crudely drawn smiley-face punctuated the message.

Jojo slapped the table. "Wow! Looks like something exciting's about to happen to Miss Sammy."

My eyes were glued to the paper, which felt like poison in my hand. I shot up from the chair and let it drop to the floor.

Jojo picked it up. "What's wrong? You look like you've seen the Ghost of Christmas Past."

"I think it's a threat."

He squinted at the message. "Seriously?"

"You haven't noticed the police circling the halls?"

"Cops? Here? What for?"

"They think Lloyd was murdered."

"What?" He gaped at the note with a new perspective. "Holy shitake!"

"Yeah."

We stared at the message as if the blood-colored words might reveal a deeper insight. All I could think about was that someone was coming for me, like in a scary horror movie. Hands trembling, I inspected the envelope. It bore a stamp, but no postmark, and no return address.

My wits slowly returned. "I wonder if the police are still around."

Jojo started for the door. "Let's find them."

On our tour of the building in search of Washington, we found Maura in the editing room. Apparently, the detective had followed my advice and interviewed her this morning, but she hadn't seen him since.

We circled back to Alicia's office. She was at her desk, swathed in one of her elegant broadcast-ready dresses—plum this time. But she was clearly not camera-ready. Her wig was askew, her face haggard.

She shot Jojo a look. "About time."

He went to her. "Sorry. I just got in." He sat on a corner of her desk and took her hand. "I'm all yours, my love. But first, Sammy needs to find a detective who might be roaming around here. Have you seen him?"

Alicia glanced at me. "He grilled me for an hour about Lloyd, but I have no idea where he is now. Have you seen Jay?"

I shook my head.

She covered her eyes with her hands and bowed her head. "Is the whole world falling apart, or just me?"

I shared her despair, but I couldn't dwell on it, or else I'd be the next to crumble. I left Jojo with Alicia and kept looking for Washington. After I rounded every corner of the station and knocked on every door, it was clear that he had left the building.

What to do with the note in my pocket? Even more important, who had sent it, and why? Was it good news, as Jojo had first thought? Or was I in danger?

I staggered back to the conference room and shut the door. Steadying myself at the table, I spread the paper out and studied it again.

If it was a threat, it could be from anyone who knew that I was now the person responsible for

Lloyd's report. My thoughts traveled back to Kyle Hysopp, the real estate developer I'd met Saturday. He'd seemed friendly, until I mentioned Lloyd's name.

The only other people who knew I worked with Lloyd were KHTS employees. Was it someone at the station, someone I said hello to every day? I ran through the staff, searching for any hint of homicidal tendencies. Except...

A chill shot through me as I recalled my on-camera interview with Alicia for the station's tribute to Lloyd. It had aired several times over the weekend. And thanks to Nandi Rudolph, it also lived on our website and in all our social media. The number of people who knew that Lloyd was in the hospital—and more to the point, that I was completing his investigation— exponentially increased to include the entire KHTS viewership. Small though it was, it was wide enough to include a possible murderer.

All I'd wanted from this job was a fresh start, and to put distance between me and my chronic knack for being in the wrong place at the wrong time. Instead, after suffering through two previous criminal investigations, I now was the potential target in a third.

Something, somewhere, had to break my way, before I broke first. I packed my work bag and headed to The Wellbourne with the words *you're next* hissing in my ears.

CHAPTER TWENTY-THREE

Reunion

If you asked me how I got to the condo, I'd have to plead the fifth. Full consciousness resumed only after a long, hot shower.

I'd phoned Washington and left a message about the cryptic note, but he hadn't called back yet. Since he would likely confiscate it, I went to the library to copy it.

The kitchen phone rang. Thinking it was the detective, I hurried back to answer.

The front-desk concierge spoke. "Ms. Newman, your friend is here. Mrs. Ka...Klas...testy? Oh, sorry. She said to say it's Gertie."

A minute later, Gertie was standing in the hall holding two sacks of food and a defiant look on her face. "If your boss can barge in unannounced, I figure I can, too. I'd say I hope you don't mind, but I really don't care."

Gertie, grouchy. A rare sight. I probably deserved it, rude as I was to her yesterday.

She marched into the kitchen and went into action. I followed and sat at the island while she filled the fruit bowl and emptied another sack into the fridge. A couple of wrapped packages and a tub of ice cream also disappeared into the freezer.

She handed me a green drink. "I know you like these nasty things. Drink up."

I took a swig of the gingery elixir. "Thanks."

She took a stool across from me and sat. "I'm here to report on what I discovered about that phone number you gave me."

"And?"

"A machine answered for something called Serenity, then disconnected."

"I knew that much already."

"Of course you did. So, I called Carter and asked him about it."

My hackles rose. I stood and paced the kitchen. "If I'd wanted to bother him with it, I could have done it myself."

"But you didn't. And why? Because you've suddenly decided to push him away. Both of us, actually, the two people in this world who care most about you. This isn't like you, Samantha."

"Maybe it's the new me."

"I hope not."

I skipped past the disappointment in her voice. "So, what did Carter say?"

"He's looking into it. He'll let you know what he finds."

"I'm tired of asking him for favors."

"Favors?" She shook her head. "I will not be a party to whatever is happening between the two of you."

"He told you?"

"He didn't have to. The minute I called that dead-end number and heard the recording, I knew. If things were right between you, you'd have asked him about it yourself. Stop circling. Come sit."

A scolding from Gertie. I halted in mid-stride, and like a good little puppy, I obeyed.

She reached for my hand. At her touch, tears sprang in my eyes. "I... I think I'm in trouble." I put my head in my hands.

As she always does when I'm upset, Gertie made tea and laid out slices of home-baked pound cake.

She joined me again at the breakfast island. "So, talk to me."

Since Gertie and Carter were obviously in cahoots, he'd probably already filled her in. But she and I hadn't spent much time together since the shooting, and her presence, even grouchy, was comforting.

Words came hard. I began at the end with the anonymous two-word message, and handed the envelope to her.

She stared at the note. "You're next? What does that mean?"

"My co-worker, Lloyd? He didn't die from the gunshot. He was murdered in the hospital. And he'd had threats like this, too."

Her face went gray. She gaped at the words. "Does Carter know about this?"

"I just received it. I phoned Detective Washington, but he hasn't called me back."

"Buron Washington? The one who hauled me off to jail last year?"

His name was certain to stir the unpleasant memory, but Gertie shook herself free. "Call him again, Samantha. Right now. I'm not leaving until you do."

"It could be a stupid prank. Maybe it's not even meant as a threat."

"Make the call."

I scrolled to Washington's number. He still didn't pick up. I left another message.

Gertie was texting someone. I didn't have to ask who the recipient was.

"Carter doesn't need to be here."

"Too late, dear. He's on his way."

I popped off the stool. "I don't want him running my life."

Gertie was unperturbed. "Considering the current state of things, I doubt he could make it worse." She poured herself a second cup of tea.

My phone buzzed. Detective Washington. I told him about the letter, and in case he hadn't looked through Lloyd's files yet, I reminded him about the hate mail.

"I'll come by on my way home."

It was shaping up to be a nerve-wracking evening after another nerve-wracking day. Nothing would stop Carter from coming, and Gertie wouldn't budge until he arrived. Add me and Detective Washington to the group, and the cast of last year's murder investigation would be complete.

I was furious with Gertie for calling Carter. But when I saw him standing in the doorway, answering yet another call to duty, I had to fight against an urge to bury myself in his arms.

In the kitchen, he and Gertie exchanged greetings. She handed him a mug of coffee, mumbled something about having to check her car, and left the room.

Carter leaned against the counter, drinking from his mug. Silence filled the space between us, until the pressure to say something became almost unbearable.

He spoke first. "I'm glad you called me—"

"I didn't."

"I meant earlier today, about the gun. I was afraid I had run you off for good."

I couldn't look at him. Instead, I spoke into my teacup. "I was wrong."

He seemed confused. "You were...?"

"The stupid things I said to you at Serenity. The way I ran out. Sorry for being such a brat."

He set his coffee down and wrapped his arms around me. "You're my kind of brat."

I could feel his breath in my ear as he whispered words I didn't know I needed until he said them. "It's okay. We'll be okay."

I mumbled into his neck. "I think I'm losing it."

"Possibly."

I leaned back to look him in the eye. "You're supposed to say, 'No you're not, Samantha. You're fine.'"

He peered down at me. "Are you fine?"

"I... I can't..." I broke away and escaped to the sink to wash the tea cups.

He stood behind me and rested a hand on my shoulder. "You've been through some very serious stuff. I've tried to give you space, but I can't stop wanting to protect you. It's not possible."

Gertie poked her head in. "You have a visitor. I ran into him downstairs."

The pinched look on her face confirmed that Detective Washington had arrived. She grabbed her purse from the counter. "He is in the living room. And I am leaving."

I couldn't blame her for wanting to escape the awkward reunion. I wished I could run away, too, because this time, the situation was worse. There wasn't a dead body next door. The danger was much closer to home.

CHAPTER TWENTY-FOUR

Whiplash

Buron Washington stood at the balcony windows taking in the glittering skyline. He didn't seem surprised to see Carter, which led me to suspect that they had discussed the situation before they arrived. Last year, the two of them had also tried to shut me out of the last murder investigation I found myself in the middle of, until they realized they couldn't close the case without me.

The detective looked as weary as I felt. "Apologies for the late hour, Ms. Newman. You have something for me?"

"Yes." I padded to the kitchen to grab my red-letter note.

On the way, my phone buzzed. Jay Patel. "Samantha, are you alone?"

I wondered if Washington had caught up with him yet. Just in case, I lowered my voice. "Where are you, Jay?"

"Long story. Anyway, what I called to say is, I'm not coming back to the station."

"Not coming back? Why?"

"Can't say right now. It will all be cleared up soon."

I was stunned. Had he been threatened, too? And if so, did Washington know?

Patel continued. "I need a favor. And I have to tell you something. There is a change of ownership at KHTS, and…"

What? A few more of my brain cells gave up and died while Patel kept talking.

"… the new guys are scheduled to visit the station tomorrow. I want you to show them around, get to know them a bit."

"Me? Wouldn't Maura be the best one to—?"

"Not Maura. You. Trust me, Samantha. They'll be taking over. It's in your best interest that they get to know you."

"But Jay, I… you… the detective is—"

"Gotta go. Sorry to leave it like this. It'll all come clear soon." He disconnected, leaving me with a thousand questions and another round of mental whiplash.

My eyes fell on the envelope that held the disturbing letter. One thing at time, I told myself. I took a deep breath and returned to the living room.

Washington had taken a chair. I handed the envelope to him. He donned gloves before sliding the paper from the envelope. "When did you receive this?"

"Today."

He inspected the envelope. "No return address, of course."

Carter rose from the sofa. "Let me see it."

The detective looked hesitant. "Best to avoid extraneous fingerprints."

"Be right back." Carter left the room and immediately returned with a plastic zipper bag. He handed it to Washington. "Put it in there."

The detective looked skeptical. "Not exactly regulation, but..." He scanned the letter again and dropped it and the envelope inside.

Carter sat beside me to look it over. "Brief." He took my hand. "Any idea who sent it?"

Washington stepped in. "We need to compare it to the others."

Carter stiffened. "Others?" He looked at me.

"Not mine. Lloyd got a lot of hate mail."

Carter studied the message again. "You could be in danger."

"Or, it may not be a threat at all. Jojo thought it might mean something like, 'Yay! You go girl!'"

Washington's eyebrows shot up. "Jojo?"

"A friend at work."

The detective frowned. "At the television station? I must have missed him on the employee list."

He made a note to himself and slid the zip bag into his briefcase. "Do you have any known enemies, Ms. Newman?"

The question startled me. Should I mention my last encounter with Maura? "I, uh, recently discovered that a person at the station may have it in for me."

All eyes turned to me. Washington spoke first. "Who?"

"I'd rather not accuse anyone without knowing for sure. Maybe your people can find something."

The detective frowned. "Ms. Newman. I've warned you before about protecting friends. Murder is serious business. If you know of someone..."

I crossed my arms. "That's just it. I don't know."

Washington and Carter exchanged glances. The detective stood. "Tell you what. It's been a long day. I have more than enough to work through. We can pick this up tomorrow."

Carter shot up from the sofa, hands on hips. "What about police protection?"

"Without Ms. Newman's cooperation, I'm not sure this letter rises to the need. As she says, you could read it both ways."

"One way being that she's in danger."

Washington blinked. "I could try to rush the forensics through. In the meantime, Ms. Newman, you might want to curtail your work activities. And think about the consequences of shielding a potential criminal."

"I have to be at the station tomorrow."

Carter looked at me like I was a crazy person. "With a possible murderer working there? No way."

I returned his glare. "Have to."

The detective intervened. "I suppose I could put an officer at KHTS for a day or two until we figure this out."

He turned to Carter. "Okay with you, Mr. Chapman?"

I bristled. Washington had learned the hard way that Carter's old connections from his undercover days—plus his recent cyber work with practically every level of law enforcement in the country—made him a formidable ally.

Still, I had to set the record straight. "Mr. Chapman is not in charge of me, Detective."

"Sorry, Ms. Newman. I only meant—"

"I don't want somebody following me around. You already said I'd be safe here, and there's a security guard at the TV station."

Carter started to object. I shot him a look. He exchanged a brief glance with the detective, then turned to me. "May I see you in the kitchen for a moment?" He marched off.

By the time I caught up with him, he was pacing angrily around the kitchen island. He stopped to face me. "Look, Sam. I don't know much about the TV business. Your job, your career, that's for you to sort out. But you're in danger. You need protection, which is something I do understand."

We traded stone-faced stares.

He broke first. "I mean it. Now is not the time for you to go it alone. I promise to back off, soon as you're out of danger." He pinned me with his ridiculous amber-brown eyes. "Somewhere in that pigheaded brain of yours, you know I'm right."

My resolve withered. "Okay, but I don't want some stranger in my face all day. And I don't want people at the station to know I'm being shadowed."

"Deal."

He headed back to the living room. By the time I caught up, he was at the front door with Washington, making arrangements.

When the detective left, Carter and I sank into another silence. He rested his hand on the doorknob. "Do you want me to stay?"

Trying to answer him was torture. *I'm fine,* I tried to say, but I couldn't form the words. I shook my head.

His eyes grew sad. He kissed me on the cheek and was gone.

CHAPTER TWENTY-FIVE

Tweedy

The next morning, I dragged myself out of bed. Over a quick coffee and toast, I briefly considered upscaling my usual jeans and blazer to something more businesslike for the new KHTS owners, but I barely had enough energy to find a clean tee.

At the station, Jojo was filling in behind the receptionist's desk. "Hey Sammy! You're looking extra wild and wooly this morning. Bad night?"

"Not the greatest. By the way, I'm supposed to show some people around this morning."

"The new owners?"

"Who told you?"

"Mr. Patel sent an email this morning. Everybody's walking around bug-eyed. How many people are we expecting?"

"Not sure. Let me know when they show up."

After a trek down the hall for more coffee, I shut my door. I had just booted up my computer when the door opened again. Jojo stood in the doorway with two men in trendy Italian suits and super-gelled hair.

Jojo ushered them in. "This is Samantha Newman. She'll show you around."

I donned a happy hostess smile and rose to greet them. "Welcome to KHTS."

They didn't introduce themselves. The taller one, in a blue-striped seersucker suit and tortoiseshell glasses, strode around the table, inspecting the room like a conquering general. Stopping where he'd started, he eyed me up and down.

"So, you're our girl guide for the day?"

I gritted my teeth. "My name is Samantha Newman."

"Sorry, I'm bad with names. Let's just call you Scout." His laugh jarred my eardrums.

His shorter pal, in a too-tight navy box-plaid suit and wire-rimmed specs, echoed with a snicker. "Good one, pal."

The seersucker guy eyed me up and down again, stopping his gaze below my collarbone. "Whatcha workin' on, sweetheart?"

Play nice, Jay Patel had cautioned. Now I knew why. "Sorry, sir, I didn't get your name, or your company."

"Scanlon. Tweedy Broadcasting Network. Your new owners."

My heart stopped. TBN was the corporate equivalent of Jojo's giant asteroid smashing into a little station like us.

I managed to recover and answer the man's question. "I'm finishing an in-depth investigation into the causes of chronic flooding in the area and its impact on—"

Scanlon raised his hand to stop me. "A local issue? We rarely do those." He shot a look at his still-nameless colleague.

"We would have to review it to see if it meets our programming guidelines," his compadre conceded.

I clamped my jaw shut.

Jojo piped up. "Gentlemen, I shall return to my duties. Ms. Newman will give you the grand tour, won't you, Ms. Newman? Why don't you start with the marketing department?"

Good idea. From their reputation, Tweedy people would be more interested in marketing than in anything resembling a real news department. I managed a smile. "Ready for a tour?"

The marketing department seemed abandoned, except for Nandi Rudolph, who handled the station's social media. Nandi was the perfect avatar for Lloyd's definition of perky. Barely into her twenties, she was tirelessly enthusiastic and eager to please. Almost all her statements ended on an up-note.

She smiled broadly, displaying a well-ordered set of shiny white teeth. "Ms. Newman, can I help you?"

"I'm looking for Missy Eton. Is she around?"

A tiny frown crossed Nandi's face. "She's still on vacation?"

Eton's absence was no great loss for the Tweedy meet-and-greet. She wasn't into friendly chitchat, as I'd discovered during my brief stint in her department. Not the best trait for a marketing manager, but apparently she was good enough to keep her job. Nandi and her bubbly personality would do just fine today.

I gestured to the Tweedy guys. "Mr. Scanlon and Mr.—?"

The box-plaid guy winked. "Jake."

"—and Mr. Jake are from TBN, our new owners. Could you fill them in on what you do and any projects you're working on at the moment?"

Nandi popped up from her chair and beamed. "I sure can!" She started right in, nattering away with our visitors.

I excused myself and stepped into the hallway to check my phone. There was a message from Carter that read:

Hope you don't mind

I had no idea what that meant. Another text came from a number I didn't recognize. Both messages would have to wait, because the conversation between the Tweedy guys and Nandi was winding down.

I pocketed my phone and composed a smile. Jake eyed me and muttered something to Scanlon under his breath. They both ogled me and nodded.

I pretended not to notice. "So, we have a window before the midday news. Want to visit to the broadcast studio now, or wait until we're on air?"

They seemed happy to speed through. I could feel their eyes on my backside as they followed me down the hall. I spun around and reanimated my hostess smile. "Let me know if you see anything you want to explore further."

Their faces turned interesting shades of burgundy.

The studio crew was preparing for the midday news broadcast. We positioned ourselves just outside the arc of light.

Scanlon pointed toward a dim corner. "Who's that guy? The one not doing any work."

I looked in the direction he indicated. At first, I thought it might be someone waiting for a live studio interview. Then I remembered Carter's insistence on a security person for me. Must be him. "He's probably the extra security we added since Lloyd's... since our colleague died."

"Why extra?"

Uh-oh. Didn't they know about Lloyd? If Patel had left that tidbit out of their conversations, no way I'd be the one. Especially since the extra security was there for me.

I shrugged. "Safety's sake, I suppose." A change of subject was in order. "So, do you want to stay and watch the broadcast?"

Scanlon's eyes swept around the studio. "Nah, I've seen enough. We'll be changing things up anyway. I'm ready to blow this place and get some lunch." He turned to me. "You come too. We're looking for a new anchor girl. You should let us get to know you a little better."

Jake grinned. "Definitely."

Definitely not. "Unfortunately, I'm on deadline with that investigative report. It's—" I stopped when I saw them chuckling. "Did I say something funny?"

Scanlon answered. "Don't fret over your little report, honey. We'll provide everything you'll need. All you have to do is sit pretty and deliver the words to the camera."

Jake chimed in. "You got a great build on you. Just upgrade the wardrobe and the makeup and... you have major anchor potential." He winked again. "Sure you won't join us for lunch?"

"Not today." And not ever, if I could help it.

After giving me another once-over, they left the studio.

Brad Hudson was at the anchor desk, preparing to deliver the midday news. While Jojo tended to Brad's shiny forehead and chin, I sulked a few feet behind the camera and pondered the future of Lloyd's report under the new ownership.

When he finished with Brad, Jojo joined me. "How'd the Tweedy thing go?"

I made a face. "Best thing is, it's over. They told me to change my look if I want to keep working here. A lot sexier, I'm guessing."

"Do you?"

"Do I what?"

"Want to keep working here."

"For them? Ick. I need this job, but I won't stoop to..." I shook my head.

"Mmm-hmm." Hands on hips, he rolled his eyes.

"No, Jojo. I won't do it."

"Pish posh. You can play their game. I'll round up some things they'll like and come over tonight. Say, seven? I'll bring pad thai."

Before I could protest again, Jojo's attention flitted to the darkest corner of the studio. "Ooh, there's that dreamy new security guy. I'm gonna go chat him up. See you at seven."

I wasn't keen on playing the game with Tweedy. However, Jojo knew more about the KHTS staff than I did, and I wanted to pick his brain as to who might have murderous thoughts about Lloyd, or at least who could have sent me the threatening note. If testing a new wardrobe was the price, I was up for it.

CHAPTER TWENTY-SIX

Bake-'n-Fresh

I'd just set my bag down in the kitchen when my phone buzzed with a call from Riva Ramirez, the pizza kid's social worker. "Good news, Ms. Newman. We were able to get Valentina's hearing postponed. Since you said you were busy this week, I scheduled your deposition for Saturday morning. I hope that works for you."

"Saturday? Okay, I suppose."

"Great! I'll text you the address. Thanks!"

Jojo arrived soon after with a couple of hanging wardrobe bags and a large sack of take-out. He carried the clothes to the bedroom while I took the sack to the kitchen. Pad thai, as promised, spring rolls, and tom kha, a spicy soup with a lime/coconut milk broth. Plus two bottles of Chang Classic. I grabbed one and was about to open it when Jojo reappeared.

He snatched the beer away. "No, no. Much too bloaty. The beer's for me."

I made a face. "I need something to help me relax."

He removed the condiments from a small paper sack and handed the bag to me. "Breathe into this for a minute."

I feigned obedience and puckered the bag around my lips. While Jojo was busy unsheathing the chopsticks, I huffed and puffed into the sack. Once it was fully inflated, I smacked it hard. It exploded with a loud pop.

Jojo jumped. I giggled.

He cracked up, too. "See, you don't need a beer to relax."

While we ate, I unspooled the questions that were bugging me about some of our coworkers. First, what did he think of Maura?

He thought for a minute before answering. "Smart. Nice skin, too. But no matter how much sparkly goop she puts on herself, she's only background noise at the station. While everybody else is circling their own sun, she makes things happen. She's kind of a dormant volcano in the emotional department, though. Could blow any minute."

No kidding. "Do you think she's capable of murder?"

He smiled. "Aren't we all, under the right circumstances?"

"I mean, do you think she could have murdered Lloyd?"

Jojo bit into a spring roll as he pondered the question. "Lloyd was a rude dude. But would Maura kill him? I don't think so."

"What about me?"

He gave me a funny look. "You didn't kill him, did you?"

"No, I mean Maura. Do you think she'd want to murder me, if she saw me as a threat?"

"Want to? For sure. You're everything she'd kill to be. But actually murder you? Nah."

"Who do you think did it?"

He took a swig of beer "Honestly, I have no idea. There are probably lots of candidates."

"What about Alicia?"

"I love you, Sammy, but I won't dish dirt about the queen. Poor woman, she's hanging onto every scrap of youth she can. Lloyd wasn't even in her orbit."

"What about Brad Hudson?"

Jojo made a face. "Conceited as all get-out. But a murderer?" He shook his head. "Although, you never know. Those good looks might be hiding something deeply evil."

I was considering that possibility when another person popped into my mind: the elusive Jay Patel. What was he up to, disappearing in the middle of a company takeover and a murder investigation? "Patel sure has made himself scarce. Do you think that has anything to do with—"

"Look, hon. Everybody has secrets. Doesn't make them killers."

"Unless they are one."

Jojo waved me off. "Enough. Ready to play dress up?"

We cleaned the kitchen and retreated to the bedroom. Jojo had laid five dresses on the bed. All were blindingly bright and looked at least one size too small.

He stepped back and assessed his arrangement. "This'll be fun!"

I wasn't so sure.

He rummaged inside one of the sacks and pulled out two body slimmers—one jet black, one skin-tone—each with a built-in push-up bra. I groaned.

He tossed them to me. "Ix-nay the attitude, hon. These weren't easy to find."

I checked the size. "How did you know?"

He batted his eyelashes. "I know my boobies. Try the flesh-toned one under this." He lifted the hot pink sleeveless frock and unboxed a pair of matching stiletto pumps. The dress was trimmed with lime green bands around the waist, at the deep vee neckline, and along the ruffled hem. It looked tiny enough to be a bathing suit.

I took it to the bathroom and shut the door, then shucked my comfy clothes and stepped into the push-up body thing. It was so narrow around my ankles, I almost toppled over. I tried to yank it up, but it wouldn't budge.

I yelled through the door. "Jojo, the underwear's too small!"

He yelled back. "Inch it up slowly, one side at a time."

I bent over, grabbed the thing again and tugged it up on the left, then the right, then the left, then right, and over again until I'd hitched it all the way up. Gave my arms a major workout.

I looked in the mirror. I liked that my waist had narrowed by a couple of inches, but my lungs protested. "I can't breathe!"

"Yes you can," he yelled. "Keep going!"

Since Jojo had invested a lot of energy into this project, I didn't want to seem ungrateful. I wrangled the dress over my head, but instead of slipping downward, it stopped at my neck. I barely managed to squeeze my arms through, but from there—except for a sharp pinch in my shoulder—the dress slipped over the body slimmer without too much coaxing.

I checked the mirror. Nestled into the plunging V-neck, my breasts blossomed forth like a pair of bake-'n-fresh rolls bursting from the can. I tucked them in as much as possible and tried on the impossibly high shoes. They left me teetering back and forth until I found my balance.

Ambulating in the heels took a whole new set of skills. To move forward, I had to raise each knee in a high-step, like a show pony. I wobbled toward the door. Mission accomplished, I steadied myself and opened it.

Jojo's eyes popped. "I think I outdid myself. Let's see the backside."

Holding onto the door, I pivoted.

"Wowza."

I turned to face him again. "These shoes are ridiculous. And my boobs are way over the top, literally."

He put his hands on his hips. "It's this or the unemployment line. Your choice."

I rolled my eyes.

He reset the dress with little twists at the waist and hips, and stepped back to check his work. "The trim brings out the green in your eyes. You look spectacular."

"I look like a hooker." I yanked the bottom of the vee upward in an attempt to cover more chest.

He tugged it down again. "Nonsense. Your bazookas strike the perfect balance between demure and shameless. The Tweedy guys will go gaga for you. Wear this tomorrow and you'll soon be the new KHTS news anchor."

"Can't you come up with something more businesslike? I still have nice suits from my corporate days. Maybe—"

"Nope, and nope. This is definitely the one for tomorrow. The others will work great, too. We can always tone things down later. Ready to move on?"

"Best thing I've heard all day. What do I owe you?"

"Nada. They're your welcome-to-the-big-show gift."

"Really?"

"Sure. They were cheaper than you look."

I laughed. "Thanks, I guess." I leaned on the doorframe to remove the pink pumps. "I'm glad that's over."

"We're not done yet. Next, we'll work on your hair."

"What's wrong with it?"

"Absolutely nothing. I'm just gonna do a few highlights to add some pop."

Except for a brief fling with a lemon juice rinse the summer I turned thirteen, I've never colored my hair. Besides, auburn suited my complexion. I made a face, which Jojo chose to ignore.

While he set up in the bathroom, I escaped to the kitchen and filled a goblet with Tempranillo. I drank half of it before I returned to the bedroom.

Jojo eyed the red in the glass. "White wine, Sammy. White wine, white teeth for the camera." He grabbed the goblet and downed the rest.

I snatched the empty glass. "You may mess with my boobs and my hair, mister, but don't ever get between me and my wine."

He laughed. "Touché. Bring me one, too. Then let's get back to work."

An hour and another glass of wine later, the hair coloring session came to an end.

Jojo stepped back to assess his work. "Yep. You're good to go. Get a good night's sleep." He kissed me on the cheek and left me with a parting word of encouragement. "Don't fret. You'll look great!"

CHAPTER TWENTY-SEVEN

Hot Pink

From the moment I opened my eyes in the morning, I deeply regretted the decision to play along with Tweedy. My shoulder pain had returned, thanks to the makeover session with Jojo. The last thing I wanted to do was squeeze into that hot pink straitjacket again.

I shuffled into the kitchen to fuel up and reconsider my options. One: quit my job without having a backup plan. Or two: hang on until they fire me. Both choices resulted in the same thing: unemployment, again.

I slumped to the bedroom, opened the closet, and gazed longingly at what remained of my old business wardrobe. I'd saved my pennies to buy well-tailored suits for my executive career. I'd even managed to rescue a few from the flood at Gertie's house.

My favorite blue one had perished pre-flood—after the ill-advised pity party—but three suits survived. I pulled out the jade green one, held it up in front of me, and checked the mirror. It still brought out the green in my eyes, but the once-trendy cut now looked stodgy. Which left a gray pantsuit, and a brown one. In the mirror, they offered all the pizzazz of a nun's tunic. Tweedy-repellent, for sure.

With a sigh, I tugged the hot pink number down over the push-up bra thingy and hot-rolled my hair into the glamour curls Jojo suggested. His highlights played in the light as planned. So did my bake-'n-fresh twins, all bouncy and pert atop the plummeting neckline. I nearly broke my ankle putting on the stilettos. Would've served me right if I had.

I ventured one last check in the mirror. It would take a sizeable amount of mental maneuvering for me to dwell inside the image that stared back. But I needed to play the game long enough to find another job. Or maybe Lloyd's killer would murder me first, though I hoped I wouldn't die looking like this.

On my way down to the garage, the elevator stopped on eleven. Pansy Gump and her husband, Hubert got on. When not lounging in her flowing caftans, Pansy often dressed as if she were heading to a board meeting for a very old and stuffy women's club. Today she was in a navy sheath with a matching purse and her ever-present strand of pearls.

I said good morning.

Her powdered, pie-crust face screwed into a frown as she looked me up and down and harrumphed. "Is that get-up supposed to be an improvement?"

"Not really. It's the uniform the new station owners prefer."

"Good heavens." She eyed me again. "I certainly hope they won't force that wonderful Brad Hudson to do the same."

An image of Brad, stuffed into the dress I had on popped into my brain. I laughed out loud.

Pansy marched out as soon as the elevator opened on their garage level. Hubert trailed behind, giving me a wink and a thumbs-up.

I felt a tiny tinge of triumph as I maneuvered in the stilettos from my parking slot all the way into the KHTS lobby without falling on my face.

Donna Sue greeted me from the reception desk. "Welcome to KHTS. May I help you... Oh! Ms. Newman, I didn't recognize you at first. You look... different."

I mumbled a thank you and high-stepped toward the news department like a show pony.

Jojo was already in my workspace preparing a supply of magic powders and creams. "Hey, gorgeous. Come sit."

I took a chair at the table and surrendered my face to his magic brush. In no time, he pronounced me ready to meet my public.

I regarded my reflection in the hand mirror. Like my hair, my cheekbones and eyes popped with highlights, as if I were lit from inside.

I made a face. "I'm not sure about this."

"Smile like a movie star. You sure look like one." Before he walked out, he offered a deep bow. "See ya later, Princess."

I attempted to walk normally to the break room for coffee. It wasn't easy, but by the time I got there I'd found a less awkward gait. Baby steps, literally.

Two boxes from Shipley Do-nuts sat beside the coffeemaker, each half-empty. Only a single glazed gem remained. Compared to the apple fritter or the chocolate crème-filled one next to it, the plain one seemed practically calorie-free. I took it as a sign that positive karma hadn't totally abandoned me and plucked it out before mincing my steps back to work.

Maura was waiting at the table. The minute I saw her, my pulse ticked up. I glanced toward my work bag, hoping she hadn't sabotaged anything. It looked untouched, thank goodness.

Doughnut in one hand, coffee in the other, I teetered in the doorway, wondering if it was safe for me to enter.

She offered a shy smile. "I won't bite. Promise."

I left the door open—just in case—and toddled in.

She seemed amused as she watched me maneuver to the table. I sat across from her, slowly sipping coffee and waiting for her next move.

She splayed her sparkly purple-tipped fingers on the table and stared at them while she spoke. "Jay Patel called me last night."

"He did?"

"Yeah. He warned me that the new management would be here again today." She studied my new look. "So, you're joining the Tweedy world. Congrats." She might as well have called me a traitor.

I started to explain, but she cut me off.

"It's okay. I know my strengths. None of which appeal to those sharks. Besides, that's not why I'm here. I want to apologize for yesterday. I spewed a lot of frustration at you, and I'm sorry."

"You don't have to…"

She stopped me again. "Jay has very gently prepared me to move on. God only knows to where, but before that happens, I wanted to clear the air with you."

"Maura, I don't want to stay, believe me, but I need the money, at least for a while."

She offered a wry smile. "Let's not compare predicaments, okay? You can work for Tweedy as long as you want, or as long as you can stand it, especially looking like that."

My face heated. "I hate that this is happening. I'm sorry."

"I'm the one who's behaved shamefully, and I need to apologize for it."

"You just did."

"No. There's something else, worse than yelling at you."

"Keeping the flood report from me?"

"Worse than that." She rested her elbows on the table, clasped her hands together, and stared at them.

My mind raced through what else she could be talking about.

She sighed deeply and raised her eyes to me. "If you haven't already, you may be receiving an anonymous letter."

"Letter?"

"In red marker?" Behind her glasses, tears sprouted. "It's from me."

"You?"

Before she could respond, my phone chimed.

Detective Washington's timing could not have been worse. I raised a finger for Maura to wait and said hello.

He sounded rushed. "Ms. Newman? I may have a lead on that note you gave me. By any chance, is the coworker you mentioned last night Maura Tustin?"

"Um, perhaps. I'm just wrapping up a meeting."

"With her?"

I looked up at Maura, who was dabbing her eyes with a tissue.

Washington must have read my silence. "I'm only a block away."

"Please speak to me before you proceed." I disconnected.

A thousand questions crowded my brain. Before Washington arrived, I wanted answers. "You sent the note, why?"

She shook her head. "Stupid, I know. But once Lloyd was out of the way, I figured I finally had the chance to reclaim my own work. Then Patel wanted you to take the credit. I thought if I could scare you off, Jay would have to give it to me."

The conference room intercom beeped and Donna Sue's monotone came through the speaker. "Detective Washington is here to see you."

Maura's damp eyes grew round behind her glasses. "Why is he here? You didn't tell anyone about the stupid note, did you?"

"I gave it to him."

"But I didn't mean anything serious! I would never..." She bolted out of her chair, panic in her eyes. "Is he coming for me?"

I needed her to stay calm. "Just to talk, I think."

"Please, you have to get me out of this. It was just a stupid prank. I only wanted..." Her voice trailed off as she fled down the hall.

CHAPTER TWENTY-EIGHT

Young Jack

Buron Washington rushed through the door but stopped halfway in. His eyes moved from my cleavage to my glam face. "Ms. Newman, you... you have, uh..." He frowned.

"Don't worry, detective. I'm still the same sweet thorn in your side."

He took the chair across from me that Maura had just vacated and set an evidence sleeve on the table. "Before I speak to Ms. Tustin, I would like you to verify something." He patted the envelope. "May I ask you to close your eyes?"

I played along.

"I am going to hold something in front of you and ask if you recognize the smell."

Eyes closed, I heard him open the envelope. I sniffed, and my heart sank. Maura's goose was cooked. The scent of her fruity bubblegum was unmistakable. I don't know how I missed it before.

"Do you need another whiff?"

I shook my head. I wanted to believe Maura when she said she wrote the note only to scare me away. But she had admitted to holding a deep resentment toward me, and Lloyd, too. If she really was Lloyd's killer, I couldn't shield her any longer.

Washington broke into my thoughts. "I take it you recognized something?"

I needed more think time. I opened my eyes and stood. "There are doughnuts in the break room. And coffee. Let me get you something."

"Can you please answer my question?"

I made my way to the door. "First, I'm getting coffee. Coming or not?"

The detective opted not to follow. I brought him a black coffee anyway, and a doughnut slathered in chocolate icing with purple sprinkles on top.

His face softened. "My daughter's favorite." A rare glimpse into the man's human side, and just the effect I hoped it would have.

He sampled the pastry and took a sip of coffee. "So, you recognized the smell."

"Yes."

"And?"

I set my mug down. "I don't want you to jump to conclusions."

His frown returned. "Ms. Newman, I've warned you about the clever little diversions you create when you're trying to protect a friend. This is no time for games. We found some disturbing emails from Ms. Tustin to Mr. Sedgwick on his laptop, and I am here to speak to her about them. I simply want to know if you can identify the distinctive odor coming from this note."

I crossed my arms and gave him my best stare-down.

He sighed and checked his watch. "Tell you what. I'll be searching the building for Ms. Tustin. If you decide to do your moral duty in the next few minutes, text me." He rose to go.

"It's Maura!" I hadn't meant to blurt it out, but there it was. "It smells like her bubblegum." My heart sank.

Washington sat again. "I thought so. I recognized it from my first interview with her. Where is she now?"

"I don't know. She ran out of here when she heard you were coming."

"She was here, in this room with you?"

"She confessed to writing the note. And apologized."

The detective rubbed his forehead and sighed. "I am going to search the building. However, given the woman's hostility toward you, I don't think you should be alone." He tapped his phone and spoke into it. "I am with Ms. Newman in the conference room. Would you care to join us?"

Less than a minute later, Carter Chapman walked in. He blinked when he saw the new me, but his face remained expressionless.

Washington resealed the evidence envelope and stood. "Ms. Newman has identified the person who sent her the anonymous note as Maura Tustin, who also has motive for the Sedgwick homicide. She may still be in the building. While I search for her, I thought you would want to keep Ms. Newman company, for safety's sake."

I rolled my eyes. "Guys, she's not a maniac. Just sad. Sad and frustrated, not homicidal."

"We'll see about that." Washington headed out.

Carter shut the door, then turned and gave me a long, slow once-over.

Part of me was glad to see him, but I was still miffed. It didn't take a genius to figure out that he'd been the security guy lurking in the shadows who made Jojo's heart skip a beat. "You're my bodyguard? The one you promised would stay out of sight?"

"You said you didn't want some stranger in your face. I haven't been near you until right now. And it's a little late to say we're strangers." His eyes traveled over me again. "Is this some kind of costume?"

With everything else going on, I hadn't mentioned my shaky employment status. "New management. The station was sold to Tweedy Broadcasting."

Carter's eyebrows raised. "To Tweedy?"

I nodded. "They said if I wanted to keep working here, I'd have to dress sexier. Like it or not, this is me, for now."

His face screwed into a frown. "Sexier? That's horseshit."

"And illegal. But Jojo talked me into hanging on long enough to find another job. He has a crush on you, by the way."

Carter shortened the distance between us until we were practically touching. "Doesn't he know I'm spoken for?"

"By whom?" I tried for a serious face, but that tingly electric flash that happens when Carter's magnetic field enters mine betrayed me.

I backed away. "You could do worse. Jojo's my best friend here. Matter of fact, he could be my bodyguard." I grinned at the idea. "You're fired."

"Not so fast. Just because Washington thinks he has a suspect doesn't mean you're out of danger. He could be wrong."

"He is wrong. Maura's not a killer."

"You're too trusting, Sam."

"And you're too paranoid."

During this exchange, we had somehow worked ourselves close together again. With his face only inches from mine, I caught myself leaning in. I backed off. "Not here."

His stepped back, too. "Agreed. This weekend?"

I was about to answer when the Tweedy guys opened the door. In case they'd caught Carter's last comment, I pivoted. "Weekend? No, I need it by Friday."

He caught the hint. "Sure. I can do that."

As Carter walked out, Scanlon's gaze followed him down the hall. He let out a low whistle. "Impressive."

His colleague nodded. "He'd be great on camera. Conservative, with a hint of danger. Very Jack Ryan."

"Sexier, even," added Scanlon.

The Jack Ryan thing came close to being accurate. But there was no way they would ever get the world's most reclusive cybergeek to perform on camera.

They shifted their focus to me. Scanlon's eyes slid over my body. "I see you took our suggestion to heart. Good girl."

"Nice," his buddy agreed.

I suppressed a shudder and summoned my happy hostess smile. "So, guys, what's on your agenda today?"

"We have to conduct some staff interviews," Scanlon said. He didn't look happy about it. "Where can we find Maura Tustin?"

The question of the hour. "I don't think she's available right now. Who else is on your list?"

"Alicia Somebody?"

"Sultana? I can show you to her office. When will you be interviewing me?"

Scanlon laughed. "Honey, these are exit interviews. You'll be staying."

CHAPTER TWENTY-NINE

The Axe

I led the Tweedies to Alicia's office, my heart growing heavier with each step. She was the soul of KHTS News, and still at the top of her game. How was it possible that the axe would fall on her today?

I stopped in the ladies room to quiet my mind. Instead, confronted with my bizarre new reflection in the mirror, I high-stepped it out again, grabbed my keys, and fled the building.

The Ferret pointed toward the nearest Whataburger drive-thru, and who was I to argue? Out of concern for my ability to breathe in the new dress, I skipped the sandwich and ordered a small fries and diet Dr Pepper. From the pick-up line, I pulled into a parking slot to eat and think.

It would be a challenge to maintain my cool and face the Tweedy men again. I longed to escape to the condo, ditch the preposterous dress, and take the rest of the day off. I sat there, chomping on fries, daring myself to do it.

When the last fry was gone, I called Jojo. "Are the Tweedy guys looking for me?"

"Don't think so. They left, just after our fearless leader showed up."

"The new guy?"

"Nope, same old one."

"Jay Patel?"

"In the flesh. He's looking for you, by the way. Where are you?"

"On my way."

I made it back to the TV station in record time. Several employees were gathered in conversation in the parking lot. Most of them held cardboard boxes filled with random stuff: coffee mugs, a trophy or two, Astros baseball paraphernalia, family photos. Sad-faced, they hugged one another and waved goodbye.

At her post behind the reception desk, Donna Sue was talking to another forlorn box carrier. I texted Jay Patel that I'd arrived. He replied by asking me to come to his office *asap*. In case something had changed since this morning and I was being axed too, I headed straight there.

Patel looked like he hadn't slept in days. "Have a seat."

He studied my new look for a moment. "I want to thank you, Samantha."

"Again? For what?"

"For keeping your cool. TNB sent us a couple of jerks, but you won them over. They definitely want you."

A mix of emotions flooded me: relief, guilt, shame.

Patel continued. "You'll be at the anchor desk very soon."

"Anchor? Are you sure I'm ready? I mean, why me, when people more experienced than I am are crying in the parking lot?"

"Strictly a business decision."

"It's not fair."

"Please, this is the first good news I've delivered today. Be happy."

"Who else is staying?"

"Can't say. I haven't spoken to everyone yet."

"Are you staying?"

"They don't need an old news hand like me. Besides, I have a network job waiting. This is my last week, if they don't kick me out sooner." He glanced at the screen. Brad Hudson was reporting breaking news about a local special election.

Patel stood. "I've got to move on to the next person, then get to the police station to post bail for Maura."

"Is she okay?"

"I'll see when I get there."

"She wrote Lloyd's report."

"I know."

"So, it's pretty much ready to go. But if she's not around, what will happen to it?"

Patel shrugged. "Keep it. Matter of fact, go home, and take whatever you've got on it with you." He offered his hand. "Good luck. I may or may not be here tomorrow. At any rate, I hope our paths cross again."

On the way out, I caught a glimpse of Alicia Sultana, still in her office. She seemed to be rummaging for something in a bottom drawer of her desk.

All of a sudden she straightened up, ripped off her wig and tossed it into a cardboard box on the floor. To my shock, she was completely bald. Without her glorious sable mane, she seemed shrunken.

I tried to scoot past, but she saw me before I cleared the doorway.

She laughed, a ragged throaty sound. "Caught me out of the clown suit, did you?"

"I... I was just passing and..."

"Come in."

I obeyed. She motioned to a chair across the desk from her.

She reached for my hand and patted it. "All good things must pass. It was inevitable that someone like you would replace me someday."

My eyes fell on the cardboard box. "I'm sorry."

"For what? Being young and healthy? Believe me, if I were your age, I'd give you a run for your money. Still could, if... " The thought trailed off.

"But, to let you go, after all your accomplishments?"

She laughed again. "Oh, baby, I wasn't fired. I quit. Retired, to be specific. With TNB taking over, I could see the writing on the teleprompter, so to speak. Besides, I'm ready to take it easy, see what my next rodeo shapes up to be. I'm fine, really."

There it was, the grin, from Alicia Sultana. I wanted to tell her how much I admired her, and that I'd try to live up to her legacy every time I was on camera. That I hoped I could inspire confidence like she had done. But all I could muster was, "I'll miss you."

She offered a twisted smile, then dove into the bottom drawer again. I had been dismissed.

Oddly enough, I dreamed of my parent's house that night. Mom was in the kitchen, whipping mashed potatoes. Her back was turned to me, but somehow she knew I was there, because she spoke.

Don't worry. Everything will be all right.

She used to tell me that whenever I was anxious about a test or something else at school. The last time she'd said it, I was about to leave for college and nervous about leaving home. Only that time, she was wrong.

CHAPTER THIRTY

Electric Blue

For Day Two of my Tweedy charade, I squeezed into the electric blue get-up, matching stilettos, and a faceful of makeup. The shoes featured a platform sole which made for a more stable base than the pink ones, so I could maneuver with less wobble than yesterday.

Normally, my little Ferret would be one of the last cars to squeeze into the KHTS employee parking lot, but after yesterday's house-cleaning, there were plenty of open spaces. I hoofed it to the news department to see if Jay Patel had made it in today. I caught up to him as he was leaving his office.

He looked me up and down and smiled. "I knew I could count on you. You're my legacy here, you know."

That threw me off. "What do you mean?"

"I hired you for your moral compass, Samantha."

"My...?"

"Your natural instinct for justice. The hallmark of a serious journalist. Can't be taught, really, but you've got it. And I'm sure you'll fight like hell against the cockamamie Tweedy system to do what's right. Somebody has to."

Quite a speech, but what was it with him and the whistleblower thing? The tag hadn't felt right when he hired me, and after struggling through Lloyd's exhaustive research and reading Maura's eloquent draft, I felt even less worthy.

"But Jay, I—"

"Follow me. I'm about to formally announce Alicia's retirement to the staff. It involves you, too."

In the break room, someone had laid out bagels and fixings. Patel gave a post-layoff speech to the remaining crew, thanking everyone for their patience and understanding during the past few days. He praised the recently departed for their work and wished them well. Then he launched into a tribute to Alicia and announced her retirement. This would be her last week.

He invited me to come stand beside him. A dozen eyeballs followed me as I worked my way to the front while he continued. "All of you in this room will officially become TNB employees on Monday. You will meet your new coworkers then. However, I am happy to announce that tomorrow, Francine Bascom will be joining Brad at the noon broadcast desk, and Brad and Samantha Newman will cover the evening news. Please give them—and your new colleagues—your best efforts."

He took a breath and continued. "Also, I'll be moving on soon. It's been a pleasure and a privilege to work with all of you, and I wish you the best of luck in the future."

In the stunned silence that followed, I spun around and followed him out. "Couple of questions, Jay."

He stopped at his office door. "I don't have much time, Samantha. Make it quick."

"Will Maura be coming back to work?"

"That was never the plan."

"But, Lloyd's report. It's really hers. Who will produce it now?"

"Take that up with your new boss. By the way, Alicia's office is available. Make it yours." He ducked into his office and shut the door.

Standing next to Patel with all eyes on me had made me queasy. What were the chances that Lloyd's murderer could be in that room, too? The urge to get away was overwhelming, but I had to stay for Alicia's big finale.

With Lloyd's report in limbo, there was little to do until then. To pass the time, I took out my spiral notebook and started listing the names of everyone still working at the station. I was pondering the list when Francine breezed in.

"Samantha! Congratulations to us! I thought I'd have to put in at least a couple of years before I had a shot at the news desk. This is so awesome!"

"I'm happy for you, Francine."

"You too, Samantha. No more Lloyd!"

Her hands flew to cover her mouth. "Oooh, that sounded bad. Sorry." She smiled sheepishly. "By the way, I'm hot on the trail of Lloyd's wife. I asked a PI friend to see if she can find a marriage record."

I tried to match her enthusiasm. "Great. Keep me posted."

"Sure thing. We're kinda like teammates now."

By five o'clock, the Tweedy guys—I'd come to think of them as Tweedle Dumb and Tweedle Dumber—hadn't bothered to show up. Apparently, I'd tugged and pinched myself into the electric blue outfit for nothing.

Almost everyone stayed late for Alicia's farewell broadcast, except Maura, of course. I still refused to believe she had anything to do with Lloyd's death.

When the hour approached, the remaining staff began to shuffle into the studio. I looked around for Carter, but didn't see him. Maybe I'd convinced him to back off a little.

Alicia made her last appearance in a stunning silver sheath. Jojo had worked his magic on her wig and makeup, and she looked fabulous as ever. As she took her chair for the last time, a hush fell over the studio. All eyes were on her, including mine.

She began by reviewing the highlights of her career, and praised the crew and the rest of the staff for supporting her over the years. She gave a heartfelt shout out to Jojo, her "special angel." Then she thanked her loyal viewers. It sounded a little like she was reciting her own eulogy. By the time she signed off, there wasn't a dry eye in the studio.

CHAPTER THIRTY ONE

Half-Peeled

On Friday morning, there was only a skeleton staff left to soldier on until the arrival of the new Tweedy people next week. Most of the technical folks had survived the blitzkrieg, but in the marketing department, only Nandi Rudolph remained. Patel's office was bare.

My costume *du jour* was a skinny yellow number in which I closely resembled a half-peeled banana. And matching stilettos, which were killing me.

Francine Bascom was about to make her noontime anchor debut with Brad. With nothing better to do, I tottered into the studio to watch.

The young woman behind the anchor desk was not last week's cub reporter. From the platinum highlights in her new pixie hairdo to her sleeveless tangerine wrap dress, I recognized Jojo's handiwork. Under her old peasant skirts and jean jacket, Francine had been hiding the muscular body of an athlete. Her melodious alto worked well with Brad's basso profondo. She nailed the broadcast.

Back in my workspace, someone had left a preliminary rundown of the evening news schedule on the table. Though my official debut wasn't until Monday, Alicia's early departure gave me less than four hours to practice being a live on-camera reporter.

THE BODY IN THE NEWS

Though Francine was almost as new to the lofty position as I was, her college communications training placed her miles ahead of me. I would be learning on the job, with thousands of strangers watching. My stomach flopped around like a fish in a bucket.

I shut my eyes and conjured up Alicia Sultana. Her smooth delivery had always seemed so effortless, it was hard to work out exactly how she did it.

Do not fidget, I told myself. *Do not stumble over words. Look confident. Breathe.*

"Hey, Samantha."

I opened my eyes to see Francine step in and shut the door behind her. "Saw you in the studio during my broadcast. What'd you think? I was so nervous!"

"It didn't show. You were good."

"Thanks. Have a minute?" She took the chair next to me and lowered her voice. "I have news about Lloyd. I finally ran into that homicide detective. He was more interested in asking me questions than in answering mine, so I didn't get much. I did, however, hear from someone else that Sedgwick did have a wife. Or, rather, an ex. But that's not the interesting part."

"Which is?"

"I was told by more than one person that Lloyd had dirt on people he didn't like. And he kept a list."

My ears perked up. "A list?"

"Like for blackmail or something."

"Who told you this?"

"Nobody seems to know anything first hand. It's only a rumor at this point."

Given Lloyd's suspicious nature, the rumor was easy to believe. Like my roster of suspects, his targets could be anyone at the station, or elsewhere. True or not, a rumor like that could drive someone to murder.

I wondered if Buron Washington had heard about it. My first instinct was to call and ask him. On second thought, he had always pooh-poohed my theories in the past, so why try? Calling him could wait until I knew more, or at least until after the looming pressure of my first TV anchor spot was over. I pushed every other worrisome issue aside and took up the rundown for the evening broadcast.

A half-hour before air time, anxiety grabbed me by the throat. On my way down the hall to the studio, I reminded myself how small the KHTS viewership was. If I flubbed up, only few thousand people would think I was an idiot.

I slipped into the anchor chair next to Brad and willed myself not to squint in the lights. I could just make out the Tweedles standing near the camera, gesturing at me and murmuring to one another.

The final script came up on the teleprompter. Most of it relied on video clips from news services, so I only had to speak a sentence or two before and after each one. The hardest parts would be sticking to my copy and not Brad's, and keeping my eyes from watering under the blazing lights. And remembering to breathe.

A moment before we went live, panic threatened again. Brad whispered, "Break a leg," and we were on.

In what felt like a nanosecond, the whole thing was over. I gasped for air. Jojo rushed over with a glass of water and gave me a hug. "A star is born!"

"At least I didn't screw up."

The Tweedy guys approached from the shadows. "You looked great," Scanlon announced.

His buddy agreed. "Love the dress. Good girl."

They didn't comment on my news-reading performance. Maybe that would be up to my new boss to handle. Seemed as good a time as any to ask which one of them it would be.

I hoped my smile looked genuine. "I look forward to working with you."

They laughed. "We're strictly transition people, honey." Scanlon replied. "You won't be seeing us anymore."

While their imminent departure was welcome news, it was ridiculous to keep KHTS employees in the dark. "Could you just tell us who it will be?"

"Not our department. We're moving on to meet the next victims. So many stations, so little time." They both laughed heartily, turned on their heels, and exited the studio.

I said a silent good riddance.

The crew was busy resetting for Brad's late night broadcast. With no one else to offer feedback, I already felt like yesterday's news. I pulled my shoes off and walked barefoot from the studio to grab my keys and leave.

All the way to the condo, my body begged for release from the banana dress. Soon as I shut the door, I ditched the stilettos, peeled everything off, and dropped it in a pile in the bedroom.

After I showered and put on my jammies, I headed to the kitchen for wine. Glass in hand, I checked my phone. It lit with calls from Gertie and Carter. I tapped Gertie's number first.

Louis answered. "Samantha, my wife's about to kill me!"

"Why?"

"I was watching the game on another station when she walked in and let out a shriek like I've never heard before! I swear, she had murder in her eyes."

Gertie must have yanked the phone away, because the next voice was hers.

"All day, I've been saying, 'Samantha's doing the evening news, Louis. Tonight's the night.' Then, the sugar cookies I was baking for his granddaughter's slumber party burned, and by the time I cleaned that up and started over, he was watching rugby on another station and the news was over. He didn't even remember to record it. I might as well be married to a turnip!"

I had to smile. "You can probably catch it on the KHTS website."

I could hear Gertie telling Louis to boot up their computer. "I'll call after we watch."

I disconnected and called Carter. He didn't say anything after hello. I had to ask. "Did you watch?"

"Yes."

"And?"

"You were fine."

"Fine?"

"You were good."

"But?"

"Not keen on the new look."

"Me either."

"That's a relief. Are you up for company? I could drive in tonight and we could celebrate your debut."

Darn. I had that deposition for the shooter kid. "I have to be somewhere with my head on straight first thing in the morning. Maybe after that?"

"Sure. I've got meetings downtown in the afternoon."

We said goodnight. I turned off my phone and finished the glass of wine while contemplating a future filled with body slimmers, bulging boobs, and tortured toes. Come Monday, our little station would feel like a whole different place. No Alicia Sultana, no Jay Patel, no Maura Tustin, no more Lloyd Sedgwick.

And if I let the Tweedy Network have its way, no more of the old Samantha.

CHAPTER THIRTY-TWO

Who Are You?

If it hadn't been for the wine, I don't think I ever would have fallen asleep. Too bad I didn't stay that way. Everything was exploding in my head like a cluster bomb. The Tweedy takeover at KHTS was worrisome, but by four a.m., it faded in comparison to Lloyd's murder. The number of possible killers gave me the creepy-crawlies.

Wide awake, I sat up and stared out at the sparkling city lights. A Life Flight helicopter, red lights twinkling, drifted across the inky sky and landed on a rooftop in the Texas Medical Center, reminding me that things could always be worse. I wished its passengers godspeed.

Around six, the sun broke over the horizon, bathing the skyscrapers in glittering pink. No use staying in bed with my pulse pounding in my ears. I crawled out and headed for the kitchen, veering slightly sideways as I went. The wine hadn't kept me in dreamland long enough, but it was still messing with my balance. I needed coffee, and lots of it, to face my deposition for the pizza kid.

The address for Salvatore Onofro, Valentina Garcia's defense attorney, was in Midtown, at the east end of a strip mall that had not yet been gentrified like the rest of the neighborhood. A tiny Korean cafe anchored the west end. Between the two, the other retail spaces looked abandoned. Peeling signs above the boarded up doors announced a tattoo parlor, the former campaign office of a city council candidate, and a tobacco vaping center.

The attorney's office looked to be only three parking spaces wide. I parked the Ferret in front of the abandoned vape shop, next to two other cars.

A bell tinkled as I walked into the entry, which held a desk and a chair that looked like they'd been salvaged from a sidewalk trash heap.

Riva Ramirez appeared from around a partition that obscured the rest of the space. She welcomed me with a warm handshake. "So grateful you've come."

She guided me past a couple of shabby, unoccupied work stations to Salvatore Onofro's office in an open space at the back.

He huffed and puffed to a standing position and rose to greet me—no small feat for a man whose girth overlapped the arms of his swivel chair. He gestured to a small round conference table. "Make yourself comfortable."

I took a seat next to a stenographer who was gearing up for the interview. We exchanged head nods and tight smiles. Riva sat across from the steno. Onofro worked himself into a chair opposite me. A pitcher of ice water and four glasses sat at the center of the table.

The lawyer nodded to the steno to begin. He formally introduced the procedure, including a caution that I was under oath to tell the truth. He asked me to state my name and address. Then he wanted me to describe what I remembered about the shooting.

After enduring other sworn statements for previous investigations, I knew to keep my answers simple. For the umpteenth time, I replayed the awful scene in my mind's eye, and spoke as it unfolded.

When I came to the part where I lunged for the gun, my pulse rate started to climb. The scene became a blur. I poured a glass of water and drank it down. Three sets of eyes watched me and waited.

Onofro offered a prompt. "What made you decide to take the weapon?"

"I tried to calm her down, and she did stop pointing the gun at us. When things relaxed a little, I realized how small she was. I thought I might be able to take the gun away."

"What happened then?"

I shut my eyes to refocus. "She lowered the gun. I went for it. I managed to grab her arm, but when I reached for the gun, we both lost our balance and fell. That's when I heard the shot."

Onofro leaned in. "Repeat that, please, just to make sure we record it accurately."

"We fell to the floor, and the gun went off."

"In that order?"

"Yes."

"Who had possession of the weapon when it discharged?"

"I... I don't think anyone did."

"What makes you say that?"

"Because the gun was on the floor between us."

"To be clear, the gun came out of her hand before you heard the shot?"

Pain in my shoulder fired up, and I caught myself twisting Mom's ring around my finger. I clenched my fist to stop it. The others at the table sat at attention, waiting for my answer.

Riva poured more water into my glass. I took a few sips until the scene came back. "It must have happened like that, because she wasn't holding the gun, and neither was I."

"So, to restate for the record, when the weapon discharged, Valentina Garcia was not aiming it at Lloyd Sedgwick?"

"Correct."

Onofro exchanged a satisfied look with Riva Ramirez. He sat back and turned to me. "Thank you, Ms. Newman. Unless you have something more to add, we can stop here."

Blazing sunlight nearly blinded me when I left Onofro's dim office. Half-stunned, I collapsed into the driver's seat of the Ferret.

Despite Carter's assurance that my actions had not led to Lloyd's death, I was tortured with second guesses, until I remembered what my long-lost, freewheeling college roommate Lista used to say whenever one of us messed up.

"What's done is done. Move on. No regrets." It has been my mantra ever since.

I shook myself and attempted the mindful breathing exercise Cassandra had taught me. Mid-inhale, my phone pinged with a message.

All it said was:

your next

I blinked at the words, trying to change them from a horror movie cliche into something positive, like Jojo had thought Maura's red-lettered note was. But in my current state, this one felt real.

Had Maura lost her mind again, or was this a new weirdo? Either way, it was too much. Somebody was messing with my head, and it had to stop. I'd read somewhere that stalkers are usually cowards, so just to shake things up, I replied with a message of my own:

Who are you?

CHAPTER THIRTY-THREE

Dirt

I arrived at the condo, shaky and hungry. There was a note from Carter on the kitchen counter saying he had come and gone.

I opened the freezer and unwrapped two of Gertie's stuffed cabbage rolls. While the microwave did its job, I checked to see if my texter had answered my callout. No reply yet.

I finished the stuffed cabbage and pulled a tub of ice cream from the freezer. I'd stayed clear of it for the sake of my Tweedy wardrobe, but what the heck? I opened the tub and removed a half-inch layer off the top, spoon by soothing spoonful.

The ice cream did a lot for my hunger, but I was still jumpy. Waiting for the police to solve Lloyd's murder was nerve-wracking. If his killer was also my mystery texter, I had to figure out who it was.

I was well-acquainted with Lloyd's mean side, and so was just about everybody else who worked with him. In hopes of remembering something important, I reconsidered the most likely candidates.

After thankless years spent propping up Lloyd's career, had Maura stepped over the line and murdered him? Or Jay Patel? His recent disappearances made him seem flaky. Was he hiding a secret worth killing for? Or Brad Hudson. The normally debonair anchor appeared unusually harried the morning after Lloyd was found dead. Did Brad have murder in his heart?

Alicia Sultana had been top dog at the station for years, and she appeared to be relatively unfazed by the murder. Then again, she was an expert at looking cool under pressure.

Francine Bascom had been unusually eager to dig into Lloyd's personal life. Perhaps there was more history between them than I realized.

I worked down to the non-broadcast employees, at least the few I knew. First, much as it pained me, Jojo.

No way.

I moved on to Missy Eton, the frosty marketing manager. Far as I could tell, she didn't have much interaction with Lloyd. But she'd been absent since the shooting, so...

As for Nandi Rudolph, she and Lloyd didn't inhabit the same planet, far as I could tell. Moe, the night security guard, lacked the cunning to plan a murder. And I barely knew the rest of the staff. I gave up and searched for possibilities elsewhere.

Someone at the hospital, perhaps, like a serial-killer nurse? And Lloyd's wife, or whoever that rude woman was who answered Lloyd's phone. Or perhaps she was just trying to protect his well-being. Understandable, I suppose.

I considered the army of haters in Lloyd's *Love Letters* file. Kyle was the only one I'd met. Did his jolly demeanor hide the heart of a killer? Or perhaps one of his real estate developer buddies did it.

I'd run out of names. Except mine. Did I have motive for killing Lloyd? Let me count the ways. I hoped Detective Washington had already ruled me out.

My attempt to figure things out was getting me nowhere. In truth, there was no proof that my weirdo texter was also the person who killed Lloyd. That lovely thought left me even jumpier than before.

Carter was still MIA. I considered going down to the gym to blow off steam on the treadmill. Then I remembered the nice swim I'd had last week, before Pansy's grandkids ruined it. Hoping I could repeat it in peace and quiet this time, I abandoned the notebook, changed into a swimsuit, and headed down to the pool.

Luckily, I had the terrace to myself. I dropped my towel on a chaise and dove into the deep end. A delicious shock of cool water broke over me . After a couple of laps, my muscles began to unclench and my breath deepened. I flipped onto my back and let the water buoy my body. The sun was warm on my face, and I floated mindlessly, suspended in time.

By the time I got upstairs, Carter was in the kitchen, in a conversation on his phone. We made brief eye contact as I passed through on the way to the bedroom. It sounded like he was talking about the murder investigation, probably to Buron Washington.

I lingered in the hall to listen, but when his voice fell below hearing range, I gave up and took a shower.

In clean shorts and tee, I returned to the kitchen. Carter was off the phone and hunched over some documents. "Top secret stuff?"

Carter made a face. "Résumés. Matter of fact, I want to talk to you about them. But first, how are things with you?"

I hit him with my issue du jour. "I got another text today."

He set his mug down. "When were you planning to tell me?"

"Soon as you tell me what you and Washington were discussing on the phone."

"A threat is not something to play with, Sam."

I met his frown with one of my own. "Does he have a suspect yet?"

"Still only conjecture."

It's easier to pry an answer from the Sphinx. "Just tell me this: it isn't me, is it?"

"You?" He laughed, until he realized I wasn't joking. "Far as I know, you're not top of the list."

"So, who is?"

He shook his head, stone-faced.

"If you want me to be safe, I need to know who to steer clear of and who to trust."

"Trust no one."

"Not helpful." We were in a staredown.

I broke first, but only because I needed his help. I fished my phone from my shorts, pulled up the creepy text and handed it to him.

He took the phone and studied the screen. "Interesting."

"To put it mildly. But I don't think it's from Maura. She was too ashamed for sending the first one."

"You may be right." He expanded the screen and turned it toward me. "Whoever sent this isn't familiar with the finer points of grammar."

Reading the message again, I saw what he meant, because it read *your next*.

In my stressed-out state, I'd totally missed the sender's mistake. They had used the possessive your instead of the contraction for you are. "It can't be Maura. She knows the difference."

"Unless it's a typo. Let me keep the phone for a sec. I'll get Ralph to check it out."

"He can do that?"

Carter smiled. "Only for very close friends." He tapped a few keys on my phone, then took his phone and tapped some more. "I sent it to Buron Washington, too. Between the two of us, we should get the I.D. pretty quickly. In the meantime, please be careful."

CHAPTER THIRTY-FOUR

The Résumés

For dinner, Carter ordered food from Hu's Cooking, and the delicious bounty was delivered in no time. Hot & Sour Soup, Three Cups Chicken, bok choy, and house combo rice. He uncapped two bottles of beer and dimmed the kitchen lights.

Jojo's rules for my on-camera wardrobe made me hesitate over the beer, but I succumbed. As we ate and talked, it felt like our recent contretemps was behind us. He brought me up to date on the progress of the retreat at Serenity. I did most of the listening. Then he asked me about the rest of my morning.

I took a swig of beer. "I gave a deposition for the child who shot Lloyd. Her social worker thinks it will help her case in some way."

"You're good at that. Helping kids."

"Not really."

"What about Lizzie and her brother T.J.?"

I'd forgotten how forlorn my little friend was when we met. "Lizzie was dealing with a lot back then, but she's a scrappy spirit. She was always going to be okay. As for T.J., somebody had to save him from self-destruction."

"Still, both Mason children were lucky to have you on their side. Which leads me to the thing I want to talk to you about."

"Can we save it for later? I'm just beginning to relax."

Carter lowered his eyes. "Tomorrow, then, for sure."

After dinner, we took a couple of Gertie's brownies with us to the library. Carter set an album on the turntable, and the soothing alto of Diana Krall began to fill the room.

He joined me on the sofa and wrapped an arm around me. I leaned my head on his shoulder, and we listened to the whole album like that.

The next morning was rainy, the gloomy kind of day that makes a person want to stay in bed until noon. But the aromas wafting in from the kitchen were too tempting to resist.

Carter was at the cooktop. "Breakfast's almost ready." He kissed me on the cheek.

I poured myself some coffee and sat at the breakfast island. "Let's stay in this morning, and you can tell me all about my co-workers' secrets."

He shook his head. "I'll do anything you want after lunch, but first, I have a couple more people to see."

I took a sip of coffee. "What's on the menu?"

"Eggs and toast. Had to keep it minimal since there wasn't much to work with. What would you have eaten if I weren't here?"

"Gertie's cinnamon sandies are in the freezer. And ice cream."

"For breakfast?"

"Why not? Flour, milk, eggs, sugar. Same stuff that's in cereal, only better."

"Not better than this." He emptied a fluffy scramble into a bowl, added a plate of buttered toast and a jar of Dottie's dewberry jam, and joined me at the breakfast island.

He handed me my phone. "Ralph has all he needs. If anyone makes a move at you, wherever you are, we'll know."

I usually balk at Carter's overprotectiveness, but given my tendency to stumble into trouble on an alarmingly regular basis, it's comforting to know that someone's watching out for me. "Thanks, I guess."

Carter smiled. "We strive to ease life's woes."

I winced. "Sounds like a commercial for antidepressant medication."

"I know. I've been working on an official name to describe what the retreat is about. I know a former high-flying marketing exec who could help with that, and a lot more, too."

"If you're talking about me, I'm afraid my wings have been clipped."

He stared into his coffee cup. "You haven't asked me about my meetings today."

"Not top secret?"

"I'll be interviewing candidates for a major role at the new retreat."

I reached for a slice of toast. "What kind of job?"

"Basically, someone to be the public face of the operation. Like what you used to do for De Theret International."

"Oh." The toast hovered in my hand. I set it down and reached for my coffee to clear a lump that had suddenly formed in my throat.

The silence in the room was stifling. I rearranged the eggs on my plate until he spoke.

"I've tried to talk to you about it, Sam, but you're so laser focused on making the TV thing work, and with everything else you've had to deal with lately..."

I blinked and looked away.

"I don't mean to pressure you, but time's getting short. I have to find someone now to start building relationships with potential stakeholders to make the place go. There are families in need. I'm committed to doing my part, but I can't do it by myself, especially with my commitment to the task force in D.C."

"What about Gertie?"

"She'll be a great support for whoever takes the job, but I need something more. I need a partner."

Silence took a deeper hold until Carter pushed away from the island and grabbed the manila folder of résumés from the counter behind him. "Anyway, I interviewed a few candidates yesterday. I'm seeing two more this morning. Matter of fact, I need to go."

After Carter left, I wandered aimlessly through the condo, trying not to fret over what might result from his interviews. Part of me hoped he'd find a really great person, because his vision deserved someone extraordinary to help him realize it. The other part of me hoped none of them would be good enough.

In the living room, I gazed out through the wide windows and tracked the progress of a heavy downpour as it slid across the city, drenching one neighborhood after another. The darkened sky brought a deep chill to the place.

My thoughts free-floated until they landed on one fact. Something is wrong. Something's wrong with my life.

A sob pushed upward in my throat. The pressure was relentless. A howl—like a trapped animal's wail—escaped and reverberated against the glass.

CHAPTER THIRTY-FIVE

The Whistle

Lucky for me, Cassandra was visiting Jojo in the city, and though she didn't have a lot of time to spare, she could see me right away.

She breezed in and went straight to the library to set up.

I followed her in. "Where's Apollo?"

"In quarantine. Denny and I are joining a group that's working to reintroduce pet sugar gliders to their natural habitat in New Guinea. Much as we love Apollo, we want him to live the way he was meant to live. Everyone needs to find the place they truly belong."

"Amen." Before we settled, I wanted to apologize. "I was a little rude to you in our first session. Afterward, I realized I'd learned a few things that helped."

She offered a forgiving smile. "Since we're short on time, is there something specific you want to accomplish today?"

"This sounds stupid, but... I want to get back to who I was before."

"Before what?"

The question jarred me. When, exactly, had I veered off course?

"I'm not sure. I've been bouncing from one place to another without a home to call my own, and from one job to another with no time to think beyond the next minute. I feel like I've been shipwrecked. I'm stranded on an island, and I can't remember where I was going in the first place." I shook my head. "Sounds crazy."

She laughed. "True crazy is beyond my expertise. But if you're only feeling crazy, let's start with where you are now."

While Cassandra scanned my body, I ran through my current stressors—the shooting, the stalker, the job, Carter. Her eyes fell on my thumb, which I'd pressed against my Mom's ring to keep from spinning it. "Tell me more about your mother's ring."

I pulled my thumb away. "I had a dream about her a few nights ago. She was telling me that everything would be all right, but—" I shook my head.

"A comforting image, isn't it? And what about that?" She pointed toward my chest.

I hadn't realized it, but I'd started sliding my silver whistle back and forth on its chain around my neck. My face heated. "This? It's... I'm supposed to be kind of a whistleblower at KHTS-TV. My, uh, friend gave it to me when I got the job."

"The boyfriend?"

"He's more than that, I guess."

"Do you ever blow it?"

"It's really loud. Just thinking about it gives me a headache."

"What do other things that trouble you sound like?"

Odd question. But I'd agreed to play along, so I shut my eyes and tried. Seconds passed until the pop of a gun jolted me. My eyes flew open.

Cassandra was watching me intently. "What is it?"

"A gunshot."

"The one that wounded your colleague?"

"Probably."

"Go there again. It may be uncomfortable, but try to hold on to every sound you heard when it happened."

I shut my eyes. In a flash, Valentina's sobs, Lloyd's moans, the squeak of the gurney as they wheeled him out—it all came back.

"Stay there," Cassandra said "Breathe in, deep as you can, and hold it. When you're ready to exhale, let go of each sound, one by one—until they fade away."

By my third breath, the scene receded. I felt light-headed. Slightly panicked, I opened my eyes.

Cassandra was smiling. "Let your breathing return to normal, then blow the whistle in one breath, hard as you can, for as long as you can."

The whole thing felt ridiculous, but I took a deep breath and blew.

The blast was even more shrill than I'd remembered. It reverberated against the floors, walls, ceiling, and every other hard surface in the library.

When the last echo died, Cassandra spoke. "What do you hear now?"

"Ringing in my ears."

"Close your eyes and listen. The silence will come."

Carter returned just as Cassandra was packing to leave. He peered into the library. "I heard voices."

He regarded Cassandra with curiosity. Without explaining who she was, I introduced them. They exchanged a few pleasantries before I walked her out.

Waiting for the elevator, I realized how much the short session had helped. "I don't know why, but I think I'm... clearer, somehow. How do you do it?"

"I just go on what you give me. You're a quick study, which makes it easier. The ring you play with feels mostly positive, like a comfort fetish, though there could be some unresolved emotions behind it. But the whistle—the way you seesaw it back and forth on the chain—seems to express opposing needs, or indecision. I thought if you used it as it was meant to be used, it might help to resolve the conflict."

Before she boarded the elevator, she offered one more suggestion. "If your mind gets jammed with worrisome thoughts again, try blowing the whistle."

Carter was in the kitchen pouring himself a bourbon. There was a stiffness to his back as he sat at the island. I sat across from him. The folder of résumés lay between us.

Curiosity got the best of me. "How'd the interviews go? Find anyone good?"

"One or two."

"Let me know if I can help." I nearly choked on my words.

He studied me for a minute. "Who was the flower-child, your astrologer?"

I laughed. "A friend of Jojo's. I don't think she tells fortunes."

"Too bad. I could use a peek into the future right about now."

"Couldn't we all." My words hung over the kitchen like a heavy cloud.

I knew Carter would want to stay, at least until we'd heard from Ralph about the texts. But it felt awkward to be together with so much between us and no words to say.

I touched his hand. "Why don't you go? I'm fine here. If you want, you can leave the résumés for me to look over."

"You sure?"

I attempted a smile. "Gives me a chance to scope out my competition."

Melancholy passed over his eyes, then vanished. "No one can compete with you." He handed me the file, kissed me on the cheek, and was gone.

CHAPTER THIRTY-SIX

Chartreuse

I had set the alarm for a super-early wakeup Monday morning so I'd have plenty of primping time for my official Tweedy debut. I ended up snoozing it twice, but by the third beep-beep, it was rise and shine.

First thing, I checked my phone. The anonymous texter still hadn't responded. Maybe I'd actually scared the bugger off.

Coffee, toast, shower. Next, the icky part: transforming myself into Tweedy eye candy.

Makeup done, I unhooked the dress of the day from Jojo's bag of tricks. It radiated a migraine-inducing chartreuse. I squirmed into it and checked the mirror. The good news was that the neckline exposed only my collarbone, and the sleeves hugged my arms all the way to the elbows. The bad? A flounce at the waist in back took my derriere to an eye-popping extreme.

I couldn't bring myself to walk out the door looking like a giant hi-lighter pen. Tweedy could either lump it or fire me, in which case I'd probably have a great case for a lawsuit. Not that I wanted to see the inside of another courtroom ever again, but a girl has to draw the line somewhere.

I peeled the dress off, returned it to the hanging bag, and tossed in the matching stilettos. Then I put on my jeans, a tee, and my trusty blazer. Tweedy may have a say about what I wear on-camera, but for the remaining twenty-three hours, I'd wear what I want.

A new security guard stopped me at the KHTS staff parking gate. Her nametag read Tamika. Short and wiry, she held a clipboard with what I assumed was the station's new employee roster. Her utility belt sported a gun, a taser, a radio, and enough other paraphernalia to fend off any marauder. It looked like it weighed as much as she did.

She gestured for me to roll down my window. A puff of warm, humid air filled the car, smelling like rain might be on the way again. "Mornin' hon. What would be your name?"

After I introduced myself, Tamika leaned in and performed a visual sweep of the Ferret. Her eyes stopped for a second on the hanging bag in the back seat before moving on. Seemingly satisfied, she straightened up and smiled broadly.

I smiled back. "Is my parking space still number eighteen?"

She consulted the clipboard. "Eighteen it is."

Before I left the car, I attempted to adjust my mental attitude before I met my new boss.

I donned my "I'm fine" smile and walked in.

At the reception desk Donna Sue was all dolled up in a Tweedy-ish, rust-colored number and a set of half-inch-long eyelashes. She looked confused, as if my presence was unexpected, or maybe the fake lashes were making her squint. Guess she needed to keep her job, too.

"Mr. Patel wants to see you."

I stopped in my tracks. "Patel? Jay Patel?"

"He said to send you straight to him, soon as you got here."

Patel was on the phone when I entered his office. He waved me in and held up a finger to indicate he'd be a minute. I dropped the hanging bag on the sofa and took a chair.

Jay was doing more listening than talking. Occasionally he'd offer one- or two-word responses. "Sure... of course... understood."

Finally, he hung up. "Sorry. Took longer than I expected."

"Last minute instructions from Tweedy?" I didn't mask my irritation.

"Not exactly." He smiled. "Good to see you, Samantha."

"I'm surprised to see you here. What's going on?"

"I took some vacation days."

"That's not the impression I got when you said goodbye."

"Well, as it turns out, that's all it was."

"What happened?"

"Long story, which I won't get into right now. Suffice it to say that I'm back, and I'm ready to keep guiding this station for as long as I'm here." His eyes moved to the clothes bag on the sofa. "Is that your broadcast dress?"

And just like that, the subject was closed. I let it go, for now.

He apologized for keeping our talk short and sent me to my new private office. Since it used to be Alicia's, my excitement was tempered by the injustice of it all.

As I scanned the space, I recalled the advice she'd bestowed on me over a year ago, when I first auditioned at the station.

"Save your money," she'd whispered as she towered over me outside the broadcast studio. "You're good-looking now, but one day you'll be old."

I couldn't help but feel awful for her. She must have sensed that time was closing in.

All her decorative touches—including the dozen or so awards she'd accumulated over the years—were gone. Only a hint of her Shalimar perfume still clung. The scent was oddly soothing, as if a touch of her glamor had remained for me to borrow.

I hooked the hanging bag over a peg on back of the door and crossed the room to try out the desk chair. Unlike Lloyd's cramped office, it took a half dozen steps to reach it. A small window let in enough light to work by without turning on the mind-dulling fluorescents.

Jojo appeared in the doorway. "Sammy in her new digs!"

I winced. "Big shoes to fill, I know."

"Pish posh. You'll do fine." He gave my blazer and tee the once over and raised an eyebrow.

"I'm saving the dress for the broadcast."

"Cool. I'll be around to help you change. Let me know when you're ready."

I made a face. "Where'd you get my dresses, Floozies R Us?"

He laughed. "I prefer to shop at Discount Divas. More upscale."

Leave it to Jojo to lighten my mood. After he left, I opened the desk drawers and unpacked the contents of my work bag into them.

I found a power strip under the desk and plugged in my laptop into to charge it, and then my phone. It lit up with a reply from my mystery stalker:

Cursity killed the cat

Another spelling mistake, but still chilling. What kind of wacko was I dealing with?

I didn't know the rules of game we were playing, but if there was a chance to smoke the creep out, I was willing to continue. I replied:

Let's meet.

THIRTY-SEVEN

Ticker

Before the noon broadcast, Patel called everyone into the studio. I noticed new faces in the technical crew, plus Brad, Francine, Nandi, and me. Patel welcomed the new people and introduced each of us by name and job title, saying how excited he was to be working with the new team and that he looked forward to doing great things together. Blah, blah, blah.

Then he dropped a bombshell. "You'll be happy to know that from now on, there is a major schedule change that reduces everybody's workload. Instead of three live news broadcasts a day, we'll have two, the noontime and the early evening."

Murmurs of surprise—and a few grumbles—circulated among the group. Patel raised his voice to be heard. "This is good news, guys. From here on out, most folks on the late crew can be home with their families at a reasonable hour."

Brad raised his hand. "What happens to my solo night slot?"

Patel nodded. "Good question, Brad. We'll be airing a rerun of the evening broadcast. If there's breaking news, we'll run updates in screen crawl at the bottom."

Hudson's voice rumbled. "A news ticker is replacing me? You can't be serious!"

Patel lost his smile. He jammed his hands into the pockets of his slacks. "Let's talk in my office." He closed the meeting and made a rapid exit.

I was about to follow the two of them to Patel's office to hear him answer Brad's question, but there were cookies on the table, which halted my progress.

Jojo caught me eyeing the chocolate chips. "No, Sammy."

Oh well. I tore myself away and scooted to Patel's office. Loud voices poured into the hall from inside the closed door. I put my ear against it to catch as much as possible, though anyone passing by could have heard Brad's thundering basso.

"... and why is *she* royally installed in Alicia's office while I'm stuck in that blasted closet of Sedgwick's?"

Whoa. I backed away and hustled to my new office.

A tall blond guy in a khaki suit, Repp tie, and enough hair gel to keep him groomed through Thanksgiving was in there waiting for me. He looked to be only a couple of years out of college.

"Hiya, Ms. Newman. I'm Evan Fentworth, your new producer." He grabbed my hand for a sweaty-palm handshake. His body spray was overwhelming. "I just stopped by to introduce myself in person and give you this, in case you're one of those people who prefers analog."

One of *those people*? How old did he think I was?

He handed me a preliminary rundown of the evening news schedule and turned to leave.

At the door, he spun around. "Um, one more thing, Ms. Newman. I'm supposed to make sure that everything goes according to company guidelines, and I noticed... I mean, I think you look nice, but..."

He eyed my tee and blazer. "You're not wearing that on the broadcast, are you?"

"There's a dress behind the door."

He checked the dress. "Oh, good. Thanks." He pumped my arm again and disappeared.

I scanned the rundown. My segments involved introducing a few pre-recorded videos. The first "package" was about a confrontation between an indigenous tribe and an oil pipeline in the Dakotas. Next came a story about how smoothly things were going at an immigrant detention center in Ohio. And a third announced a record day on Wall Street. After one or two short sentences, all of them cut to video. I hoped I'd get a chance to preview the videos to see what I'd be talking about on air.

The thought that I would be a professional television anchor in just a few hours left me queasy. On the positive side, I had time to practice. And with such a light load, there were fewer chances to get tongue-tied on camera.

Five o'clock came fast.

Jojo knocked on the doorframe. "Ready for your finishing touches?"

I set the rundown aside and hauled myself up on the stilettos. "Ready as I'll ever be."

After Jojo worked his magic, I scurried to the studio. My entire body buzzed with a mix of excitement and terror.

The last game show of the day was playing on the monitors as I slid into my chair behind the broadcast desk. Once the script appeared on the teleprompter, I practiced it over and over while the crew performed a light check.

A new tech person fitted me with a microphone and earpiece. The booth did an audio check and made adjustments. Jojo swooped in for a fresh dusting of color on my cheeks and a dab of lip gloss.

Evan Fentworth appeared from the dark to tell me that Brad would not be joining me. He handed me Brad's pages, but there was no time left for me to practice. Reading unfamiliar words on live TV with the lights boring into my eyeline would require supreme concentration, and luck.

The chartreuse dress squeezed against my diaphragm. I could breathe okay standing up, but sitting down was another story. Hopefully, I'd be able to suck enough oxygen into my lungs to keep from passing out on camera. I caught sight of Jay Patel beyond the lights. He gave me a thumbs-up, which helped a little.

Time flew, and suddenly—three, two, one—the red button lit, and I was on.

I made it through the broadcast without a major mistake. From the smile on Jay Patel's face, I must have done pretty well. Soon as a tech guy unburdened me of my equipment, Fentworth reclaimed the paper back-up scripts and gave me another sweaty handshake.

I kicked off the stilettos and padded barefoot down the corridor toward Patel's office to ask him about Brad's no-show, but he had already left the building.

Jojo was waiting for me in my new office. "See? Nothing to it."

"At least I survived. Do you know what happened to Brad?"

"Nope." He returned my dress and shoes to the hanging bag.

I thought back to the heated exchange I'd overheard between Brad and Jay earlier. Had Jay fired him, or had Brad quit over the loss of his late broadcast?

Jojo helped me into my blazer. "What's wrong, Sammy?"

"I think I have a new enemy."

"Brad Hudson? He lives to be on camera. He'll show up eventually, I guarantee. Wanna grab a bean?"

CHAPTER THIRTY-EIGHT

Squiggles

Instead of eating out, Jojo invited me to his place, and since he didn't own a car, I ended up driving him home. I hadn't realized that he rode the bus every day. For the first time, I considered what little money he must be making at KHTS.

On the way, we stopped to pick up Korean food. Jojo ordered a cold noodle dish. I asked for fried chicken, extra-spicy.

Jojo frowned. "Sure you don't want something, um, less filling?"

I repeated my order. "Nobody's messing with my food choice tonight." The woman behind the counter smiled and entered the order.

We moved to an empty table to wait. Jojo looked worried. "Eat like that and you won't be able to squeeze into your little dresses."

"I've been thinking about those. The camera only sees me from the waist up, right? I could be wearing cutoffs and flip-flops behind the desk and no one would know. Plus, the fatter I am, the bigger the boobs. That should keep them happy."

He laughed. "Seriously though, Tweedy doesn't joke around."

"I know. Ditching the late news? Not only are they purveyors of prefab soundbites, but they're cheap to boot. Those dresses make me feel cheap, too. What if you find a couple of tops that cover more than half my chest?"

Jojo frowned. "That may be a problem."

"Because?"

"I don't work for KHTS anymore."

I stared at him. "Back up a minute. You quit?"

He shook his head. "Nope. Apparently, I was on the list to get axed last Friday, but they never got around to me. Just before you went live tonight, Patel lowered the boom."

Our food order was ready. I paid, and Jojo carried it to the car. As I fired up the Ferret, my anger boiled over.

I turned to Jojo. "You can't leave. I'll talk to Jay."

"It's no use, Sammy. Tweedy is a juggernaut. You can't fight 'em."

"Then I'll quit in protest."

"No. You have to stay. At least there'll be one decent human left around there."

The place Jojo called home turned out to be a dilapidated two-story duplex on Vermont Street in the Montrose district. He lived on the ground floor.

As we climbed the rickety steps up to the front door, he must have read my shock at the disrepair. "At least it didn't flood last time," he muttered.

He unlocked the door and turned on a light to reveal an amazing wonderland. Random swaths and squiggles in rainbow hues covered the walls, as if he'd been testing new colors of paint. "You're redecorating?"

He laughed. "No, this room's finished."

I considered the walls again. The overall effect was actually quite cheery.

We took the food to the kitchen, where paint splatters decorated the counters, the table, two chairs, the ceiling, and the floor in random Jackson Pollock-like dribbles. It was like being inside a crazy kaleidoscope.

Jojo dragged two bottles of Shiner Bock from the fridge and handed me one with a wink. Once we settled in at the table, he raised his beer. "A toast to new beginnings!" We clinked our bottles together and dug into the food.

My thoughts returned to his job status. "I can't believe Jay Patel had the guts to fire you."

"It's okay. I needed a kick in the pants."

I ached for him, but he seemed upbeat. "What will you do?"

"Line up a few odd jobs, I guess. But I've always dreamed of becoming a full time artist. Now that I'm unemployed, I'm gonna give it another try."

I glanced around the room. "And do art like this?"

"I've dabbled in almost every medium. It may take a little time to find a direction. But that'll be half the fun." He took a swig of beer. "Wanna see some of my old stuff?"

He led me to a spare bedroom and turned on the overhead light. The room was chock-full of art in practically every style and medium. Dozens and dozens of pen and pencil sketches covered the walls. Most were portraits of people and anatomy studies that could easily be been mistaken for Michelangelo's.

A work table in one corner was jam-packed with elongated plaster-of-Paris sculptures that resembled alien beings. Next to that sat a table with fabric swatches and a sewing machine. Another table held strips of painted paper and piles of dyed cloth that looked like a collage work-in-progress. In the center of the room stood an easel holding an abstract acrylic in deep reds, soft pinks and bright yellows, and shades of green I never knew existed.

"Wow." I turned to Jojo. "You are unbelievably talented! Some of this should be in a gallery."

"It's a lot, I know. I have a hard time picking a single direction."

I picked up a pencil sketch of a man's torso from a pile on the floor. "I love this."

"Take whatever you like. I can always make more."

I liked almost all of them, but I didn't want to be greedy, especially since I didn't own a home to hang them in. But I did have walls my new office. I pored over the pile in earnest and picked out three.

I would have stayed longer, but my eyelids were starting to droop, along with my energy. I apologized for ending the evening so soon and made Jojo promise to keep in touch.

He smiled. "You bet. Matter of fact, if you're not doing anything Saturday, a friend is opening a new light show in the old city cistern, and there's a private preview that morning. I invited Mr. Patel, and he wanted me to mention it to you and a couple of others at the station. Are you up for it?"

I had never been to the cistern, but I'd heard it was an amazing place to visit. "Sure. Sounds like fun."

Jojo helped me carry my new art collection to the door. There were no streetlamps on his block, and it was pitch dark outside. In the off-chance my stalker was lurking nearby, he walked me to my car and set the art in the back.

I got in, and locked the doors. As I cranked up the Ferret, my phone pinged.

My stalker was at it again.

I had really hoped my suggestion that the two of us meet would scare the weirdo away. Instead, the game continued with this:

Alredy have.

We had met? Who was this person?

I dropped the phone and sped away, my pulse racing faster than the little Ferret's engine. I don't think I took a breath until I was inside the gated garage at The Wellbourne.

CHAPTER THIRTY-NINE

Rundown

First thing the next morning, I headed to Patel's office. He was studying the monitors on his wall.

I stuck my head in. "What happened to Brad last night?"

"He wasn't feeling well."

That sounded like a fib, but I moved on to something more important, which was to plead my case for keeping Jojo employed. "He's a good guy, Jay. One of the few ones left around here."

"It's not about who likes whom, Samantha. We have a job to do, even if we don't like parts of it." He sounded none too happy to be here, either.

I took the chance to ask him about it. "You'd said you were moving on. Now you're back. What happened?"

His face darkened. "Long story."

"I have time." I made myself comfortable in the chair across from him and watched the monitors, too. A paid advertorial was running with a pumped-up guy in a tight red bodysuit selling exercise balls.

At last, Patel gave up and swiveled his chair to face me. "I *was* going to a new job. The minute I heard about the Tweedy purchase, I put my résumé out there. When an offer came, I jumped on it."

"How long ago did you know?"

"If you're asking if I knew about the sale before I hired you, it was only a rumor then."

"So, my future here was pretty much doomed from the start?"

"I'd like to think I gave you an opportunity."

"What happened to your new job?"

His forehead knit. "Lloyd's murder."

The conversation came to a halt, but I couldn't let him dismiss me. My anonymous texter's last message said we already knew each other. If I was ever going to ask the question that begged to be asked, now was the time.

"Did you text me last night?"

"Text you? No." He turned his chair and focused on the monitors again.

It occurred to me that he'd never answered an earlier question of mine. "What about Lloyd's computer? It disappeared after the shooting and didn't show up until days later. I keep wondering where it had been and how it ended up in my credenza."

"I don't think we should be discussing the investigation."

"But it might be tied to whoever killed Lloyd. Doesn't it bother you that there could be a murderer among us?"

He stood. "Drop the subject, please. This meeting is over."

I tried one more question. "What about the flood report? Will we ever air it?"

Jay raised his hand, his palm pushing at the air between us. "Please, Samantha."

"Lloyd and Maura put in a lot of work into it. I've done some, too. This story is more important to our audience than one about a water park in Iowa, for Pete's sake. Aren't you afraid we'll lose viewers if we don't tell them what's going on in their own back yard?"

"I'm always concerned about our viewership."

"Then why not tell Tweedy we need more local stuff."

Patel pressed his hands against the top of his desk as if to stop it from levitating. "Tweedy has never strayed from their centrally-controlled programming. There's almost zero possibility to do local reporting anymore. Especially something that smacks of controversy."

"How is chronic flooding controversial?"

He didn't answer, but I pushed on. "This is a major issue facing our area and I think it's our duty to—"

"I said no!" He pounded the desk so hard that a wave of coffee splashed over the rim of his mug and onto the desk. He dabbed angrily at the spill with a napkin. The subject was closed.

Getting your own office is not always all it's cracked up to be. In the days when I was a hot-shot executive, I enjoyed the privacy, and having my stalwart assistant, Gertie, nearby. But at KHTS, I felt isolated, especially since Jojo wasn't around anymore.

Without the flood story to work on, there was nothing to do until the rundown for the evening broadcast was posted. I wandered into the kitchen for coffee. To pass the time, I took a seat at a table and scrolled through my phone. The text from last night popped up first.

Alredy have could only mean one thing: I'd met the creep. But where, and when?

Somehow, they had my phone number. The only other clue was that they were bad at spelling. Unless they were faking it.

I was running through possibilities when Brad Hudson entered the break room. When he saw me, he hesitated, then puffed himself up and proceeded to the coffee bar. After the shouting match I'd heard through Patel's door yesterday, and his no-show for our first shared broadcast, I engaged with caution.

"Hi, Brad. Feeling better?"

Busy with packets of creamer and sugar, he kept his back to me and mumbled a reply I didn't catch. Probably just as well.

I tried again. "How's your noon broadcast shaping up?"

He harrumphed. "Any idiot could read that guff."

"Any idiot, like me?"

He spun around, sloshing a spot of coffee onto his tie. "I didn't mean—"

"It's okay. If I had your years of experience, I'd be pretty miffed if I had to partner with a clueless sidekick like me."

He sputtered a few syllables before recovering his voice in all its operatic roundness, along with a pained smile. "I have no idea what you're talking about, little girl. I wish you nothing but the best. And, should you care to seek my advice, I would agree to teach you a thing or two about your job."

I gritted my teeth. "Generous of you."

"You're welcome."

With a curt nod, Brad vacated the kitchen, and I returned to my office, dreading the hour when we'd be on camera together.

Back in my office, my computer beeped. Evan Fentworth had sent the rundown for tonight's evening news.

I printed it from the desktop copier on the credenza behind my desk—a perk of moving into Alicia's former domain. No more traipsing down the hall to make copies.

As the pages rolled out, I took in the emptiness of the space. The walls had once been covered with photos of Alicia, dressed in golf clothes, team jerseys, or evening wear, and smiling for the camera next to local and national celebrities. Her shelves were filled, too, with family photos, trophies, awards and citations, and knickknacks from exotic travel adventures.

Now, the walls and shelves were barren. I didn't have famous friends, and the few pictures of my family that had survived the fire still made me sad to look at. I made a mental note to get Jojo's drawings framed so I could hang them.

When it was time to get ready for the broadcast, I squeezed into the last dress from Jojo—a cabernet number with a fringe of fake grapes at the neck and around the cap sleeves. In an unsteady pair of purple toe-torturers, I high-stepped into the studio.

Taco Day

The Tuesday broadcast played out much the same as yesterday's, except that Brad had condescended to join me at the anchor desk, which was sort of the good news and bad news. I hoped our lack of chemistry didn't show through the camera.

I was on my way out when I ran into Jojo, who had come in to pick up his final check. I asked how his first day of unemployment had gone.

He beamed. "Best day I've had in a long time."

"What'd you do?"

"Anything I wanted! I shopped for you, and then I shopped for me."

"And you bought... ?"

"New tops for you, and for me, a couple of sketchbooks and a huge set of drawing pencils in pretty much every color in the universe. And I lined up a part-time bartending gig."

"Sounds like you're on a great new adventure."

"Feels like it, too. How was your broadcast?"

"You were wrong about Brad. I think he really hates me."

"Pish posh. Say, it's ninety-nine-cent taco day. How 'bout I pick some up and come to your place with your new clothes?"

After my downer of a day, did I really want something cheesy, meaty, greasy, and with zip nutritional value. "Yes, please."

Wednesday at KHTS was a mirror of Tuesday, but for one thing: I was comfy in my jeans. Along with the tacos, Jojo had delivered my new tops and some bib necklaces to go with them. I'd also located a few possibilities in my closet, including a wrap-around, collared shirt in fuchsia, and a royal blue one in the same style. For today, I paired that one with one of the necklaces, and I ditched the heels for flats. I felt pretty good.

An idea had come to me during the night about how to get Brad to warm up to me and improve our on-camera time together. I stopped at Jay Patel's door and stood quietly until he acknowledged me.

"What is it now, Samantha?"

I took that as an invitation to enter. "I get that you're under pressure, Jay. I'm sorry if I've added more."

"Apology accepted." His end-of-conversation paper shuffling started up. When I didn't leave, he looked up. "What?"

I ignored the pique in his voice and pushed on. "I was just thinking about Brad, and I had an idea. How possible would it be for us to sneak in just one local special? Not about flooding. Just something light, like the piece about the Iowa water park, only local to us. Something Tweedy could share with its other stations, like they did with the water park in Ohio."

Patel's face brightened.

Since he didn't appear to hate the idea, I continued. "And Brad could be the host. It might soften the blow of losing his late broadcast."

"I can't push anything on Tweedy too soon."

"Just think about it." I walked out before he had time to say no.

Thursday felt pretty much the same as the day before. I was breathing easy in one of Jojo's new purchases, a pink long-sleeved leotard top under my trusty blazer, and a crystal bib necklace. Before I made it to my new space, Jay Patel sent a message that he wanted to see me as soon as I got in. I headed to his office.

He motioned me to a chair across from him. I perched on the edge of the seat, wondering if he was about to put me in wardrobe hell again. Or fire me.

He looked happy. "What you said about how the new format could lose us our loyal viewers... I lost a lot of sleep thinking about it. I've made some mistakes in my career, and I may be making one now. Might even cost me this job, but I'd rather crash and burn with Tweedy than ruin my reputation with everyone else in this business."

He splayed his hands on his desk and leaned forward. "So, I am willing to produce a test segment that would feature a local event or place of interest, like the ones Alicia used to do. I still have to figure out how we can afford it, given our minuscule budget. But if I can pull it off, I want you and Francine to tape the pilot."

"Not Brad?"

"Let's see how the chemistry works with two women. Lots of morning shows do it, and I think Tweedy will like it more that way."

"But the whole idea was to give the gig to Brad Hudson."

Patel's face darkened. "Don't press me on this, Samantha."

No use arguing, for now. As I rose to go, he lifted a paper from the top of a pile and handed it to me. It was a memo from Tweedy Inc., Office of Human Resources.

You are hereby instructed to remind your female evening anchor of the Tweedy dress code. Men are to wear ties and structured jackets. Women must wear dresses that showcase their femininity.

I chucked the memo onto his desk. "Really, Jay? How did they know I wasn't in a dress?"

"Your new producer. I told him not to be concerned, but he took it over my head. I've asked Jojo to come up with a few new dresses that might suit you better."

"He's back on the payroll?"

"Unfortunately, no, but I'll make sure he gets paid."

I was glad to get to see Jojo again, especially since my list of friends at the station had shrunk to almost no one. On top of dealing with my pompous stiff of a co-anchor, I now had a new frenemy: my producer, Evan Fentworth.

Some things were looking up, though. Not only was I not fired, Patel had actually agreed to produce a local story. Or, try to, if he could get Tweedy to bless it.

In the afternoon, Jojo showed up at my office door, breathless with excitement. "Man, did I score! Power dresses! They're expensive as all get-out, but Patel gave me a little shopping allowance. Lucky for us, the ladies who lunch only wear these once, then toss 'em down to my favorite resale shop. Try the red one first."

He removed the dress from its hanger and held it out to show it off. Like the ones before it, it looked two sizes too small.

"Am I supposed to get into that?"

"You're gonna almost love it, I promise."

While he went to get his full-length mirror, I stripped and pulled the thing on. It was remarkably easy to get into, owing to a zipper opening, which my previous instruments of torture had lacked. The lining was thin, but amazingly sturdy, and sculpted to fit a woman's torso.

Jojo returned with his mirror and zipped me up. Instead of pinching and squeezing, the dress gently hugged me. One look in the mirror, and I understood what he'd meant by power. The color popped like the red on the Lone Star flag. And it fit like some kind of magic armor. I definitely looked powerful, and strange as it sounds, I felt more powerful, too.

Two more dresses—one blue, the other green— were variations of the red one. All three provided more skin coverage than the slutty ones had.

I couldn't help but smile. "Not bad."

Jojo grinned. "Are you kidding me? You look like the next President of the United States!"

Despite Brad's cold shoulder, the red dress buoyed my spirits through the evening broadcast. And though I still didn't feel like a real news anchor, at least I was beginning to look like one.

Back in my office, I was changing into my regular clothes when another idea for how to get on Brad's good side popped into my mind. Patel had nixed him for the local story, but I could go straight to Brad with this one.

I ran into him just as he was leaving. "Say, Brad, do you have a minute?"

He scowled. "What is it?"

"I've been thinking about your offer to mentor me. Sitting next to you at the anchor desk, I realize how much I still have to learn. So, would you? Mentor me, I mean, if the offer's still good."

A stunned expression crossed his face. Clearly, I'd caught him off-guard. Ever the pro, he recovered quickly. "I have a very busy schedule, as you know."

"Of course. Any time you could give me, I'd be honored."

"In that case, I shall consider your request."

I nearly made myself nauseous pandering to his vanity, but I had a feeling Brad would say yes. If it led to a better on-camera partnership, I hoped it would be worth it.

I was on my way out the door when my phone pinged with a message:

u look nice tonite

The message ended with two blue crying emojis and three red-faced devils.

Whoever the creep was had just hit my last nerve. My first attempt to call the bugger out had failed, but I decided to double down.

I replied:

so do u.

CHAPTER FORTY-ONE

Chicken Soup

I sped to The Wellbourne with one eye on the rearview mirror. Once inside, I forwarded the text to Carter and poured myself a glass of wine.

The manila folder of applicant résumés was still on the counter. I'd managed to avoid them, but I needed something to do with myself, so I opened the packet.

Almost all the candidates were women close to my age. Two of them had experience and skills that looked promising. I did a web search to see what they looked like. They were both knockout gorgeous.

My phone lit with a message from Gertie:

Don't eat dinner. On my way with food.

She must have been downstairs when she texted, because she appeared two minutes later at my door, carrying a large thermal bag. She excused her sudden visit with a straight face. "Louis is under the weather again, and I made too much of everything."

Only one thing would oblige her to leave her sick husband. "You spoke to Carter?"

"I was glad he called, because my freezer is too full."

She pushed past me to the kitchen, where she busied herself emptying the tote. A wrapped casserole dish came first. "Lasagna. Easy to reheat. And..." She drew another container out. "Chicken soup."

When the tote was empty, she sat across from me at the island looking especially stern. "What's going on with you?"

"I'm fine."

"So you say."

"Did Carter tell you about the latest text?"

"I just thought that maybe you needed—"

"Soup?"

She flushed. "Truth is, Samantha, I miss our talks. I want to know how you are with your new job and, you know, that terrible shooting. That young hooligan nearly ended your life!"

"Actually, she's kind of a victim herself. I gave a deposition on her behalf last week."

Gertie looked puzzled. "You're helping her?"

I shared what I knew about Valentina's predicament: her mother's sudden deportation, the homelessness, turning to a gang for shelter, and the threat of rape, or worse. "And to top it off, she's only twelve. I don't want to be the one to ruin her already blighted life. Actually, I wish I could do more."

Gertie's eyes welled up. "You've done it before."

I had no idea what she was talking about.

She smiled. "What about Lizzie Mason?"

Carter had mentioned Lizzie, too. I'd met her when she was a forlorn ten-year-old, living at The Wellbourne with her brother T.J., and taking care of their invalid mother. We bonded over ice cream. After T.J. got himself in trouble, their dad Tom retired from life as an Army Ranger, moved the family to Serenity and went to work for Carter. "It's great to see how happy she is now."

"And you? When will you be happy, Samantha?"

"Me?" The question hit like a punch to the chest.

Gertie took my hand. "You were once a lost girl, too, remember? And you worked so hard to overcome it. But if I could give you just one piece of advice..."

I shut my eyes. "Not now, Gertie."

"I'm sorry, dear, but some things must be said. You think your life belongs only to you. But when other people love you, you are part of them, too. It hurts to see you run from things that make you happy."

"I'm not sure what makes me happy anymore."

She held up an index finger. "One, helping people, especially young ones like Lizzie and her brother. And apparently, this new little hooligan, too."

Another finger went up. "Two, doing work you believe in. I've seen you in action when you're passionate about something. You're unstoppable."

And a third finger. "People who love you."

Hot tears threatened my eyes. "Even so, I need to make a living. I have to keep this job."

Gertie looked sad. "What good is it, if it doesn't bring you joy?"

Gertie's visit left me more depressed than ever. She had come into my life when I was at the top of my game. Decisive and determined. Unstoppable, she'd called me. And now? Faking it.

It was almost time for the rerun of the evening news broadcast. I heated some chicken soup and took it to bed with me while I watched myself play news anchor next to Brad.

Jojo was right. The red power dress nearly popped off the screen. I looked like the real deal—professional, self-assured—or at least, a close facsimile.

I hoped tomorrow's emerald one would transform me into that person again. I texted Jojo:

Thanks for the magic dress.

He sent back a smiley face and a beating heart.

I felt energized. And I wanted to hear from Carter. I tapped in his number.

He answered on the first ring. "Hey, Wonder Woman."   '

Like his touch, the sound of his voice could change my pulse rate, and sometimes take my breath away. While I searched for words, he filled the gap.

"You looked amazing tonight."

"Thanks."

"Everything okay?"

"I miss you."

He took a moment to respond. "The weekend's coming up."

"Can we have a do-over at Serenity?"

"No."

My heart froze until he added, "No need for you to come here. I have meetings in the city tomorrow."

CHAPTER FORTY-TWO

Pheromones

The power of the red dress lingered Friday morning as I slid the Ferret into its parking slot at the station. Carrying a clothes bag with the emerald green one inside, I marched straight to Jay Patel's office and I poked my head in.

He greeted me with a smile. "Hello, Samantha. Good broadcast last night."

"Thanks. I think I'm getting the hang of it. Did you like the dress?"

"Jojo does good work."

"He said you paid for them."

"Thank our new owners. They may scrimp on some things, but they doubled our promotions budget. I used some of it for your wardrobe. And, I can also cover the cost of a local segment. So, let's talk next week about what we want it to be." He grinned. "I almost feel like a freedom fighter."

I took advantage of the moment. "So, can we also find a way to produce Lloyd's report?"

His smile disappeared. "Tweedy has nixed it, permanently. Consider it dead."

Clearly, it would take more than a magic dress to open that subject again.

After I set my stuff in my office, I went for coffee in the break room. Brad was just leaving.

"Ms. Newman, in regard to your request, I have decided, in the interest of improving the quality of our broadcast, I would be willing to teach you a few things."

"Great."

"I shall prepare a curriculum. We can begin on Monday."

I took Brad's acceptance as a good sign. He'd already softened up a little, which boded well for our on-screen partnership. If I learned something from him in the process, so much the better.

Carter surprised me by showing up at the station just before the evening broadcast. I caught sight of him out of the corner of my eye as he stood next to Jay outside the camera's sight lines. I was so shocked to see the two of them sharing a friendly chat, I almost missed the opening countdown.

They were still yakking when the broadcast was over. I slid out of my chair and approached them, my head full of questions. Had the oh-so-private Carter actually revealed himself to my maddeningly evasive boss?

"You two know each other?"

They exchanged a look.

I turned my eyes to Carter, daring him to tell the truth. He didn't blink. "We were just talking about you. You were great, by the way."

The three of us had an awkward moment before Patel excused himself. Something felt hinky between them, but I'd wait to grill Carter on it when we were alone.

I left for my office to shed the magic dress, change out of the stilettos, wipe off the makeup, and don my jeans and tennies. Without the butterfly glam, I was comfy as a caterpillar.

In a corner of the lobby, Carter and Evan Fentworth were deep into a serious conversation. Evan's cheeks turned as red as yesterday's power dress when he saw me. He offered a hasty, tight-lipped hello and retreated out the door.

I turned to Carter. "You know him, too?"

"Just met."

"Looked like you were angry at him."

"Did it?" He shrugged. "Meet you at the condo?"

I could tell there was more to the story, but I let the subject die, for the time being. We had the whole weekend to sort it out, among other things.

By the time I arrived at the condo, Carter had Gertie's lasagna in the oven and a bottle of Sangiovese ready to pour. He'd also turned off the overhead lights and lit a couple of candles. In the warm glow, my worries temporarily slid to the background.

He sliced a bite-sized wedge of cheese and fed it to me. When his fingers brushed my lips, I tamped down a pesky rush of libido and changed the subject.

"How do you know Jay Patel?" My fingers drummed on the table while he worked out his answer.

He popped a nugget of cheese in his mouth, chewed and chewed and chewed, and swallowed it with a chug of wine. "I just ran into him at your TV station."

From his early undercover career, Carter was a trained dissembler. I'd never known him to flat out lie to me, and yet, it was obvious he was holding something back. I renewed the stare down.

His eyes met mine straight-on. "I did some research on him when you first started working there. Given your previous employer's record, I wanted to make sure you weren't walking into another lion's den."

I took a sip of wine. "So, what did you find?"

"At the time, he seemed to be an upstanding guy."

"And now?"

"Buron Washington hit a dead end in the murder investigation. He asked if I'd dig a little deeper into a couple of people. Patel is one of them."

Now we were getting somewhere. "So, maybe you can tell me why Jay's been so flaky lately."

"Flaky?"

"He yo-yos from good boss to bad boss and back again on an hourly basis, and he disappears and resurfaces like nothing happened. I don't need more than one mystery man in my life."

Carter's eyes turned sad. He took my hand. "I don't want to be a mystery to you, Sam. You know me better than anyone."

I willed myself to ignore the puppy dog eyes and the proximity of his pheromones. "Who else?"

"Pardon?"

"Who else have you investigated for Washington?"

"Can we save that for after dinner?"

If I were as unyielding as Lysistrata, I would have pried an answer from Carter right then and there. But lately, I'd ruined so much of our time together, and his request seemed reasonable. "Okay, after dinner, but definitely then."

After we cleaned up the kitchen, we carried our glasses and the half-empty wine bottle to the library, where I expected to hear more about the mystery that was Jay Patel.

With Miles Davis's *Kind of Blue* album filling the air, we sat together on the leather sofa. Carter wrapped his arm around me. A lot of kissing followed. Soon, the questions he'd promised to answer blurred and slipped away, and there was nothing left but the music and the two of us, still hungry for each other.

Saturday morning, I ambled into the kitchen to find Carter already dressed in slacks and a button-down shirt. I sat across from him at the breakfast island.

He handed a mug of coffee to me. "Morning, sleeping beauty. I was just about to leave you a note."

"Going where?"

"A couple of second interviews. I'm almost ready to make a decision. Have you had a chance to look over the résumés?"

My heart thudded. "Happy to discuss them when you get back."

In truth, I wasn't feeling happy at all.

He rinsed his cup, kissed me goodbye, and left.

Alone with my coffee, a huge case of the grumps settled in. The image of Carter in an intimate conversation with a potential new hire took over, and by the time I finished my coffee, I was miserable to the max.

And then I got angry. Carter still hadn't said what he knew about Jay Patel's flaky behavior, or why he'd scolded Evan Fentworth, or if Ralph had identified my stalker. If he wanted to know my opinion of the candidates for the job at Serenity, he'd have to answer my questions first.

I had just refilled my mug with fresh coffee when the phone buzzed.

Jojo. "Sammy! Glad I caught you. You don't have to pick me up this morning. I'm already here."

The cistern. I'd completely forgotten about the light show. After all Jojo had done for me, I didn't want to disappoint him.

I checked the clock. If I left now, I'd make it just in time.

CHAPTER FORTY THREE

Inner Sanctum

Deep underground near the north bank of Buffalo Bayou, the cistern had served as a reservoir for the city's drinking water nearly a hundred years ago. Its subterranean vault was just west of downtown. Outmoded by technology and outgrown by the city, it languished for decades, abandoned and all but forgotten.

In recent times, the vast concrete cavern had been reimagined into a historical site and a public showcase for changing artistic installations.

I left the Ferret by the neighboring skateboard park and took a walkway past walls of colorful graffiti art. Outside the cistern's entrance, I saw Jojo talking with an older man dressed in baggy khakis, a guayabera shirt, and a straw hat.

Jojo waved me over and introduced me to Alejandro, the artist whose exhibit we were there to see. The man's sun-weathered face broke into a wide smile.

"*Encantado,*" he said, and kissed my hand.

The three of us walked inside, where we were each given a white nylon cloak to wear over our clothes. "To capture the light," Alejandro explained. He led us into a dimly-lit descending passageway, then excused himself to make sure his installation inside the chamber was ready.

Twenty or so white-cloaked people had already formed a line. Someone at the front poked a head out and looked back toward us. As he approached, I recognized Jay Patel, cocooned inside his white smock. A woman and two little girls trailed behind. He introduced his family and stepped into line behind us.

Patel leaned in and spoke into my ear. "From what I've heard, we're going to be wowed by this show. Could be the subject of our local report for the Tweedy network. Francine is here, too, so you both can assess the possibilities."

The doors to the underground opened, sending a whoosh of cool air over us from inside the vault. Still descending, we plunged into deeper darkness and silence, except for the sound of our shuffling feet. Once all had entered, the doors shut behind us and the show began.

An ethereal melody filled the air. Soon, multi-colored lights cast rainbow stripes that undulated all around us, playing over the walls and over our white cloaks and astonished faces. A collective "Wow!" echoed through the massive space as the vault's extraordinary proportions were revealed, more vast than a football field, and as tall and deep as a natural cave.

Hundreds of graceful columns rose from the shallow pool below us all the way up to the lofty ceiling above like smooth man-made stalactites and stalagmites. The sight took me back to a long-ago family trip to Carlsbad Caverns.

Beside me, Jojo whispered. "Spooky cool."

A child's voice arose from behind. "Awesome!" The word echoed through the chamber. I turned to find the Patel girls and their parents still behind us.

Jay smiled, his face striped with wavy rainbows of colored light.

I seized the moment. "Let's definitely feature this for the local piece."

He gave me a thumbs-up. For once, the future of KHTS seemed a tad brighter.

With ever-changing colors and patterns rippling over the walls, columns, and our smocks, we proceeded along the elevated walkway that circumnavigated the inner sanctum. Soon, the music's rhythm became more upbeat, and the lights deepened to primary colors and thinned into laser grids and geometric shapes that swept through the vastness.

Another loud "Wow!" echoed and reechoed, zig-zagging across, up, down and around the expanse, eliciting additional hoots and whistles. People pulled out their mobile devices to record the phenomenon.

I heard Brad's deep baritone rumble, "Wonderful." From somewhere behind me, Jojo laughed and shouted. His cheery "Hello... *ello... ello... lo... lo...*" joined Brad's undertone, and the harmony echoed around and around until the music took over again.

Francine caught up and grabbed my arm. "I have news about Lloyd's ex-wife. I know who she is." She drew me aside to the railing and leaned in so no one else could hear. "She's here, and you won't believe who it is."

Before she could say more, someone screamed—more like a roar, really—and a body slammed into us, shoving us into the rail. Francine went airborne. I reached out to grab her, but it was too late. She tumbled over the top and down the steep concrete slope to the bottom.

Our attacker tried to pry my fingers off the rail. As the lights and the music played on, the woman's earsplitting screams exploded in endless echoing waves. I heard Brad Hudson's thunderous voice shout "No, Miss... i*ss*... stop, *op... op... op*!"

The crazy woman did stop for a second before she punched me in the face. By the time I recovered, she had thrown herself over the rail and plummeted down the slope.

Through the darkness, I saw her land in an awkward position near Francine. Without thinking, I scrambled over to help. The slope was steeper than I'd counted on, and I ended up skidding and sliding and skidding again to the bottom.

I landed in the shallow water next to our assailant, who was face-down and not moving. I managed to work myself up to a sitting position and leaned her head on my lap so she could breathe. Then I must have blacked out.

When I came to, Buron Washington's image swam through the darkness, colorful lights playing over his face. I thought I was hallucinating, until I heard him yell, "I need light... *ight ...ight*! And ambulances... *lances... ances*!" By the time his echoes died down and the music stopped, the colors had disappeared in a glare of utility lights.

Someone, maybe Brad, lifted the woman off me. The detective offered his hand. "Can you try to stand, Ms. Newman?"

I was soaking wet, and too shaky to move.

Jojo had scrambled down to help. "I've got you, Sammy. Just lean on me."

By the time the EMT's arrived, Jojo had me upright.

We made slow progress through the shallow water while murmurs from the group above filled the cavern. I looked up toward their startled faces. Someone shouted my name. It sounded like Jay Patel. I waved and called out, "I'm okay." The echoes ushered me the rest of the way: *okay... ay... ay...*

CHAPTER FORTY-FOUR

The Fritz

I awoke in bed at the condo, though the memory of how I got there was a little hazy. My head pounded, my jaw felt like it wasn't hinged right, and my right eye seemed to be on the fritz.

A grinding noise coming from the kitchen told me I was not alone. I gurgled out a weak "Hello?"

"I'll be right there." Carter.

I attempted to boost myself up, but my left arm balked and began to throb. That's when I discovered the bandage on my elbow. Red and purple flesh peeked out at the edges. I rolled to my right, a simple enough maneuver, except for the pain in my ankle.

Carter appeared at the door with something pink and frothy in a ginormous tumbler. A smoothie. "Happy Sunday. Do you know where you are?"

"Neverland?"

"Close enough."

I one-eyed the tumbler. "Is that for me?"

"Yes. The ER doc said to start with soft foods. You managed to loosen a few teeth. Best to let them settle down, unless you want to risk losing them."

"Charming. Is there something wrong with my right eye?"

"You have a beauty of a shiner under that eye patch." He set the drink on the night stand, hooked his arms under mine and hoisted me to a sitting position on the bed. I was in my jammies, which he must have put me in at some point.

Reaching for the drink, I discovered that my assailant had successfully mauled the backs of my hands. Under a clear plastic bandage, patches of skin were scraped raw from wrist to fingers.

I cradled the drink gingerly between my palms and tasted. A mixed berry concoction, thick with vanilla ice cream, and soothingly cool in my mouth. "What happened to the crazy woman?"

"Recovering."

"Why attack me? Or was it Francine she was after?"

"Washington's unscrambling that question now. He had to wait until she was conscious."

"Francine okay?"

"Messed up, like you."

My head hurt, and my arm, and my ankle. "Did they give me something for pain?"

"You're drinking it. I knew your head was too hard to sustain permanent damage, but in case you decided to brave through without meds, I pulverized two pills and mixed them into the smoothie. Enjoy the trip."

I took a another pull on the straw. "Delicious and nutritious."

The simple act of drinking wore me out. I handed the empty tumbler to Carter and scooched down the mattress until my head rested on the pillows. I think I mumbled thanks before I shut my good eye and drifted off again.

Carter's voice roused me from a druggy sleep. "You up for company?"

I raised my head off the pillow and opened the good eye. "Who?"

"Your pal, the makeup guy."

"Jojo? Sure." I rolled over, wiped drool off my cheek and lowered my feet to the floor. Before I stood, Carter slipped a brace over my ankle and strapped a sling to my shoulder. I took a few tentative steps. So far, so good.

It was dark outside, which told me I'd slept the entire day. I considered changing into something more guest-appropriate, but Jojo had seen me in less. I shuffled down the hall on my own steam.

Jojo was taking in the view through the balcony door. When he saw me, he made a sad face. I lowered my stiff body to the sofa.

He sat beside me and squeezed my hand. "I could wash your hair, if you want. And maybe cover up a few bruises."

I hadn't looked at myself in the mirror. "Is it that bad?"

"An eye, a cheek, and your nose and chin."

Carter had taken a chair. "Not as bad as it sounds," he offered.

I looked to Jojo for confirmation. "Giant asteroid bad?"

He nodded.

Just what a girl wants to hear. I changed the subject. "What happened to the light show?"

"Alejandro was worried that people wouldn't come after the news got out. But it got a great review in the Chronicle, and tickets sales are taking off."

"Glad we didn't ruin things." My back and hips began to bark. I winced and shifted my position a little. "I'd like a rematch with whoever attacked us."

"From what I hear, Missy got the worst of it."

I wasn't sure I heard him right. "Did you say Missy? Missy Eton? She was hurt, too?"

Jojo frowned. "Well, she brought it on herself."

"Are you saying *she* was the woman who attacked us?"

Jojo covered his mouth. "Oopsie. You didn't know?"

"It was so dark, and those wavy lights and white shrouds made it hard to recognize anybody. Patel told me Nandi was invited, but I never saw Missy." I looked at Carter. "Did you know and not tell me?"

"I was waiting until you were fully awake." He stood. "Time for another smoothie?"

"No pills this time. They make me fuzzy in the head. I just need to lie down for a minute."

Jojo jumped up. "Probably best if I leave. I brought some Thai basil soup for you. It's in the kitchen, ready to eat."

He bent down, kissed the top of my head and headed to the door. Halfway there, he turned. "Almost forgot. I'll be moving soon, and I'm throwing myself a party at Axelrad. It's tomorrow. Hope you'll be ready to bop by then."

"Moving? But, your house is so... you."

"Old me. I'm ready to move on, see how the rest of the world lives."

"River Oaks?"

He laughed. "Slightly less posh, and a lot farther away. New Guinea."

"New Guinea?"

"Yeah. Cass is taking Apollo back there to help him find his own kind, and hopefully, a sweetie he can shack up with. And Denny's band got a gig in Papua, so meanwhile, I'll look for a place to live. On the beach, if possible, where I can do my art. If it was good enough for Gaugin, it's good enough for me."

"I think that was Tahiti."

"Close enough. Who knows, maybe I'll find true love there, too."

After Jojo left, Carter helped me into the dining room and served up the Thai soup, along with the bottle of pain meds and a glass of water. "You seem lucid enough to regulate your own drugs."

"No drugs until we talk about Missy Eton. She was never nice to me, or anyone else, far as I can tell, but—"

Carter's phone buzzed. "Chapman here. Who? Hold on." He looked at me. "Your boss is downstairs and wants to come up."

Patel probably came to see if I'd be camera-ready by tomorrow. I could easily camouflage the bad arm, but my asteroid-stricken face might be a problem.

"Tell him I'm sleeping. I'll see him at the station in the morning."

"The bruises may look worse tomorrow."

How bad did I look? I had to see to for myself. I gripped the coffee table with my good arm, hoisted myself off the sofa, and limped to the bedroom to check the mirror.

An unrecognizable human stared back at me. It would definitely take more than a day to undo the damage.

CHAPTER FORTY-FIVE

Move On

I changed into jeans and a tee, pulled my bed-head hair into ponytail and removed the eye patch.

Yikes! A Halloween mask of a face gaped at me from the mirror. Thanks goodness I found a pair of Carter's sunglasses in his side table. I put them on and took a few practice steps until my limp was under control.

Patel rose from the living room sofa when he saw me and organized his face into a stiff smile. "Hope you don't mind the intrusion."

"Not at all. I'm fine."

An arm chair next to the sofa looked like the least painful place to land. I lowered myself with as much grace as I could summon.

Carter and Patel exchanged a look. For the second time in recent days, I got the feeling that they were more than new acquaintances. I used the awkwardness of the moment to steer the conversation.

"I've been meaning to ask you guys, how long have you known each other?"

Another look, another awkward moment.

Carter spoke first. "Jay and I worked together on a couple of projects back in the day."

Back in the day. That was code for Carter's undercover career, the one he'd sworn off of after we met. Somehow, I couldn't see Patel doing that kind of work.

Jay spoke. "I was only a desk jockey. Ran an information department."

Carter had developed a wide-ranging network of contacts from his previous career, but before Jay Patel, I'd only met one other: Roland Birney, the producer at *Front & Center*, the popular television news magazine. Alleged producer, I should say. In my early days of getting to know Carter, Birney had swooped in, said hello, and minutes later, the two of them swooped out together. Carter was gone for days with no explanation. It wouldn't surprise me if they still teamed up on secret stuff together from time to time.

Slivers of a new insight began to crystallize. I turned on Jay. "Did you hire me because Carter asked you to?"

Carter exploded. "Good grief!"

I ignored him and continued to skewer Patel. "Did he?"

"Absolutely not. I had no idea you two were connected. You were great in your stints as a guest expert, so when you came on the market, I snapped you up, plain and simple. Until this week, I hadn't seen or talked to Chapman since his wife and kids' funeral."

Carter sprang out of his chair and stormed out. A second or two later, I heard the front door slam.

I wished I could chalk up my behavior to the pain, but truth was, I'd hurt Carter, again. Patel and I remained seated, both of us mute.

Jay spoke first. "I don't know what's going on with you two, but I swear, until last week, I hadn't seen or talked to him in years."

"I jumped to the wrong conclusion. Sorry."

Jay stared at his hands. "Forget it."

Easier said than done. I had to find Carter and apologize. I stood, attempting to control the pain in my ankle and hips as I rose. "See you tomorrow?"

"Not tomorrow. Francine's bunged up too, but only from the neck down. Jojo can fix her well enough to cover noon and evening until you heal. You're her hero, you know."

"Glad she's mostly okay."

Another awkward silence. Patel rose and headed for the door. "I should go."

I'd missed the chance to ask about Missy Eton. I tried to catch up to him, but couldn't get there fast enough. I made it to the entry just as Carter appeared in the doorway, glaring.

I lowered my eyes. "Jay left."

"Saw him at the elevator. He called me a lucky guy."

Ouch. No way Carter was feeling lucky right now. "I'm sorry."

"You can trust me, Samantha. I'm on your side. Always."

"I know. But when you said you'd checked out Patel as a murder suspect, why didn't you tell me you knew him? Or even last year, when he first hired me? I've been working for an old colleague of yours, and you never mentioned—"

Carter strode past me and spun around, his face hard. "Let's be clear here. When I knew Patel, we were not in the habit of acknowledging each other in public. We fell out of the same circles years ago. He had no clue that you and I even knew each other until last week."

"But you knew, and didn't tell me."

"I never disclose the identity of colleagues, past or present. Besides, it wasn't relevant."

"It's relevant to me. You ask me to trust you, but you don't trust me to keep a secret."

We were back to glaring at each other again. And again, I broke the silence.

"Jay said not to come back for a week."

"He told me."

Normally, this would be when Carter would suggest that I stay with him at Serenity while I heal. But he didn't. Instead, he asked if I was hungry.

I turned away. "Is there any Thai soup left?"

He brought the steamy, fragrant bowl to the dining room and set it on the table. Then he left the room, saying he'd be right back. I hoped he wasn't packing up to leave.

A few minutes later, he returned with a great looking chicken salad sandwich.

I felt like I needed to clear the air. "Can we have a do-over?"

"For what?"

"For you and me."

"Us?" He shook his head. "Look, I know I'm not the easiest person to live with sometimes. But lately, neither are you. I'd rather not repeat the past few days. So, no. No do-over. I'd rather move on."

CHAPTER FORTY-SIX

The Prophet

Move on? "What does that mean?"

"I'm tired of going round and round."

"And?"

"And nothing. Let's just change the subject. How's the soup?"

"The soup? It's good."

"Maybe I'll try it next time."

Next time. Felt like I'd just dodged a bullet.

We ate in silence for a while, until my thoughts circled back to Jojo's visit.

"It's puzzling about Missy Eton. Did you know she was the one?"

"I was about to tell you when Jay Patel showed up. Ralph had identified some of those text messages as coming from her phone."

"From Missy?"

"Not all were from her, and it took a while to separate the two. Since Washington was already investigating the KHTS employees, Ralph passed the info to him. The detective promised to put eyes on you until he figured out who was who."

"So, that's why Washington was at the cistern yesterday."

But Missy Eton? When I first started working at the station, I endured a less-than-inspiring stint in her marketing department. Between her sour personality and my pitiful trainee wages, my initial enthusiasm for the job had ticked down a notch even before I moved on to Lloyd. But, why had she been harassing me? And why attack Francine if it was only me she was after?

Carter interrupted my thoughts. "Want know who the other texter was?"

"Another co-worker?"

"Evan Fentworth."

"My new producer? What does he have against me?"

"Nothing. Matter of fact, seems like he's got a crush on you. Once Ralph separated Eton's texts from what turned out to be the ones from Fentworth, it was easy to tell her veiled threats from his lame attempts to flirt with you. Read them again and you'll see."

"No thanks. At least it explains why you were fussing at him the other day. My poor secret admirer. I'll be kinder next time I see him."

"You might reconsider that. He sent similar texts to your co-workers, Francine and Nandi."

So much for feeling special.

Carter eyed the résumé stack. "I'm heading back to the ranch. Are you up to talking about those before I go?"

My heart sank. Carter wasn't staying over, and he wasn't inviting me to come with him. My appetite for the soup vanished. I slid the bowl away and replaced it with the résumés. No use avoiding the subject any longer. I was about to tackle the first applicant when Carter interrupted.

"Before we start, I need to update you on a few things." He took his time clearing the table before he sat and pinned me with those soulful eyes. I braced myself for what looked to be a difficult conversation.

"You know that I manage most of my interests myself, with the help of Ralph and Tom Mason."

"And Gertie."

"And Gertie, of course. However, a new, important project will be taking more of my time for the foreseeable future, just when the retreat requires day-to-day attention. Tom can handle the facilities and most of the operations, but I'm hoping that the person who takes the Executive Director job can step in immediately to run it and the foundation, too."

It took a moment for me to unpack what he was saying. His new client had an issue so urgent that Carter was willing to put the retreat and his charitable foundation into someone else's hands?

"Is this the prelude to another disappearing act?"

"Not like the old stuff. I've been asked to join a new cyber security task force in D.C., and I've accepted. Between that and my other clients, I'll have a full plate for a while."

"Sounds like you need a clone."

"Not sure there needs to be another me. Just someone who can execute the foundation's mission, including the new retreat."

"You'll be reachable?"

"For this person? Yes."

I ran through the job applicants to refresh my memory. "You have a favorite?"

"I do."

My heart twisted. I caught my breath and put on a brave face. "Which one?"

He nailed me again with his big browns. At first, I thought he wanted me to guess, but as his stare deepened, I got a different vibe. Heat rose in my face. I had to say something.

"I have a job."

"A job you hate."

"I don't hate it exactly, I just..."

Carter waited for me to finish the thought. I couldn't.

He broke the silence. "I've tried to talk to you about this so many times, Sam. But you kept changing the subject. When you got the TV job, I truly wanted you to thrive there, if that was what you wanted. But I don't think that's happening."

"Is this another one of your pity moves?"

"Don't be ridiculous. We both know you're more qualified than anyone else. You love a meaningful mission, you're already accomplished in most everything needed to run this one, and despite the misguided notion that I hide things from you, you know me better than anyone."

"The timing just seems so convenient."

"You worry about the strangest things." He pushed away from the table, gathered the résumés, and took his sandwich with him to the kitchen.

I stared at his empty chair, wondering why I kept trying to drive him away. My ankle balked as I struggled up from the table. Pain meds in hand, I hobbled after him.

He was standing at the sink finishing his sandwich. He glanced at me and looked away.

I leaned against the island and set the pill jar on it. "I need to take one or two of these, but before I get loopy, I want to say something. Two things, actually. First, I'm sorry. I'm an idiot and I don't know why. Two, can I have few days to think it over?"

He dropped his empty plate in the sink with a loud clank and washed it, then tossed the towel onto the counter and turned to me. "I never wanted to pressure you, Sam, but I have to have a person in place before I fly to D.C. If I don't have your answer before then, I'll assume it's a no, and hire someone else. In the meantime, I'll be at the ranch."

After Carter left, I considered switching from pain pills to wine. But I had deep thinking to do, so I poured myself a tall glass of water and carried it to the library for some serious introspection.

As I stretched out on the sofa, a book of writings by Kahlil Gibran winked at me from the coffee table. I'd first encountered the poet/philosopher in college when I read *The Prophet*. Fresh from losing my family, and with no other guidance at hand, my resolve to stay strong and independent was largely informed by that book.

I opened the book to a random page. The words I found there hit my chest like a crash-triggered airbag.

Between what is said and not meant, and what is meant and not said, most of love is lost.

Was that what was happening to Carter and me?

All at once the world quit turning. Or, maybe it was my heart that stopped.

Every part of me wanted to climb back into bed and shut out the world. But Carter deserved an answer. I had to make a decision, and soon.

It would be a challenge to keep my sanity if I stayed with the Tweedy bunch. On the other hand, if I stuck it out long enough, I might be able to parlay it into a better offer and a fascinating career. Or, I could be murdered at the station in a matter of days.

But if I moved my entire life to Serenity, would I lose what little remained of my independence?

CHAPTER FORTY-SEVEN

Family Secrets

My phone buzzed. Alicia Sultana was calling? Curious, I quickly connected.

Her rich alto voice was unmistakable. "How are you, Samantha? I heard about the weekend kerfuffle."

"I'm fine, really, just sitting around waiting to get back to work and driving myself crazy over who Lloyd's killer could be. The usual."

She let out a throaty laugh.

I pursued the subject. "You didn't want to speculate before, but now that you've distanced yourself, do you think someone at the station did it?"

"You mean, among the many of us who at one time or another wanted to throttle him?"

"You, too?"

"Guilty as charged. In thought only, however."

"Anyone who might have actually done it?"

"I wouldn't want to cast blame on the wrong person."

"Neither do I. But do I have a question about Missy Eton."

"Missy? Very private. Difficult, sometimes, but I never really got to know her beyond conversations about my public appearances or photo shoots, things like that."

"What about Maura and Jay Patel? Something's off with them. What am I missing?"

It took her a while to respond. "Well, they were the ones who worked most closely with Lloyd. I knew that Maura did the heavy lifting on his reports, for which he took a hundred percent credit. Could be she'd finally snapped."

"And Patel?"

A longer silence followed, so long that I thought the line had dropped. "Alicia?"

"Sorry, you reminded me of something Jay mentioned a few days before Lloyd was shot. Something about Lloyd threatening to expose dirt on someone at the station. It sounded to me like Sedgwick's usual bluster, so I forgot about it."

"I heard the same thing from someone else. Do you know who Lloyd's target was?"

"We all have things in our past we'd rather not have aired in public."

I wanted her to go further, but she wouldn't budge. With a 'nice talking to you,' she wished me well and said goodbye.

The whole conversation left me frustrated. Too many people remained question marks. I needed to talk to someone who would know more.

I called Maura. Her phone rang half a dozen times. In case she was staring at my caller ID, trying to decide whether or not to connect, I hung on for a half-dozen more rings.

She picked up. "Why are you calling me?"

Not a great beginning. I pressed on anyway. "Just wanted to see how you are. You heard about the incident over the weekend?"

"Yes."

"Well, I'm stuck at home, bored out of my gourd and thinking about you. Everything okay?"

"Why do you care?"

She wasn't making this easy. I abandoned the indirect route and went with the truth. "I have a lot of respect for you, and I think you've been treated unfairly."

"Cut the crap. What do you want?"

"I mean it, Maura. You're good at what you do, and you deserve a fresh start."

"Got one for me?"

"Not at the moment. But I do have a question. Who do you think killed Lloyd? I just spoke to Alicia and asked her the same thing, by the way."

"What did she say?"

"That just about anyone who knew Lloyd could have done it."

"Sounds right. So, why ask me?"

"He may not have been anyone's favorite person, but he still deserves justice. You knew him best. You must have your suspicions."

Maura blew out a breath. "I'm the most likely suspect, according to the cops, but they don't have enough evidence to charge me. Yet."

"I don't think you did it. So, besides you... who else?"

She took a moment before answering. "Maybe Brad Hudson."

"Brad? What makes you think it was him."

"Family secrets."

"Meaning?"

"His sister was married to Lloyd."

Wait, what? "Say again?"

"Brad's sister is Missy Eton, Lloyd's crazy ex-wife."

Lloyd and Missy, married? What an unhappy match that must have been. It occurred to me that it could have been Missy at the other end of Lloyd's phone at the hospital. "Did you tell this to the police?"

"Yes, but they only care about keeping me in the hot seat."

"How did you find out?"

"I was one of the few people around during the divorce. Nasty. Lloyd and Brad almost came to blows a couple of times, and Missy was vindictive as hell. Wouldn't surprise me if one of them finally did him in."

I'd always considered Missy Eton to be a cold fish, but after her unhinged behavior at the cistern, it was easy to believe she was crazy enough to kill. But, Brad Hudson?

I tried to wrap my brain around the possibility that my new mentor—the man whose good graces I'd wheedled my way into—could be Lloyd's killer. However, if Patel also suspected him, it would explain why he'd slashed Brad's air time.

As Missy's husband and Brad's brother-in-law, Lloyd had access to any number of family secrets. Perhaps he'd weaponized what he knew, creating bad blood between them that ended in homicide.

Talking to Maura and Alicia had only raised more questions. If I wanted to get to the truth, I had to pursue the person who probably knew more about Lloyd than anyone: Jay Patel.

My on-camera duty was on hiatus, but no one said I couldn't show up at the station.

CHAPTER FORTY EIGHT

Briar Patch

By dawn Monday morning, I had a plan. I sat up in bed and tested my arm and my ankle. Both seemed mostly workable.

I peeled myself out of bed and gingerly tugged up my jeans. As I bent over to wrap the brace around my ankle, my ribs balked, but my bandaged arm slipped easily into a roomy tee shirt. I dabbed cover-up on my bruised face and grabbed the sunglasses, then checked the mirror to make sure I looked reasonably put together.

Taking my time in the kitchen, I made a pot of French press and looked for something soft enough for my jaw to handle. Oatmeal seemed about right, with butter and brown sugar. Unsure if my hips were ready for the barstool, I filled my mug and ate standing up. Then I hauled my work bag to the breakfast island.

As I rummage through, the sight of my own laptop reminded me that Lloyd's was gone forever. Which raised the old question: who had it before I found it in my credenza, and why had they put it there?

I made myself crazy with that for a while until my phone beeped with a call from Buron Washington. "Ms. Newman, I'd like to see you as soon as possible about the Sedgwick case."

Twenty minutes later, the detective was at my door. His usually inscrutable expression dissolved when he saw my bruised face.

I tried a little humor. "It's not as bad as it looks."

I limped into the living room and lowered myself to the sofa. He followed and took a side chair. Before he started in about the murder, I had a pressing question. "Can you tell me what happened to Missy Eton?"

Washington frowned. "She's currently being treated for her injuries, as well as her mental state."

"Did she kill Lloyd?"

"Sorry, I am here only to discuss Lloyd Sedgwick's computer. You were the last person to possess it, correct?"

Washington and I must have been on the same wavelength about the laptop. "It just showed up out of the blue inside my credenza. I only used it to search for material on the report I was working on. Far as I know, yes, I was the last one to have it."

"Any idea where it might have been before you found it?"

"No. And no idea why or how it ended up in my credenza."

"Did you delete any files while the device was in your possession?"

"Delete files?"

The detective's eyes drilled into mine. An uncomfortable thought struck. "Am I a suspect?"

"Until a crime is solved, everyone is."

"I did not delete any files, and I did not kill Lloyd."

"Noted. Besides yourself, would it be odd for anyone else to have used the device?"

I pondered the question. Clearly, someone had moved it into my credenza. But why would they need to mess with it, unless, like me, they were searching for something inside, an email, or a document, maybe, like...

"Oh!"

Washington sat up. "Something I should know, Ms. Newman?"

"I wonder if it had anything to do with the rumor about Lloyd's dirty secrets list."

The detective was staring at me. "Dirty secrets?"

"I heard that Lloyd kept a dirty secrets file on people, like for blackmail."

Washington's expression changed ever so slightly. "Thank you, Ms. Newman. I'll be in touch."

I followed him to the door. "Wait. Do you think I'm right?"

"That is best left for another day."

I started to chase him to the elevator, but my body balked. If I was going to function at all today, I'd need pain meds to see me through.

Back in the kitchen, I swished one down with the rest of my coffee and considered Washington's question about a deleted file. Whatever he was looking for was likely deleted before I got my hands on it. But maybe I'd overlooked something.

I refilled my mug, plugged the thumb drive into my laptop and watched the files populate the screen.

I'd almost forgotten how deep Lloyd's research had been. And how mind-numbingly detailed. I scrolled through to make sure I hadn't missed anything that looked like it could be a dirty secrets list. When I came to the report Maura had written, I got sidetracked.

Patel made it clear that the fate of the flood report was in my hands. Knowing the breadth and depth of the material Maura had to work from, the finished product was practically a work of art. It would be a shame to let it languish in limbo.

Too many lives had been upended, too many homes destroyed. Not enough was done to restore what was lost, and not enough to prevent a future disaster.

I didn't have it in me to bury the story forever. But, what to do with it now?

Slowly, an idea took shape, but to get it done, I needed information from Carter. I'd behaved badly the last time he was here. Now I had a reason to call him and apologize.

He picked up right away. But with so much to say, I was too tongue-tied to speak.

"Sam, are you there?"

I swallowed hard. "I have a question."

"Just one?"

"For starters. It's about your friend, Roland Birney."

"What about him?"

"Is he really affiliated with Front & Center?"

It was Carter's turn to hesitate, and I knew why. When we first met, Carter had posed as Birney—a producer for the weekly TV news magazine—saying he wanted to interview me for a segment on the show about the region's employment outlook. It turned out to be a ridiculous ruse he was using to investigate my old employer's criminal activities.

Eventually, I met the real Birney, just before the two of them disappeared together on a secret mission. Later, Carter promised me he wouldn't take on anything too dangerous anymore. But Birney could still be in the game.

"What do you want him for?"

"The flood report. It's a great piece of reporting. Tweedy will never air it, and it's too important a subject to let die. I'm hoping a show like Front & Center will pick it up."

"I'll send you his network contact information. He may pass it on to someone else, though."

"Thanks."

"That all you need?" A loaded question.

"Sorry I was such a cow when you were here. Can we talk later? I took a pain pill and I'm starting to feel kind of fuzzy."

Carter didn't press, which felt like good and bad news at the same time. Was he giving up on me and really moving on?

Once upon a time, I had my life under control, or thought I did. Nowadays, everything was falling apart, including me. I normally operate on the assumption that the longer you postpone a decision, the thornier it gets. True to form, this one was starting to feel like a great big briar patch.

CHAPTER FORTY-NINE

Scrambled

One good thing about the pain meds. They knocked me out, but they also helped me sleep the kind of sleep where worries do not exist. It was almost noon when I awoke.

My original goal for the morning had been to quiz Patel about Lloyd's enemies. Now, there was also Washington's question about a deleted file to ask about. I felt pretty good after my nap. No reason why I couldn't go to the station this afternoon.

The employee parking lot was only half full. I steered the Ferret into its usual spot and gingerly peeled myself out, one limb at a time. In the lobby, the receptionist's chair was empty. With no one to stop me for a chat, I toddled straight to Patel's office.

He was on the phone with his back to me. Normally, I would wait to be invited in, but this time I entered and sat opposite him at his desk. When he caught sight of me, he seemed to levitate off his chair a fraction of an inch.

He terminated his conversation and spun around to face me. "I thought I told you not to—"

"Easy, Jay. I'm feeling good enough to work."

"You can't be on camera with that eye."

So much for camouflage. "But I can get started on the local cistern story. And since it doesn't look like we have a receptionist today, I'm happy to sit up there and answer the phone while I work. But first, I need your help with something that's driving me crazy."

"Which is?"

"Lloyd's murder. I'd sleep better at night if I could do something to help catch his killer. Who do you think it is?"

Patel began rearranging items on his desk.

I pressed on. "When I brought you the idea of producing a local spot, you didn't want Brad Hudson to be part of it. Does that have anything to do with his relationship to Lloyd?"

He answered with a steely glare. "I prefer not to discuss an employee's private life."

"Maura clued me in about Missy and the wife/sister thing. And I've heard talk about a dirty secrets file. So I'm wondering, do you think Brad killed him because of the file? Or Missy?"

Patel shot up. "You have no idea what you're talking about!" He turned a scary mahogany red. Between Lloyd's death and the Tweedy takeover, it's no wonder the poor guy was crumbling under the pressure. I had probably just made it worse.

"Sorry to upset you, Jay, but the sooner Lloyd's killer is caught, the safer we'll all be, don't you think?"

He covered his face with his hands. "No more, Samantha. Please, just go away."

Not wanting to give the man a heart attack, I backed off. "Tell you what. I'll be at the front desk while I work on a few ideas for the cistern spot. We can talk later when you're feeling better." I gathered my bag and retreated to the lobby.

Stationed at the receptionist's desk, I booted up my laptop. Instead of starting with research on the cistern, I decided to follow up on Maura's shocker that Brad and Missy were siblings and see what the internet had on them. Maybe I'd find a biography with clues about Missy's marriage to Lloyd. Or a news article hinting at some other juicy piece of personal history.

LinkedIn appeared to be the only site Brad was active on. His profile revealed only his alma mater and a list of the stations he'd worked for before coming to KHTS. Nothing about his private life. And nothing on Missy, other than her employment here.

The vast implacable internet: so handy with meaningless trivia, so unreliable for the really important questions. I slammed the laptop shut. Just like Lloyd's computer, its passive-aggressive indifference was infuriating.

Then it dawned on me: I'd meant to ask Patel if he knew who had Lloyd's laptop before me. I was dying to run back and ask, but given his current emotional state, it seemed best to postpone another round of questioning.

Thank goodness I had the thumb drive. It was still possible I'd snagged something in Lloyd's files that was relevant to his murder. I plugged it in and was starting to scan through documents when the main phone line lit up.

I answered with my best receptionist singsong. "KHTS. May I help you?"

A familiar voice asked if Jay Patel was in. I ditched the melodic affectation. "Detective Washington? It's me, Samantha."

"Ms. Newman? I thought you were staying home this week."

"I came in to talk to Jay Patel."

Washington audibly sighed. "You shouldn't be there."

"So I've been told. But as it turns out, they needed a receptionist today. If you want to speak to Jay, fair warning, he's a little upset right now."

Just then, Patel walked into the lobby. He appeared to be on his way out.

"Oh, here you are, Jay. You have a call from—"

Washington yelled into the phone. "No! Do not tell him it's me!" He disconnected.

Patel had stopped in the center of the lobby. I put the handset down slowly and tried to make sense of Washington's panic. "I guess he'll call back later. Are you leaving?"

Jay stared at me, an odd glint in his eyes. Without warning, he charged the desk. I barely had time to jump away before he changed course and came after me again. I managed to sidestep him. By now, we were both in the middle of the lobby, staring each other down like prizefighters in the ring.

He was coiled and ready to lunge at me again, but instead, he straightened and looked around, wide-eyed, as if he suddenly didn't recognize where he was. When his eyes fell on me, he screamed. "You! Why is it you!"

He sprang forward and grabbed me by the shoulders. Wrestling for control, we both fell to the floor. Somehow, I ended up on top of him, my face smushed against his.

He began to whimper. "I tried to protect you! I just wanted everybody to be okay."

I pulled my head back to see him more clearly. His eyes were open, but unfocused, and he was babbling incoherently as sweat beaded his forehead.

In that moment, I realized what was happening. Jay Patel was having a mental breakdown.

Eventually, Jay stopped struggling. His body went limp.

I spoke as calmly as I could. "It's okay, Jay. It's me, Samantha. You're safe."

Wrong move. At the sound of my voice, he screamed again and tried to push me off him. With my arm and leg weakened by the attack at the cistern, I lost the struggle. The minute I rolled away, he leapt up and shot out the door. I hauled myself up and limped after him fast as I could. By the time I caught up, he was staggering toward the parking lot.

Just before he reached the lot, he stumbled and fell. I launched myself forward and landed on top of him again. This time, I dug my hands underneath him, clasped them together, and held on.

Sobs racked his body. Slowly, his resistance ebbed until at last, he stopped struggling and moaned. "Why did it have to be you?"

I didn't grasp what he meant at first. Then it hit me. It was dreadfully possible that Jay Patel had killed Lloyd Sedgwick. My body went cold.

Faint at first, the blare of sirens grew louder. In that distracted moment, my grip loosened, and Jay wriggled free. He popped up and stumbled toward his car.

A squad car squealed to a halt at the curb. Two policemen jumped out and rushed toward Jay. Another car arrived, this time unmarked. Buron Washington emerged from the driver's seat. He gave me a nod and joined the group around Patel. I followed him to get a better view.

The two officers had cuffed Patel. He and Washington seemed to be having a relatively calm conversation, though occasionally Jay would shake his head in response to something the detective said. After a few minutes, the officers led him to a squad car not far from where I was standing.

Patel and I briefly caught eyes. His face was dark and wet with tears. Hanging his head, he let himself be lowered into the back seat of the cruiser. It was the saddest sight I'd seen, almost ever.

CHAPTER FIFTY

Monkey Bread

$\mathbf{M}$y nerves were shattered. The receptionist's phone could answer itself, for all I cared. I limped down the corridor to my office.

I had to talk to someone who could help me make sense of what had just happened. Detective Washington would be tied up for a while. Not that he'd be telling me anything anyway.

Only one other person could shed some light on the situation. The one who was always wired in: Carter Chapman.

He answered on the first ring. The sound of his hello sent my pulse into overdrive. I still hadn't given him an answer about the job at Serenity.

First things first, I told myself. "I need to ask you something. When did you know that Jay Patel killed Lloyd?"

It took him a couple of beats before he replied. "Where'd you get that idea?"

"Buron Washington just hauled him away in handcuffs."

"Is that why you're calling?"

Of course, he'd expected me to start a different conversation. "Not entirely. I was planning to call you about that other thing, and then all hell broke loose around here."

"You're at the TV station?"

"I came in to talk to Jay. We spoke for only a minute before he had some kind of mental breakdown, then Washington showed up and took him away. The whole thing is bewildering as all get-out."

"Go back to the condo and get some rest."

"I don't want to go back to the condo. I need to talk to you."

"I'm with someone right now."

With someone? Oh, geez... Had time run out for me to give him an answer? Had it run out for us altogether?

Now or never, I had to make a decision. I hobbled to my car and headed to Gertie's.

The Kleschevsky estate in River Oaks stood among the many mansions in that grand Houston neighborhood. It was hard to see from the street, due to the dense plantings in the acre of front lawn, but once you made it up the driveway, you were facing a chateau that rivaled those in Loire Valley.

I pressed the call button at the security gate and showed my face to the camera.

Gertie's sweet voice answered. "I'm just making coffee. Come in!"

By the time I reached the stone-paved apron in front of the house, she was standing in the open door, looking every bit the River Oaks matron in a long caftan of silk, with red poppies splashed over a wash of pale green and white. As I climbed the few steps to the entry, she opened her arms. "I'm so happy to see you, dear."

"My face is a little messed up."

"Thanks goodness it wasn't worse!" She took me by the hand and led me into the kitchen. It was four or five times the size of the one in her little lost bungalow, but I recognized a familiar cinnamon-sugar aroma.

I sat at the cooking island while she donned two mitts, extracted a Bundt pan from the oven, and set it on the granite counter to cool. As she busied herself with tea fixings, my mind flashed to the last time I'd seen her in a housecoat. Before she met Louis, she had favored quilted gingham robes, the kind you might find at JCPenny. Not anymore.

"Love your caftan."

She huffed. "Louis! Every time I turn around there's a delivery from Neiman's or Tootsies at the door."

"He has good taste."

"Expensive taste. I nearly fainted when I saw the price tag. I didn't marry him for the money, and I told him that if he didn't stop this nonsense, I would most definitely leave him for it."

"What did he say?"

"He said, 'No problem. Exchange it for something you like.' Never thought I'd be spending almost four hundred dollars on a housecoat, but it was a bargain by comparison. At least it goes in the washer."

I tried to hide a smile. "He's a generous man. And he loves you. Let him pamper you."

Gertie brought two cups to the bar. "I admit, it is wonderful to be pampered. You should try it sometime."

I swear, she's a mind reader. She hadn't bothered to ask me why I'd showed up unannounced. She didn't have to.

Tongue-tied, I sat and watched her ease a thin knife around the edges of the cake, place a platter on top and invert the whole thing. Then she turned her attention to me. "You're not working today?"

"No."

When the tea was ready, she carefully coaxed its contents out until a monkey bread rested on the plate. Cinnamon-sugar peeked out between each pillowy, butter-glazed section. She took a stool across from me, and studied my face. "How bad is your eye?"

I removed my sunglasses to give her a peek at the purple, green, and yellow still decorating my eye socket and cheek.

She made a face. "Mardi Gras colors. Too bad it's not February. How's the rest of you?"

"Sore, but everything will heal, thank goodness."

"Everything?"

See what I mean? Clairvoyant. Might as well get to the point. "I suppose you've spoken with Carter about the person he's trying to hire at the retreat?"

"Several times."

"I have a decision to make."

"Indeed you do."

"I was hoping we could talk pros and cons, like the old days."

"Those were business decisions. This one's more than that, don't you think?"

I lowered my eyes. "How close is Carter to hiring someone?"

"Very close. I love you, dear, but we're all tired of waiting. It's time for you to decide."

I didn't have to ask her what she would do. It was obvious whose side she was on.

She was right, of course. The decision was only mine to make.

We chatted a while over warm monkey bread and tea, talking about her cruise with Louis before his stomach issues took their toll.

Small talk is hard when there are heavy things on your heart.

I rose to leave. Gertie walked me to the door and hugged me. "Be kind to yourself," she said. "For once in your life, choose to be happy."

As I started up the Ferret, my phone buzzed with a text from Riva Ramirez. I'd nearly forgotten about her quest to save the pizza girl from a life of misery.

Her message was a long one, essentially outlining the progress of Valentina's case. There were still a lot of hurdles to get over, but it ended on a positive note:

Judge gave time to evaluate Val. Fingers crossed no juvie record. Million de gracias.

Though the child's stupid actions had put Lloyd's life on a downward spiral, I couldn't help but be glad that her life might be redeemed. I texted back:

De nada.

At least I'd done something good for a change.

CHAPTER FIFTY-ONE

Axelrad

On the way back to the condo, Jojo called. "Hey, girl. Hope you're coming to my going away party."

"It's today?"

"Yep. Starts at five, at Axelrad. Last chance to see my pretty face. I'm leaving in the morning for Palau, but I'm here setting things up if you wanna come early."

Exhausted though I was, I had to put in an appearance for Jojo. But wallowing in the dirt with Patel demanded that I clean up first.

Soon as I got to the condo, I fished out a pain med from its container and swallowed it down with a green drink, then took my wreck of a body down the hall to shed my scruffed-up clothes.

At Axelrad, I spotted Jojo out back by the bandstand. He waved and came over. "Hey! Glad you're early. I brought party favors for everyone, and I need help figuring out where to put them." I followed him to the side of the stage where stacks of his brightly painted canvasses leaned against a black equipment case.

"You're selling your artwork?"

"Giving it away. First come, first dibs. I don't need to take it all with me. I can always make more."

I helped him tilt some canvasses against the front of the bandstand and we used the rest to cordon off a few tables down front. Once all the canvasses were placed, I sat alone and ordered a beer and a pizza.

People started drifting in, asking for Jojo. Aside from Alejandro, I didn't know any of them. I would have been more social, but this morning's wrestling match had taken the stuffing out of me. I was happy to stay put.

Alicia showed up, carrying a huge cake box. When she saw me, she came over and set it on the table. "I wasn't sure I'd know anyone, but I had to come to say goodbye."

I nodded. "Same here. What's in the box?"

She opened it so I could take a peek. The sheet cake had been iced to resemble one of Jojo's lively paintings. In the center, the words *Bon Voyage!* arched above remarkably accurate portraits of Jojo and Apollo. It smelled like chocolate heaven. While Alicia went in search of a knife, my pizza arrived. Famished as I was, I dug in.

Alicia returned with the knife and a glass of red. "Pizza looks good." She sat and tore off a slice. "Did you hear about Jay?"

"I was in the thick of it. Pretty awful."

"They're letting him go, you know."

"They are?"

"Yes. He called and asked me to scoot over to the station and help calm everyone down until the end of the day. Left me just enough time to pick up the cake."

I wondered if what Jay told Alicia was true, or if he was merely getting out on bail. "Why was he arrested in the first place? Did they think he killed Lloyd?"

She looked at me as if I were an idiot. "Of course not. If you thought Jay Patel was a murderer, you don't know him very well. He wouldn't hurt a fly."

"So, if Jay didn't do it, then who?"

"Beats me. I'm sure we'll all know in time."

The band started tuning up for their first set. Denny left his keyboard and moved to the center stage microphone. "Friends and neighbors, tonight we're celebrating our good buddy Jojo, who's coming with us when we take our furbaby Apollo to his rightful island paradise. Come on up here, fella."

Jojo waved off the invitation until people started chanting, "Jo-jo! Jo-jo! Jo-jo!" forcing him to climb onstage and say something. "Thanks, guys. I'll miss each and every one of you. Love you all." He hugged Denny and jumped off again.

Alicia leaned close to me. "You know, if I didn't know better, I'd say leaving the country is a pretty suspicious move for Jojo. Perhaps *he* is Lloyd's killer."

I looked at her in horror.

She burst out laughing. "I'm joking! We both know that's absurd."

"You had me going there for a second. Actually, I'm tempted to ask Jojo to take me with him."

"I know the feeling."

The sun was gracing the horizon with a glorious, blazing finale while the band played and Jojo worked his way through the crowd, saying hello and goodbye along the way. When he reached our table, Alicia hugged him and handed him the cake box. "To share or eat all by yourself. Your choice."

He peeked inside. "Never realized how much Apollo looks like me! Thanks, my queen."

Then he turned to me. "As for you, Princess, promise me you'll call Cass if another giant asteroid hits. I won't be here to square your shoulders anymore."

Alicia's joke about escaping to avoid arrest for Lloyd's murder popped into my head. Jojo was the one person I'd never suspected. I had to ask. "Are you running from the law?"

He laughed. "You've been talking to Alicia."

My eyes teared up as I hugged his skinny body.

The minute I parked the Ferret at The Wellbourne, my phone lit up with Alicia's on-camera face. I could hear Denny's band playing in the background as she spoke. "Guess who showed up at Axelrad right after you left?"

"Who?"

"Jay."

I wasn't sure I'd her heard right. "Jay Patel?"

"Sitting right next to me. Well, he was until he got up to speak to Jojo. He looks beat, but says he's okay. I think he took something to smooth himself out, if you know what I mean."

"Did he say what happened after the police took him away?"

"You know Jay. Not much of a sharer when it comes to personal information. Anyway, I'm guessing the whole thing plays like a soap opera." She chuckled. "Tune in tomorrow..."

I was amazed at her blasé attitude, which made me wonder.

In the elevator, my mind worked to fill in the blanks. If Detective Washington had let Patel go so soon, perhaps Jay wasn't the prime suspect in Lloyd's murder. Maybe he's only driven himself crazy trying to protect someone else.

Deep into my ruminations, I lost track of where I was until I realized I was still standing inside the elevator in the garage. The doors were closed, but I had failed to push the button to go upstairs.

CHAPTER FIFTY-TWO

Unscrambled

More questions cycled through my mind, too many to get a good night's sleep. All was not lost, though, because I'd managed to make at least one decision by morning. I chugged some coffee, washed down two ibuprofen and hurried to dress.

Jay Patel's red Porsche was in its usual spot when I pulled into the parking lot at the station. A good sign, since he was the one I'd come to see.

I stood in the doorway to his office and waited until he finished reading something on his desktop. I wasn't sure how I should feel about him, not knowing if he was involved in Lloyd's murder. But he didn't look scary, only more ragged than the day before.

He looked up and saw me. "Samantha?"

"I promise I haven't come to torture you."

He offered a weak smile. "Why are you here?"

"I want to return these." I unzipped the wardrobe bag with the floozie dresses inside.

"Are you quitting?"

"Depends. I would like to keep my job, but I will not wear these awful things anymore. If Brad doesn't have to show up on camera nearly topless, I shouldn't have to, either. The rest is up to Tweedy."

The last thing I wanted to do was risk setting him off again, so I said a quick goodbye and left his office. As I was walking out the front entrance, Brad

Hudson was coming in. I hadn't seen him since the cistern fiasco.

I was dying to ask him about Missy. On second thought, I kept it causal. "Hi, Brad."

He stopped short, looking stunned to see me. He pointed at my face.

I laughed. "Yes, you'll be anchoring solo for a while."

We stared at each other, unsure how to disengage. Finally, he cleared his throat. "I am late for a meeting with Jay Patel." He headed for the hall.

My curiosity got the better of me. "Before you go, could I ask you something?"

He reeled around, red-faced. "What?"

Maybe it was too soon to broach the Missy subject. Changing gears, the only thing I could come up with was, "Can we start my training today?"

His face relaxed a tiny bit. "My office. Half an hour."

Oh joy. If only I'd just said hello and left him to his meeting. Kicking myself all the way, I reversed my direction and slumped to my office to wait for his meeting with Patel to end. In the meantime, I checked my messages.

Roland Birney's contact info had arrived from Carter. I booted my laptop and plugged in the thumb drive. I set up a message to Birney and dragged Maura's report into it, adding a short synopsis of the report and my reason for sending it to him.

I also suggested that if *Front & Center* ended up producing a segment from the material, they should consider giving credit to Lloyd Sedgwick for the research and Maura Tustin for the writing. I added a plug for Maura's competence as a news producer, in case the network was hiring.

Immediately after I hit *Send*, an unexpected twinge of regret came over me. Had I just given away the story that could have launched my career as a bona fide whistleblower?

But the report was really Lloyd's and Maura's. Someone had to speak up for their work, and for the tens of thousands of flood victims in the area. As for me, I'd be satisfied if the report found a wide audience, with or without my name on it. Maybe this time, serious solutions to our chronic flooding could be implemented.

I still had a few minutes before meeting Brad in his office, which was the former icy domain of Lloyd Sedgwick. I shuddered at the prospect of being in there again. To distract myself, I started discarding the few remaining paper copies that were still in my work bag.

At last, only Lloyd's cryptic ledger sheet remained. I studied it for a moment, but I still couldn't decipher the scribbles. I set it aside.

As soon as it was out of my hand, Lloyd's chicken scratch suddenly began to unscramble in my mind. I snatched the page back to take another look.

This time, each pair of letters appeared to be the same as the initials of KHTS employees: ME for Missy Eton. AS, Alicia Sultana. BH, Brad Hudson. MT, Maura Tustin, JP, Jay Patel, and so on. Once they came into focus, the numbers beside them that I'd first thought were Lloyd's expenses, began to look like money of a different kind.

The last two initials at the bottom stopped me cold: SN. Did they stand for me, Samantha Newman?

No dollar amount was included, which left me to wonder what Lloyd had planned for me.

At any rate, I knew I was holding Lloyd's blackmail list. And a strong motive for murder. I set the page down and tapped Detective Washington's number to alert him to what I'd found.

At that moment, Brad Hudson opened the door and strode up to my desk.

"I believe I said to meet me in my office, not yours. This is not an auspicious beginning, Miss Newman."

"Sorry. I was going through some of Lloyd's old notes and lost track of time."

His eyes fell on the ledger sheet. "Oh my God! Where did you get that?" He tried to snatch it, but I grabbed it in time.

"It's just a bunch of scribbles," I said. "I was about to throw it away when you walked in." I crumpled it up and tossed into the can under my desk.

He shoved his hand in my face. "Give it to me."

My pulse kicked up, but I held my voice steady. "It's just trash, Brad. Somebody's old expense report or something."

Brad's face purpled. "I know exactly what it is! Hand it over now!"

He pounded the top of the desk so hard I could feel it in my molars. As he rounded the desk, he tripped and stumbled backward, and fell against the wall.

He sat up, slightly dazed, and scrambled toward me. I kicked at him, but he managed to grab my ankle and pull me to the floor with him. I swung at him best I could, but I was no match for his size. He held me off with one arm, and reached for the trash can with the other.

"Is there a problem?" At the sound of Evan Fentworth's voice, Brad froze. He loosened his grip on me, straightened up, and peered over the desk. "Just looking for something under here. Nothing to worry about."

Taking advantage of the distraction, I reached in and plucked the balled-up page from the can. I shot up, gripping it tightly. "Got it!"

Brad sprang to his feet and bellowed, "It's mine!"

"No it isn't!" I yelled. "It was Lloyd Sedgwick's, and I'm pretty sure Detective Washington should see it. It may be a clue to Lloyd's murder."

I tossed the crumpled ball over Brad's head to Evan, who caught it with a triumphant grin. "Whatever this is, I'll hold it until the police arrive."

"The police?" Brad's face lost color. He started breathing hard. "But it's got nothing to do with... it's got nothing to... Oh, what's the use?" He collapsed into my chair and hid his face in his hands. "I'm ruined. That bastard ruined me and my poor sister, Missy. He got off easy, and I'm left to pay..." His voice trailed off.

Buron Washington stood in the doorway. "I'll take that." I'd been so astounded by what Brad was saying, I hadn't noticed the detective's presence.

Evan handed the crumpled ledger sheet to him. Two policemen entered the room. They yanked Brad upright, handcuffed him, and sat him down again. He hung his head and quietly wept.

"Take him to the car," Washington said. "And send another car here. There may be one more person to take downtown as well."

CHAPTER FIFTY-THREE

Between the Lines

While one officer marched Brad out, Washington kept his eyes on me, leaving me worried that the second transport he'd ordered was meant for me.

Another anxious moment passed before he spoke. "Ms. Newman, please explain what the commotion over this piece of trash is about."

I replied, calmly as I could. "I believe it's Lloyd Sedgwick's dirty secrets list in his own handwriting. It could also be the original source of the digital file that was erased from his laptop."

Washington frowned. "Who told you about that?"

"You asked me if I had deleted anything from the device, remember?" I smiled. "Give me some credit for reading between the lines."

The detective carefully smoothed the paper and studied the sheet. As he raked his eyes over it, his stony expression cracked a little. "This wasn't turned over with the rest of Sedgwick's files."

"I thought it was just scribbles until a few minutes ago when I found it. Look: the two letters in the first column match initials of KHTS employees, and the numbers in the second column look like dollar amounts. It must be the blackmail list, and the killer's initials are probably on it."

As soon as that was out of my mouth, an awful thought stopped me in my tracks. My initials were on there, too.

Three words leapt into my brain: *Means. Motive. Opportunity.* The trinity of crime-solving. My visit to Lloyd's hospital room—the crime scene—was in itself proof that I had the opportunity. My name initials on the ledger sheet offered a motive. And the means? I had no idea exactly how Lloyd was murdered, but I hoped it was something I could not possibly have accomplished.

I held my breath as Washington continued to study the sheet.

Finally, he blinked. "I'll take this with me." He walked out.

I hurried down the hall after him. "Please, Detective, just tell me, am I still a suspect?"

He spoke over his shoulder as he quickened his pace. "I will speak to you later."

I couldn't limp fast enough to catch him. I stopped just outside Patel's office. Jay wasn't there. Then I remembered the police transport the detective had asked for. If it wasn't meant for me, it must have been for Jay.

I hobbled through the lobby and out the door and arrived outside in time to see Jay being marched in handcuffs to the second squad car.

At the sight, an entire scenario played through my mind like a TV crime drama, and answers to my biggest questions began to fall into place.

Washington was just getting into his vehicle. I flagged him down.

"Ms. Newman, do not try to impede me, or you'll risk being arrested for hindering a police action."

"But I think I've just solved the whole thing!"

The detective sighed. "One minute. That's all you get before—"

"I'll talk fast. Jay Patel was the most likely person to have taken possession of Lloyd's computer after the shooting. I'm sure he'd heard about Lloyd's dirty secrets file, and looked for it in the laptop. If he found it, he'd surely have deleted it, because he's all about protecting his employees. So he deleted the digital file and then put the laptop in my credenza so I could finish Lloyd's report."

Washington got in his car and lowered the window. "An interesting speculation, Ms. Newman. But my job is to bring Sedgwick's murderer to justice. So, unless you know who that person is—"

"Brad Hudson! He was confessing when you walked in."

The detective offered a wry smile, raised the window, and drove away.

I turned back toward the station and immediately bumped bodies with Evan Fentworth.

I'm not sure who looked more uncomfortable, me or him. After his rash of annoying texts, I had expected to have an awkward conversation with him the next time I saw him. But now, the socially inept man-child had become my rescuer.

Evan broke the ice. "You okay?"

I managed a nod. "How did you happen to show up at my door?"

"I was asked to keep an eye on you if you came to the station, so..." A triumphant grin spread on his face. "Mission accomplished."

"Who asked you?"

"That security guy, the one who chewed me out the other day for—" His face turned a deeper pink. "You know him, I think."

"Carter Chapman?"

"Yeah. He asked me to—sorry, I'm not supposed to tell anyone."

I was too beat to care. My nerves were shattered, and my whole body throbbed from wrestling with Brad. I limped inside to get my things.

Evan followed.

I grabbed my things and returned to the lobby.

Evan came, too.

In the kindest way possible, I had to stop his new annoying behavior. "Your guard duty is over, Evan. I'm going home. Thanks for everything."

As I hobbled to my car, I could feel his eyes following me. At least he was keeping his distance.

I sat inside the Ferret, stewing. The day had started so well. I'd dumped the floozie dresses and found a good home for the flood report. And I'd tried to befriend Brad. Then things went wrong again.

In truth, I'd been stuck in the same pattern for years, ever since I lost my family. Despite little successes along the way, I was still rootless.

Before I returned to the condo, I detoured through Gertie's old neighborhood in hopes the new house would feel homier than it did last week. From the street, the place appeared move-in ready. Nice and new, but still completely lacking the charm of the cozy little bungalow I loved.

At Serenity, I'd blubbered like a pathetic child over the old place. But not Gertie. Her life had changed in ways she never would have imagined, yet she was happy. It was time for me to let go, too.

I needed to hear Carter's voice. Before I left the old neighborhood, I called him.

He picked up immediately. "Sam, are you all right?"

"More or less. Your appointed watchdog saved me, by the way. I guess I'm lucky you're such a snoop."

"You sound tired."

"I'm whipped, but I just wanted to let you know that I... I'm fine, and I haven't forgotten about..." My breath gave out.

"Get some rest. Tomorrow, if you're up to it, come to Serenity. There's someone here I want you to meet before I leave for D.C."

CHAPTER FIFTY-FOUR

The New Hire

I couldn't have asked for a more beautiful day for a drive—just me, alone with my thoughts as the Ferret scooted down the highway. Traffic wasn't too bad going west, and in less than a half-hour, I had left the metropolitan sprawl.

When I first visited Carter's ranch, the route beyond this point was bordered by fields of sorghum and corn, and open meadows dotted with grazing cattle. Now, barren, unplowed fields took over, posted with billboards touting new real estate developments.

Eventually, the urban prairie gave way to the rise and fall of rolling hills that marked the threshold of Central Texas. From there, it seemed like no time before I peeled off the main road and entered the winding, oak-bowered drive that led to the great house at Serenity.

Halfway in, I slowed to a crawl and rolled the windows down to take in the dewy-fresh morning. A mockingbird greeted me with a song so lush, I braked to listen. A second bird replied with its own morning repertoire. I could have stayed there longer, but there was another piece of unfinished business for me to take care of.

I rounded the last curve and stopped the Ferret next to another car in front of the house. Carter must have seen me approach, because the front door opened, and there he was.

Every part of me wanted to jump out of the car, run up the steps and fall into his arms, but if the other car belonged to the "someone" he said he wanted me to meet, and if that person was the one he was "with" two days ago, it could be the new executive director. I had to keep things cool.

He studied my face. "You're looking better."

Under his tender gaze, keeping cool was hard. "Thanks."

He took my hand. "Come in. There's someone waiting to meet you."

Inside the foyer, a woman stood at the bottom of the grand staircase. Raven black hair. Smiling almond eyes. Clear tan skin. Darned good-looking. I tamped down a twinge of alarm.

Carter walked over to her and put his hand on her shoulder. "Samantha, this is Kim. She'll be working here at the retreat."

Breath left my body. So this was Carter's choice.

Kim smiled, showing dimples and a mouthful of beautifully straight teeth. She said hello. I choked out a reply. After an awkward moment, she added, "Nice to meet you."

I fought to keep myself together while Carter walked her out to her car. They must have had a lengthy conversation outside, because it felt like an eternity before he bounced back in. "Let's talk for a minute, and I'll tell you all about her." He led me to the library.

We sat on the sofa, and he took my hand. "Sure you're okay? You look a little pale."

"I'm fine." I gave him the smile. "So, Kim is your new person?"

"Yep. Crossed that decision off my list. She'll be great too, with her background."

I struggled to clear the lump in my throat. "I don't recognize her from the résumés. Background in what?"

"She's an equine therapist."

"A what?"

"She's a friend of Tom Mason's, or rather her brother is. The two men reconnected at an Army Ranger meet-up last week, and Tom told the brother what we're creating here. The brother told his sister, she flew in to see the retreat and... well, she'll be ready to move here soon as we're ready for her. FYI, she and Tom may have a future together, from what I've seen."

It dawned on me that Carter and I might not be talking about the same thing. "A horse therapist. Not the executive director?"

He turned serious. "I had to postpone that decision. I could really use your help with it before I leave. Matter of fact—" He reached for a manila envelope on the table beside him and handed it to me. "Here's one more excellent candidate."

I set the envelope aside. "Before we get into this, I want to clear something up."

"Which is?"

"An apology, mostly, for behaving so badly after the shooting. I let myself obsess over things that made me crazy, and I pushed you away."

Carter squeezed my hand. "Sometimes it's—"

"I'm not finished. I told Jay Patel I wouldn't wear those stupid outfits anymore. I'm not sure what he'll do with that, but I'm either going to be a real journalist, or none at all."

"A whistleblower?"

"Not the kind of whistleblower Lloyd was, always looking for the worst in people. I'm afraid I was heading that way, too. I'm sorry for being such a pain in the patoot lately."

"Lately? More like historically, since the day we met. It's part of your charm."

"Gee, thanks."

"Now then, before I leave for D.C., I'd like to show you what you've missed at the retreat. Or we could discuss the new candidate. Which one are you up for first?"

"When are you leaving?"

"Day after tomorrow."

The reality of Carter's imminent departure sent my pulse racing. There wasn't much time left for us.

Instead of stopping the Jeep at the retreat's reception building, Carter circled around it and drove toward the duplex cottages where client families would be staying. All appeared to be ready for business, and the clinic that Gertie and Louis were funding was almost complete.

As we traveled deeper into the property, we neared a larger cottage in the last stages of framing. Carter parked in front and bounded up rough-cut limestone steps. He waved at me to join him.

In the center of the first room was a makeshift table with a sheet of plywood resting on two sawhorses, and on it, a set of blueprints. Carter unfurled the drawings. "Come, take a look."

The top page represented an elevation of the exterior, similar in style to the duplex cottages we'd just passed. The second page was the floor plan. Instead of a duplex, it seemed to be designed as a single residence.

"What's it going to be?" I asked.

He rolled the plans up and took my hand. "Let's do a walk-through."

At this stage, the front rooms looked fairly unremarkable. But the back side was a big open space. Newly-installed floor-to-ceiling windows spanned the back wall, offering abroad view of an open field, blanketed with wildflowers and bordered by oak trees.

Inside, the space itself was plumbed for a kitchen and bar at one end. The adjacent living area sported a double fireplace that straddled a common wall between the room we were in and another, which turned out to be a spacious bedroom that shared the same pastoral panorama.

I looked out over the flowered field. A few yards past the deck, a bunny was nibbling its way through a patch of buttercups.

He squeezed my hand. "So, what do you think?"

"I'm not exactly sure what I'm looking at, but this is definitely the prettiest site on the property."

"There's a natural spring just beyond the trees that could feed a pond or a well in the meadow one day. Want to see it?"

He slid the glass door panel open. When the cottontail heard the noise, it froze. We stopped, too. After a moment, it returned to nibbling again.

Carter led me across the meadow and into the trees. From the cloudless sky, sun streamed through the canopy above us, dappling the ground with bright shards of light. When we emerged on the other side, he pointed to a slight dip in the land where a healthy trickle of water burbled from a narrow, half-buried pipe. I'd never seen a natural spring before. The sight of it inspired an idea.

I turned to Carter. "Does the retreat have a name yet?"

"Only a working title: Serenity Family Retreat. You have a better one?"

"I may."

A silly grin appeared on Carter's face before he wrapped his arms around me and kissed me. Not just any kiss: a long, deep one that told me I was forgiven for being a patoot.

He kissed me again—a short one this time that made me wish for more.

As we retraced our steps, I paused on the deck for another glance at the glade we'd just walked through. "The view from here is gorgeous."

"I hope the new Executive Director likes it. That's who I built it for."

Oh. My throat constricted, making speech impossible.

Neither of us spoke on the drive back to the mansion. While Carter went off to confer with Ralph inside their secure third floor office hideaway, I wandered into the library. It was my favorite place in the big house, grander and brighter than the one at the condo, and with even more books.

Light spilled in through the leaded windows that overlooked the front lawn. I retreated to the sofa and eyed the manila folder with the new candidate's info in it.

The job offered someone an opportunity to do good things in the world, and I sincerely hoped the new person was up to the challenge.

On the other hand, I really hoped Carter hadn't made a decision yet, because I wasn't sure I was ready to hear it. If I told him I'd take the job, would I be choosing the easy path like I had before, only to have it lead to the wrong destination? And would I be risking what was left of my independence?

My phone pinged with a message from Evan Fentworth:

Need u to anchor today

I replied:

I'm out of town.

Evan:

u r my only anchor

His only anchor? I picked up the phone and called him. "What about Francine?"

"She's got the flu, and Patel and Brad are... well, you know." There was panic in his voice. "I had to play anchor at noon, but I need you for the evening broadcast."

Through the front windows, I caught sight of Tom Mason's truck making its way toward the house. It had barely come to a stop when the rear door opened and his little daughter Lizzie popped out and charged up the steps.

She shouted my name from the foyer. "Samantha, are you here?"

I spoke into the phone. "Evan, I'll have to call you back." I disconnected.

THE BODY IN THE NEWS

Lizzie peeked into the library. When she spotted me, she raced for the sofa and almost knocked me over with a hug. "I saw your car and I got so happy!"

"Glad to see you, too, Lizzie."

"We only had a half-day at school, so T.J. drove Dad's truck here for lunch. I'm supposed to be setting the table. Can you come, too?"

"Well, I..."

Carter had appeared in the doorway in time to hear Lizzie's question. He answered for me. "Good idea, Lizzie. Why don't you go tell Dottie there'll be an extra place at the table? In the meantime, Samantha and I have a few things to talk over in private."

Lizzie happily zipped off to the kitchen.

"You have a lifetime fan in that girl," Carter said.

"The feeling is mutual. She's a special spirit."

Carter sat beside me. "You okay, Sam?"

"I just spoke to Evan Fentworth. He begged me to come back to the station today."

He lowered his eyes. "You're not actually thinking about going, are you?"

FIFTY-FIVE

Redacted

Carter sighed. "Before you go, would you please look at this last candidate? I really think this is the one." He opened the manila envelope, extracted a sheaf of papers, and passed them to me.

On the cover page was a large gray official seal that read *Department of Justice Federal Bureau of Investigation.* In the center of the seal were thirteen stars and a shield. The remaining pages were titled *Office Memorandum – United States Government.* Names, dates, and other identifying information were blacked out, leaving only random words and numbers visible.

I stopped partway through. "Are you hiring a secret agent?"

"Maybe."

I flipped through the heavily redacted pages to a sheet with the blurry photocopy of a driver's license on it. It took a moment for me to recognize a face from years ago.

It was my own. "What is this?"

"Remember when we met?"

"Worst first date ever."

"You taught me a lesson that day that knocked me sideways."

"Which was?"

"People are more than their résumés."

I scanned the pages again until all at once, I realized what they were: my own FBI file, from back when I was moonlighting as a part-time receptionist to pay my way through college. Too naïve for my own good, I had thought I was making appointments for a 24-hour physical therapy clinic. As it turned out, my employer was actually running a prostitution business, and when he was brought to trial, I had to testify in court.

I knew a record of the trial existed, but I had no idea that there was also an official file on me. Carter must have found it before we met, when he was investigating my ex-employer's evil deeds.

I wondered if Lloyd had also discovered the file. It could be the reason why my initials were on his blackmail list. My mind traveled along that path until Carter's voice brought me back.

"Earth to Samantha…"

"Why are you showing me this?"

"I first uncovered it when I investigated your old boss, Vinson De Theret. Since you were pretty high up on the food chain in his company, I looked into your background, too."

"Not your finest moment."

"Except, look here…" He turned the papers to the back of the last page where handwritten notes had been added. I recognized Carter's bold script and the heading *De Theret International.*

As I read, he continued to explain. "It's a pretty detailed look at your business accomplishments, which happen to fulfill everything the retreat needs in an Executive Director. 'Helped fledgling business grow into powerhouse. Managed budget in the millions.' And so on."

"What about this one?" I pointed to the last note at the bottom where he'd written, 'Can she be turned?'

"That was before I met you. C'mon, Sam. Look it over and tell me who the best candidate is."

"Not me."

"Why not you? You were damn good at your job. If you could make a lowlife like De Theret look like an angel, you can do this job standing on one foot."

"But I... I..."

"You really should see a specialist about that stutter."

"You should mind your own business."

"Exactly what I am doing."

My face heated to an unsustainable temperature. The urge to flee propelled me off the sofa. I started pacing. "You're trying to make me say yes."

"Impossible. I've never been able to make you do anything you didn't want to do."

Carter's phone beeped. He looked at the screen. "Damn. Gotta take this." He left the library and reappeared on the front veranda, pacing while he conversed with his caller.

Meanwhile, I paced around the room. After a couple of circuits, my eyes came to rest on the spine of a book. *Beloved Prophet: The Love Letters of Kahlil Gibran and Mary Haskell.*

Gibran again. Hoping to find something in the pages to help calm my mind, I pulled it from the shelf. It was full of intensely passionate love letters between the poet/philosopher and the woman he loved. I took the book to the sofa and started reading.

After a few paragraphs, I realized I was peering into the real-life story of two star-crossed lovers. I kept going until I came to a line that stopped me cold:

One day you will ask me which is more important? My life or yours? I will say mine and you will walk away, not knowing that you are my life.

Of course, Carter would pick that moment to walk in, just as I was dabbing my damp eyes with the back of my hand.

I couldn't look at him. "Please, just go away."

"I live here, remember?" He frowned. "Is it something I said?"

I pointed to the book.

"Ah, Gibran, that tear-mongering scoundrel. Gets to me every time, too."

"I've never seen you cry."

"Look closer."

I never should have. The moment my eyes met his, I started tearing up again.

Carter sat next to me. "I hate to break the spell, but I have Buron Washington on the line for you, if you're up to talking to him."

I grabbed the phone. "Detective?"

"Ms. Newman. I've been told that my lack of transparency has caused you some distress. I only have a moment, but perhaps I can explain a few things, if you're interested."

"I'm all ears."

"First, about the ledger sheet you found. We checked the people on the list against some bank records, and were able to narrow the field of suspects. It was an important key for us."

I felt a rush of excitement. "So, tell me, was it Jay Patel or Brad who killed Lloyd?"

"That has to wait until after formal charges are filed. However, I can reveal that you also provided us with the murder weapon."

"I did?" I raced through mental images of the things I'd handed over. Lloyd's voice recorder didn't seem substantial enough to kill somebody with, unless it was deployed by the clenched fist of a heavyweight champion. Everything else was just a bunch of papers. Except...

"Lloyd's laptop?"

"Yes."

"How on earth does a laptop kill someone?"

"At first we thought the victim had simply fallen out of bed. However, on autopsy, his head wound had settled into a distinct pattern that indicated he'd been struck by an unknown object. We were able to match the pattern at his temple to an edge near the thumb drive port on his computer, where the screen hinges to the cover. Physical material containing the victim's blood was also found in that area."

What? A piece of Lloyd was lurking on the laptop the entire time I was using it? How did I not notice? My stomach hurled upward.

My fingerprints were all over the laptop, too. No wonder Washington had me feeling like a suspect. If I didn't know better, I'd have come to the same conclusion.

The detective broke into my thoughts. "I have to go. I hope this puts your mind at ease. And thank you for your cooperation." He disconnected.

I handed the phone to Carter. "That was interesting."

"You look a little shaky. Did he tell you about the murder weapon."

"Kind of a shock. I carried that laptop around and worked on it for days, with a piece of Lloyd still lurking in the cracks." I shivered. "I would've thought the man's head was hard enough put a dent in the thing, not the other way around."

"If a blow to the head is in just the right place—or the wrong place, from Sedgwick's point of view—it could, with enough force, cause harm. He'd been on blood thinners, which made things worse. The internal bleeding wasn't detected until he was too far gone."

Lloyd, killed with the tool of his perverse and misguided revenge, like in a classic Greek tragedy.

CHAPTER FIFTY-SIX

Where Were We?

My conversation with the detective had cleared up almost everything, except the most pressing question of the moment. I turned to Carter. "Did Washington tell you who killed Lloyd?"

Before he answered, my phone lit with a call from none other than Jay Patel.

"Jay! What's happening?"

"Nothing at the moment. I'm out on bail, but before things get really crazy, I feel like I owe you an explanation. I got you involved in a bad situation, and I'm sorry."

"Which one?"

"After the shooting, I took Lloyd's laptop to the hospital and told him you would be finishing the flood report since he'd said it was almost ready. When I asked for the password to access his files, he went ballistic. I was worried he might blow a gasket, so I left.

"The next day, I went back to get the computer. Brad was there, and they were arguing over the laptop. At one point, Brad grabbed it, and for a minute they both had a grip on it, until Brad yanked it away and hit Lloyd with it. Lloyd lunged for Brad and fell out of bed. At the time, I didn't think Brad had done much damage. Anyway, I grabbed the laptop and left."

"And you put it in my credenza?"

"You needed it."

"Did you delete any files?"

"I can't get into that."

"Why were you arrested?"

"I held off telling the police what I'd witnessed, until my lawyer convinced me to cooperate. I'll have to answer for that, and for messing with some evidence, but I had no idea Lloyd would end up dead. Hopefully, they'll go easy on me."

"I'm sure you were trying to protect Brad and everyone else, as usual."

"It's okay. Gives me some time to rethink the rest of my life."

I wished him well, and we said goodbye.

Carter had been watching my reactions. "What did he say?"

"Brad Hudson. I told Washington yesterday that Brad had confessed, but he ignored me. It sounded like Lloyd had been blackmailing him or Missy. It's easy to imagine someone being angry enough to kill Lloyd, but maybe Brad only wanted to stop the harassment."

"What Hudson's intent was will be up to the prosecution, and eventually, a judge and jury. At any rate, nothing to be done now but wait for the outcome."

Carter was right. Nothing to do about it now. I shook myself out of that useless loop. "Where were we before the Lloyd saga cropped up?"

"We were right here, talking about your excellent qualifications and how I'm making it hard for you to say no." He took my hand. "I'm not going to swallow you whole, Sam. I'll be totally hands-off unless you need me. I'm just hoping you'll see that you're perfect for the job."

Words failed me. I took a deep breath and pushed through. "Would you excuse me for a minute?" I bolted from the sofa and strode past the entry and out the front door.

I didn't stop until I reached the horse barn. Hollywood's stall was toward the back, across from Remington's. I headed that way.

She whinnied when I called her name and poked her head through the open top of the Dutch door. I held my hand out to give her a whiff. Her nostrils flared, taking me in.

"Hello friend," I said. "It's good to see you, too." I patted her face and rubbed her muzzle. We communed in silence, until I heard Carter's voice behind me.

"Asking Hollywood for advice?"

"She's very wise."

"Horse sense?"

"Goes a long way." I stopped petting Hollywood and turned to Carter. "I've come to a conclusion."

"And?"

"Well, first, about leaving to help Evan out at the station—"

Just then, Lizzie burst into the barn, breathless. "Hey, people, you're late for lunch. The food's getting cold and Dottie's getting really grouchy!" She zipped out again to announce our arrival.

I hesitated, a little unsteady from the weight of my decision.

Carter touched my shoulder. "You can't go now. Lizzie set a place for you."

As usual, the kitchen held a delicious potpourri of the best home-cooking aromas in the universe. Everyone was gathered around the big farm table:

Lizzie, her brother T.J., their dad Tom Mason; Kerry, his big sister Courtney, their dad Ralph Velasco, and Ralph's mom, Dottie.

Lizzie pointed me to the chair next to hers. Carter took his seat at the head of the table. "Sorry for the delay. Now that we're all here, let's eat."

Fried chicken, corn on the cob, green beans, and mashed potatoes were already set out. Dottie added a basket of fresh rolls from the oven. Bowls and platters were passed. I put a drumstick/thigh quarter on my plate, added all the vegetables, and slathered a roll with butter and honey.

After much talk and laughter, Dottie and Courtney rose to serve dessert: homemade Texas peach pie—which I knew from experience would be a slice of heaven—and a tub of delicious vanilla ice cream from the creamery down the road in Brenham.

Looking around the table, I realized that each of us had survived deep personal loss, including the children. Yet to an outsider, we might look like one big, happy family. And in a sense, we were.

Lizzie and Kerry helped clear the table before running off to play, and everyone else left to tend to their afternoon chores.

Carter and I moved outside to the veranda at the back of the house, where the willows lining the natural lap pool offered shade. Side by side, we stood at the railing above the water.

Neither of us spoke, until Carter reopened our conversation. "So, are you taking Hollywood's advice?"

"About that. Your horse therapist, Kim. I'm thinking I may need her services."

"You said you were feeling better."

"I am better. I just need a reason to spend more time with Hollywood."

"Are saying yes?"

Was I? I looked up at Carter. We both stood there, gawking at each other, until Carter spoke. "Occurs to me that you haven't heard the rest of my sales pitch."

"Lay it on me."

"First of all, about the new Executive Director's house. I left it unfinished inside on purpose, so the person who lives there can turn it into whatever makes them happy. Cozy, like Gertie's old place, or something entirely different. And we can add a trail from the springs to the horse barn to make it a shorter walk. As for Kim's services, you'll have to negotiate those with her."

"You're making it hard to say no."

"I'm trying to make it easy to say yes."

"Easy for who?"

"For you, Sam. Easy to see that we're meant to drive each other crazy for the rest of our lives, or at least until we're too tired to butt heads anymore. You think I'm trying to do you a favor, but I need you to do this for me, too. I need you in my life, period."

"But I—"

"You love a good cause."

"But I don't know much about non-profits."

"You've handled multi-million dollar budgets and helped build a company from scratch. You'll learn the other stuff in no time."

"Maybe, but—"

"You know you want to do it."

"Yes, but—"

"Yes? You said yes!"

My face was burning. "I... I..."

"There's that stutter again. Maybe we should add a speech therapist to the list of new hires."

"But, I—" I what? Why was it so hard for me to say?

Carter eyes brimmed with hope. "Just nod if the answer is yes."

That made it easier. I nodded and fell into his arms.

The sun had worked its way to the veranda where we stood. Golden rays filtered through the trees, reminding me of the sunset I'd seen from this spot when I first visited Serenity. It was the first time we kissed.

Carter turned to me. "Looks like it's going to be a nice evening. Let's stay out here for a while."

We moved to the railing that overlooked the back stretch of the lap pool below. Once I regained my voice, we started talking through a mutual vision for Carter's charitable foundation, including the retreat and the music education program he'd created before we met. The possibilities seemed endless.

"I'll need Gertie's help," I said.

"Hire anyone you want. Just promise you'll stay out of trouble."

I laughed. "I'll have to work on that. But I can promise you one thing."

"Which is?"

"I'll be the best executive director you ever had."

"You're the first."

"Exactly. What do you think of calling it Serenity Springs?"

"For the real spring here?"

"And because hope springs eternal."

We stood there, grinning stupidly at each other until Carter wrapped me in his arms.

"Welcome to Serenity Springs," he whispered. His breath tickled my ear.

We stayed out there at the café table, talking for hours. As the sun began to dip below the horizon, Carter disappeared into the kitchen and brought back two glasses of bubbly. We drank a toast to the future of Serenity Springs, and another to Carter's important work with the U.S. Cyber Commission.

After a while, we fell silent, listening to the cicadas and the frogs and the rustling leaves perform an evening serenade. Eventually, the sun gave way to a clear night sky, full of stars, and not a giant asteroid in sight.

About the Author

G ay Yellen began her working life as a stage and TV actress, then happily moved behind the camera at The American Film Institute (AFI) as Assistant to the Director of Production. A former magazine editor and national journalism award winner, she was the contributing book editor for *Five Minutes to Midnight* (Delacorte Press), an international thriller and a *New York Times* "Notable". Her Samantha Newman Romantic Mystery Series includes *The Body Business, The Body Next Door,* and *The Body in the News.*

Gay loves connecting with book clubs and community groups in person and online. You can contact her through her website, GayYellen.com.

Gratitude

Much of my research for this book came from the excellent reporting in *The Houston Chronicle* about the devastation wrought by Hurricane Harvey in 2017. In 2023, many residents have still not recovered, and some never will. Investigative journalists are my heroes. Our democracy needs them. May they live long and prosper.

Thanks to my readers, who kept asking for more and who waited patiently while I crafted this story. Special thanks go to those who post reviews and recommend my books to their friends and book clubs. You have my sincerest gratitude.

Speaking of patience, I am forever grateful to my husband for his patience during all the days and months and years of waiting while I toiled away at this book.

Many thanks to SkipJack Publishing for embracing *The Samantha Newman Mystery Series*.

I am especially grateful to Pamela Fagan Hutchins, Saralyn Richard, Patty Flaherty Pagan, and Lois Winston for taking time away from their own writing to read the unfinished manuscript of this book and for cheering me on in difficult times. It's a gift to have such cherished writing colleagues. Thank you to all.

Now that you have read *The Body in the News,* would you please consider taking a moment to leave a brief honest review on the book's Amazon.com or BookBub.com or Goodreads.com page? It's a great way to share your thoughts and help other readers decide if they might enjoy the book as well.

The author would greatly appreciate it. Thank you!

Have you read these
SAMANTHA NEWMAN MYSTERIES?

Book 1: **The Body Business**
Book 2: **The Body Next Door**
Book 3: **The Body in the News**

Want to know more? Follow Gay on:

Amazon
BookBub
Facebook
"X" (Twitter)
Instagram
Goodreads

For inside info about Gay's books, sign up for her newsletter at GayYellen.com.

Made in United States
Orlando, FL
27 November 2023

39461261R10176